DEC 2019

## GREETINGS FROM THE FULLERTON VALLEY!

Dear Charlotte and Lydia,

Whose idea was it, anyway, to look up our first loves?

Guess what? I've already found mine, and Ryan's just as gorgeous as I remember and, better yet, he's still single!

He lives on a ranch near Stoney Creek with his aunt (a sweetie), his brother, Cameron (who's really kind of a mystery man), and his darling little niece.

Guess what else? The hotel here is closing for the winter, so I'm going to be staying at an apartment the Donnellys have at their ranch. I should be there till Christmas.

Wish me luck! Will let you know how it all turns out.

Love,

Zoey

P.S. See you both on New Year's Eve!

Dear Reader,

Have you ever sat around a table with your best friends, talking about old times, and someone's said, "Hey, I wonder what happened to so-and-so?" The first guy you had a crush on, the first love of your life. Did he become the doctor or astronaut or bus driver he always wanted to be? Did he get married? Have children? *Does he ever think of me*?

Three best friends—Zoey Phillips, Charlotte Moore and Lydia Lane—take up the challenge in my new miniseries, GIRLFRIENDS. We start with Zoey's story, when she's invited back to the small town in British Columbia she'd once called home. She's there to help with a friend's wedding. And she's bound to run into the boy she lost her heart to at sixteen. What happens then? I think the results may surprise you!

Like girlfriends everywhere, Zoey keeps in touch with Charlotte and Lydia while she's away—and discovers that Charlotte has set out on the same quest, while Lydia... Well, you'll see.

I hope you enjoy GIRLFRIENDS, the stories of three best friends who met as eighteen-year-olds just out of high school while working at a wilderness resort in the Rocky Mountains. Now, ten years later, they set out—each on her own—to track down that elusive first love.

And all the while, their friendship remains an important part of their lives. *Old friends, best friends*...GIRLFRIENDS!

Warmly,

*Judith Bowen*

P.S. I love to hear from readers. Write to me at: Box 2333, Point Roberts, WA 98281-2333 or check out my Web site at *www.judithbowen.com*.

# Zoey Phillips
## Judith Bowen

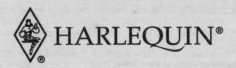

**HARLEQUIN**®

TORONTO • NEW YORK • LONDON
AMSTERDAM • PARIS • SYDNEY • HAMBURG
STOCKHOLM • ATHENS • TOKYO • MILAN • MADRID
PRAGUE • WARSAW • BUDAPEST • AUCKLAND

ISBN 0-373-71020-8

ZOEY PHILLIPS

Copyright © 2001 by J. E. Corser.

# Zoey Phillips

# *PROLOGUE*

WHOSE IDEA HAD IT BEEN to look up everyone's first love, anyway?

First love, first crush…whatever.

The challenge, as Zoey recalled, had been tossed out last spring at the ten-year reunion of the Jasper Park Lodge female summer staff. Zoey and her best friends, Charlotte Moore and Lydia Lane, both of whom she'd met at the lodge that long-ago summer, had flown from Toronto to Calgary for the big event, rented a car and driven through Banff and the glorious Alberta Rockies to Jasper. Last time they'd been there, they'd been swabbing out bathrooms, changing sheets and peeling vegetables. This time, they were paying guests.

About twenty girls had shown up. Someone—Jenny Springer?—had announced that they all ought to look up their first crushes, just for the fun of it, even if he'd been the cute guy with the freckles in kindergarten. Simple curiosity. Just to see what had happened to that first heartbreaker in a girl's life. Probably bald, boring and hopelessly unappealing now. Then—here was the test—they'd all report back at next year's reunion.

Zoey hadn't given the suggestion a thought, but

later, when she and Charlotte and Lydia were floating under a clear midnight sky in the outdoor pool overlooking Lake Beauvert, the topic had come up again. Lydia, naturally, had sneaked in a bottle of bubbly and some plastic glasses and they'd each had a glass or two. There were so many events and memories to toast....

"I've made up my mind. I'm going to do it." Charlotte raised her glass to the others. "Wish me luck."

"Do what?" Zoey had been idly watching the tattered balloons of her breath hanging in the cold air over the heated water and thinking of bears. Wondering if they were still hibernating—it was late April—and if they ever came out of the woods and wandered down to the lodge pool to check out the contents.

"Look up my first crush." Charlotte was delicate and fragile in appearance, with blue eyes and perfect skin—in fact, everything about Charlotte was perfect—but Zoey knew what kind of energy was hidden beneath that remote, hands-off exterior. The three of them had run a business together, the Call-a-Girl Company, nearly eight years ago. They'd done children's birthday parties, house-sitting, gardening, last-minute catering, pet-walking, what-have-you—and no one had put in more hours or devised better, more off-the-wall money-making schemes than Charlotte.

"Yeah, and who would that be?" Lydia asked. She was a tawny blonde, a little taller than the other two, whose lazy, sensual looks hid a razor-sharp mind.

"My first?" Charlotte gave a throaty chuckle. "Liam Connery. He was in my sister's class at school when I was in grade five. A loner type. He'd just moved to Toronto from somewhere else, the East coast, I think, and I remember he had a big brown dog. All I know is that I was desperately in love and that he wanted to fly airplanes when he grew up. He was so handsome, at least I thought so at ten, eleven, whatever I was.''

Zoey and Lydia laughed.

"My sister hung out with him," Charlotte continued dreamily. "I'm not sure we ever even spoke! The age difference is huge when you're in grade five and he's in high school, but—" She shrugged and raised her glass. "Oh, what a heavenly feeling, just to know he was looking at me. Once in a while, anyway!''

Lydia laughed and raised her glass, too. "To first love. Drink up!''

They all repeated the toast solemnly and downed the champagne. Zoey felt silly. First love? That would be Ryan Donnelly, the handsome track star at Fullerton Valley High who'd taught her what a French kiss was and then laughed at her when she wanted more.

"That's it?" Lydia asked. "No more juicy details?''

"That's it." Charlotte smiled through the ghostly mist that undulated on the surface of the pool. "I have no idea what happened to him. They moved, I guess.'' She laughed and took a sip of her champagne. "Probably married and living in Scarborough and the closest he's ever come to flying is taking his kids on the Sky-master at the CNE each year.''

"So why look him up?" Zoey asked. She was perplexed and yet genuinely interested. Charlotte was a smart woman. She had a boyfriend, a handsome, successful lawyer type on Bay Street. Why would she waste her time on this?

"Oh…just because," she'd answered dreamily. "Don't you ever wonder what happened to *your* first guy?"

She hadn't. Then, six months later, Zoey accepted a childhood friend's invitation to help plan her stepmother's wedding. Until then, she hadn't thought she'd see Stoney Creek or the Fullerton Valley again. Or Ryan Donnelly. But on the drive up from Vancouver to Williams Lake and north, to Stoney Creek, she'd thought of little else. Did he still live there? He was from a large, well-established Chilcotin ranching family. Was he still handsome? The eighteen-year-old had been both a football hero and a track star. And, even more puzzling, how exactly had a sensible girl like Zoey ended up head-over-heels in love with him in the first place?

As she recalled the situation, Ryan had suggested in their last year of high school that he and Zoey pretend to be an item so he could make another girl jealous, the class beauty, Adele Martinez. Zoey already secretly adored him so she'd jumped at the chance. Surely any girl of that age would be forgiven for believing that events might turn out differently. She certainly had. In her preferred version, Ryan concluded that, *of course,* Adele wasn't the one for him; Zoey Phillips was.

Or, Joey Phillips, as she'd been then. Joey was short for Josephetta Antonia. There were six Phillips girls and every one of them had a feminized male name: Thomasina, Frederica, Roberta, Frances, Josephetta and the baby, Stephanie. Harvey Phillips had clearly wanted a boy, but after six girls, he'd given up.

Stephanie was the only one who got off relatively easy, Zoey thought.

Joey, another boy's name, was bad enough. Everyone knew exactly what it was short for, the weird Josephetta, which was the name teachers read out for roll call and the name typed out in full on her report card. She'd dumped Joey her first year away from home, part of the calculated distance she wanted to put between who she was now and who she'd been then, at least in the eyes of Stoney Creek. *Zoey* was glamorous. Mysterious. Different. And so was the second-youngest Phillips girl, Zoey had decided. She'd tried *Chloe* for a while, but no one could spell or pronounce it, so she'd tossed it for Zoey.

Stoney Creek was the closest she'd come to having a hometown. It was the longest the Phillipses had stayed in one place, first in the run-down house across the tracks and later, as Harvey Phillips's fortunes improved, in the white-painted clapboard house with the lilac hedge and the big maple trees at the top of the hill. They moved a lot. Zoey remembered leaving one elementary school after only two months—finish school on Friday, gone by Monday. Her father was an inventor and a dreamer, always searching for the perfect place to live, always losing or quitting his job. Luckily, her mother was a nurse and could get work nearly everywhere they went.

There was no money for education but Zoey had made up her mind she was going to college. She put herself through with summer jobs and the money she

made with Call-a-Girl Company, which she and Charlotte and Lydia ran year-round, even during the aca-
demic year. Charlotte, from an upper-crust Rosedale
family, had the contacts and no shortage of good ideas.
Lydia, a dreamy girl with a lot of imagination and a
soft heart, was an excellent cook and organizer and
had taken charge of most of the catering they'd landed.
Her goal was to earn enough to travel to Australia.
Zoey, who claimed no particular domestic or culinary
skills, pitched in wherever help was needed, dealing
with the advertising and promotion for their little company as well.

After graduation, Zoey had managed to turn her En-
glish major into a successful editing and book packaging career, first in Toronto, then in New York for a
couple of years and now back in Toronto. Her time
was her own and she made good money now that she
worked exclusively with bestselling mystery writer Jamie Chinchilla, whipping the author's convoluted
manuscripts into shape before Chinchilla's publisher
saw them.

As a single, independent woman, she now moved
when *she* wanted to—not when there were too many
bills to pay and the most attractive option, according
to Harvey Phillips's modus operandi, was simply to
leave town.

Zoey Phillips had—in her estimation—arrived.
She'd worked hard to get where she was today. Per-
haps it was time to return to Stoney Creek for a visit.
She'd changed—had the town?

# CHAPTER ONE

"THAT'S HIM— over there!"

*"Where?"* Zoey rolled her eyes and made a little face. Obviously, Elizabeth didn't expect her to turn right around and stare.

Her friend leaned across the table and wagged her spoon meaningfully in a direction that was behind Zoey and slightly to her left.

"There! By the window. He's having dinner with his aunt and his brother and—" Elizabeth craned her neck delicately "—and his niece. And maybe someone else, I can't tell." It was just past six, but the Gold Dust Café, the restaurant on the main floor of the Fullerton Valley Hotel was packed, mostly with families. People dined early in Stoney Creek, British Columbia. Zoey had been dragged along by her schoolfriend, Elizabeth Nugent, formerly Jonkers, when she could have been ensconced in the privacy and quiet of her room upstairs, starting work on the manuscript she'd brought with her to edit. She had to admit, though, that dinner with the Nugents, a precursor to making an appearance later in the evening at the volunteer firefighters' dance, had been pleasant so far.

*Ryan Donnelly.* Zoey held her breath, suddenly seventeen all over again—*be still my trembling heart.*

Was that really him? She artfully dropped her paper napkin, which skittered a surprising distance, and reached to pick it up from the carpet, sliding her eyes to the left as she did. Disappointment washed through her. Rats! That wasn't *him*—that was the man she'd seen in the shoemaker's shop this morning. The man who'd picked up a bridle that was being fixed.

"Who's that, hon?" Arthur Nugent asked his wife, eyes on the lettuce leaf he'd turned over on his salad plate.

"Ryan Donnelly. Zoey's high-school heartthrob. Oh, Arthur! Don't you remember them going out together, back when Ryan was trying to make Adele Martinez jealous? Zoey's still half in love with him." Elizabeth giggled. "She told me last night. Isn't that *romantic?*"

"Lizzie!" Zoey shushed her friend. "Don't be silly. I just wondered if he was still in town, that's all—"

"What's wo-mantic, Mommy?" five-year-old Tessa asked innocently. Zoey wished Elizabeth had kept her big mouth shut. She loved her dearly, but Elizabeth was an inveterate fixer—anybody's relationship problems were fodder. Of course, Zoey had no relationship problems, but she *had* confessed to Elizabeth when she'd arrived in Stoney Creek the day before that she'd love to run into her old high-school crush. The boy who'd seen her as an enthusiastic partner-in-crime, a fellow road warrior, when she would've preferred he see her as the love interest.

"Never mind, honey," Elizabeth soothed her youngest, then inexplicably reversed herself. "Well, guess what? Auntie Zoey likes Lissy's uncle, that's all."

"Oh." Tessa covered her mouth and grinned. "Are they in love and getting married, like Barnaby's mom and dad?"

"Not yet!" Elizabeth's eyes twinkled and Zoey would have elbowed her if she'd been closer. "You eat your salad now, Tess. Yum-yum. It's full of vitamins and minerals that little girls need to grow up strong and pretty and smart like Zoey who's come to visit us all the way from Toronto! Isn't that wonderful, girls? I still can't believe it!"

Zoey smiled. Sometimes Elizabeth made her feel like she was another member of the Nugent brood, in need of constant management and encouragement.

"But Daddy isn't eating his," Becky observed calmly. At six, nearly seven, she was eons more sophisticated than her sister. "I think there's something in it. Maybe something bad." She glanced at her sister. "Maybe a worm."

Tessa dropped her fork with a clatter and gave her mother a pained look, mouth open. *"Aaaah…"*

Elizabeth's attention lit on her husband. "Arthur, *what* are you doing? That's only radicchio and you're not setting any kind of example for the girls, playing with your food like that."

Arthur, a partner in the Nugent family insurance business, was a large, quiet, thoughtful man. Zoey remembered him vaguely from high school. He'd been a year or two ahead of Zoey and Elizabeth and their gang. As she recalled, he'd been large and thoughtful then, too, with untamable stand-up hair. His hair, thinning a little on top, was nicely combed now.

"I don't think I care for these designer greens,

Lizzie.'' He smiled at his wife and put down his fork, directing a quizzical glance across the table. "Hey, Zoey, want me to take you over and introduce you, see if he remembers you?"

"Ack!" She let out a tiny shriek, which amused the girls highly. "No, definitely not. I'm in town until Christmas." It was nearly the end of November. "I can wait. Besides, that isn't Ryan over there, anyway."

"It is!" Elizabeth insisted.

Fortunately, their main courses arrived then, diverting Elizabeth, and the subject was dropped, to Zoey's enormous relief. But Arthur's comments lodged in her heart. *Would* Ryan Donnelly remember her? She'd been poor and skinny, with horrible carrot-colored hair. As untamable as Arthur's, if the truth be told. And Ryan had never been in love with her at all— only used her in a ruse designed to make the town's teen queen jealous. As if anyone would envy Zoey Phillips!

She, pathetically, had gone along with everything he'd suggested: dances, dates at the local cinema, kisses, trips to the Dairy Queen. When Adele Martinez had finally deigned to notice him after a month or so, Ryan had disappeared from Zoey's life. Thank heaven, it was the spring before graduation, and Zoey had landed a plum job that summer, working at Jasper Park Lodge in the Alberta Rockies. No more boring, dusty, small-minded Stoney Creek, she'd thought. The pain of that first love, never returned, had faded, as she'd known it would. Wasn't that the way with first love?

You always fell for the wrong guy, the one who broke your untried teenage heart.

Now, ten years later, she'd come back, after all. To see Elizabeth and Mary Ellen Owen and her stepmother, who was getting married, and some of the other people she still cared about. To look up that aging charmer, Ryan Donnelly—maybe. To have a working holiday in British Columbia's interior, a place she thought she'd left behind forever.

Deep down, she knew she'd come for another reason, too: to rub the town's nose in her success. Just a tiny bit... No one in Stoney Creek, except Elizabeth and Mary Ellen and Mrs. Bishop, the school librarian, had ever taken her seriously.

She'd been a skinny, scared, brainy brat when she left. A good education, a terrific job, hair that was a nice ordinary dark-auburn now, with a little assistance—everything had changed in her life. She was no longer one of the six gawky Phillips girls, all red-headed, all wearing hand-me-downs and living in a ramshackle house on the wrong side of the tracks. She'd even lost most of her freckles.

Times had changed. Zoey Phillips was definitely *somebody* now. And, with the exception of the freckles, she'd done it all on her own.

RYAN DONNELLY *WAS* sitting at the large table near the window.

At one point, Elizabeth got up to help Tessa take a trip to the bathroom and Zoey saw her smile and wave. She gave Zoey an exaggerated wink.

Zoey glanced toward the table in question to see

that a man, who'd had his back to them, had turned slightly and was staring at their table. *Ryan Donnelly.* Her heart nearly stopped in her chest. She smiled but to her shock he didn't respond, his gaze moving to Arthur and Becky before returning to her for a few seconds. He smiled uncertainly and Zoey made a tiny gesture, a sort-of wave.

Ryan leaned toward the other man, the one she'd seen in the shoemaker's. He turned and Zoey caught the glimpse of recognition as he noticed her. She smiled distantly; what else could she do? Ryan never looked her way again.

She would've known him anywhere.

Well, that was that. She'd seen him and he was as handsome as he'd ever been, maybe more. Zoey quickly scanned Ryan's table. Besides the man who'd recognized her from their brief encounter that morning, there were two women—one of them a blonde, one of them quite a bit older—and a young girl.

Zoey felt oddly let-down as she resumed eating her cherry cheesecake. Her cheeks were hot. What had she expected—that Ryan Donnelly would rush over and fall onto his knees and exclaim that *she'd* been the girl he'd loved all along? She, Zoey Phillips, and not the gorgeous Adele. That she'd broken his heart when she'd left Stoney Creek, that he'd never married because no other woman had quite measured up to her…

Zoey found herself smiling. A girl could dream, couldn't she?

She'd been on pins and needles ever since she'd arrived the day before, thinking she might run into him—on the street, in a café, in the hotel. Okay, so she'd seen him now. Next step was actually talking to him. She could handle that.

"You up for an hour or so at the firemen's dance—oh, excuse me, it's fire*fighters* now, I forgot," Arthur said with a cheerful smile. Zoey realized he was addressing her. "We've got a couple of women on the roster so maybe it's fire*persons,* I don't know. Should be fun. I promised the girls a few dances."

"I'm looking forward to it," Zoey said, surprising herself. Well, she was…now. Would Ryan be there? Idiotically, she wished she'd dressed up a little, worn a skirt, paid more attention to her makeup.

Elizabeth hustled back to the table, red in the face. Tessa's bottom lip stuck out stubbornly. Now, what was *that* all about? Some kind of mother-daughter disagreement. Zoey loved to visit her nieces and nephews, but motherhood was a total enigma to her. She didn't know what she thought about kids; sometimes she yearned for a family of her own, a husband and children, and other times she wondered what all the fuss was about.

"Finish your dessert, honey," Elizabeth told her daughter, then straightened and sent another quick smile toward the Donnelly table.

"Whew!" She sat down. "Okay, everybody ready to go?"

Arthur went over the bill, item by item, refusing to let Zoey contribute. There was an error in the addition and by the time he'd figured it out, paid, and carefully counted out a generous tip, Elizabeth had her daughters' coats on and was trying to convince Tessa to wear her woolen cap. No luck.

Zoey glanced toward the table by the window again. It was empty. Ryan and his friends were already gone.

They'd dated, they'd held hands, they'd kissed in the Rialto. They'd danced together at the spring prom. Sure, it was all a big joke. And it had been ten years ago, nearly eleven. Still, she couldn't understand why he hadn't walked over to their table to say something. *Hello. Having a good life? Where've you been? Nice to see you.* Anything.

What was she—invisible? Zoey swallowed her disappointment. So much for first loves. Just as she'd always maintained, they were better forgotten.

ZOEY HAD ARRIVED in Stoney Creek the day before— Friday—to a mix-up with the hotel. She'd thought she had a room for the full five weeks, but the man at the desk told her they were closing for the winter after hunting season, the end of the following week. She'd have to find another place to stay.

The Fullerton Valley Hotel was old but charming, with sloping floors in the corridors and a creaking, slow-as-molasses elevator. She'd remembered it as being quite a bit more charming and a whole lot less old, but that was the way memory seemed to work. Between a high-school basketball tournament and hunting season, the place was full. They'd put her in the top-floor honeymoon suite.

*Honeymoon suite.* She'd wanted to giggle. Well, at least she'd get a peek inside one, since it was starting to look as though she might not get there in the usual way. She'd dumped her most recent boyfriend, Chad Renwick, Jr., when she discovered him attempting the horizontal mambo on the office sofa with his new receptionist four months ago, and she'd had absolutely no prospects since. Not even bad ones.

First things first. Zoey had changed out of the fleece pants and jacket she'd traveled in and stretched out on the giant-size bed, propped up by half a dozen soft pillows. There was a large mirror on the ceiling that she decided to pretend wasn't there. She called Elizabeth to say she'd arrived, accepted the invitation to join the Nugents Saturday night, then called down for room service only to discover it didn't exist.

Figured. She found the phone book and dialed a pizza joint two blocks away that said they'd deliver.

Dawson, Dodson, Donaldson… Zoey leafed through the phone book and let her eye stray down the columns. Donnelly. Hmm. Five Donnellys. The schools were probably populated with all kinds of cute little Donnellys.

Fielding, Furtz—wasn't that the shoemaker who'd been so kind to her father? She'd definitely go see him the next day.

Hanson, Hoare—she recalled how the poor Hoare girls had been teased—Hopewell, Hoskins, Jenkins, Jones, Jonker. That was Elizabeth's mother and dad.

Probably a whole lot of the kids she'd gone to school with had stayed in Stoney Creek. Maybe, with Elizabeth and Mary Ellen in tow, she'd visit some of them while she was here.

As soon as the stores were open the next morning— cold, bright and crystal clear, with the snow-capped Coast Mountains majestic in the west—she'd headed for Mr. Furtz's Saddlery and Shoes. It was exactly as she'd remembered it. Various pieces of dusty leather paraphernalia adorned the street-front window, along with some fancy-stitched cowboy boots, children's sandals, a few samples of out-of-style high-heeled shoes, leather dog leads and harnesses and several trade publications—she made out *Canada Shoe and Boot* and *Leather Forever*—fanned artfully near the window to entice the passerby, their covers pale and sun-bleached.

She pushed open the door with the old-fashioned jangling bell.

"Joey Phillips! My goodness." Mr. Furtz had actually remembered her before she'd had to introduce herself. Zoey felt a warm rush of gratitude. Until then no one she'd seen in town had recognized her. Mr. Furtz pronounced his *j*s with a *y* sound, in the German way, so even the name she'd discarded didn't sound too bad. Yo-ey. "My, my, such a beauty, too," he went on, eyes twinkling. "All you Phillips girls were lovely girls, just like your mother. How is your father, my dear?"

"Just fine. Dad's got a new job, with a municipality in Saskatchewan. Rosetown."

The old man nodded his head vigorously, making the few hairs he'd wound across the top of his mostly bald pate bounce dangerously. "Oh, yah, yah! Good for him. He's a good man, your father. A very fine man."

Zoey felt her eyes water slightly. Most people had regarded her father as a hopeless loser. Mr. Furtz was still smiling broadly when Zoey heard the bell jangle again.

"Oh!" The harness-maker looked up toward the door. "Ah, *there* you are!"

Zoey turned. A tall, dark-haired man, obviously a cowboy of some sort from his dress—worn Wranglers, a broad-brimmed hat, chambray shirt, sheepskin vest, scuffed boots on his feet—had entered the store.

"You mind, my dear?" Mr. Furtz whispered loudly. "A customer—?"

"Please! Go right ahead," Zoey said, stepping back as the customer approached the counter. He seemed vaguely familiar but she was quite sure she'd never met him. One cowboy looked pretty much like another, in her view, and Stoney Creek was full of them. "No hurry. I'm staying in town for several weeks," she said into empty air.

Both men were bent over a piece of equipment on the counter. A little embarrassed, Zoey moved away to inspect the articles on display. Purses, more shoes, Birkenstocks, a whole rack of boots of various kinds. She could feel the stranger's gaze on her back. Her cheeks burned. She turned quickly toward the counter, but he was absorbed in examining whatever piece of horse equipment the shoemaker had repaired for him. She must have imagined it.

"Nice job, Raoul. Very nice work. Hell of a note getting it caught in the binder like that and tore up. I figured I'd have to throw it away."

*Raoul?*

"Never! Something's made of leather, it can be fixed. No problem. That man-made stuff, vinyl, plastic, now that's another story. I—"

"How much?" The stranger reached in his back

pocket and removed several bills from his wallet. He tossed them onto the counter. "That do?"

"Oh, yah. Maybe too much," the shoemaker said doubtfully. "It was an easy job."

"For you, maybe. Take it." The stranger laughed and Zoey felt the sound echo along her ribs. She glanced at him again. He was attractive, in a rough-hewn, serious way. Not knock-down handsome at all. But attractive, nonetheless.

"Yah, yah! Good joke. Ha, ha." The shoemaker rang up the transaction on his old-fashioned cash register. "'Easy for me,' *yah!*"

He handed the customer a receipt and the man slung the bridle onto his right shoulder, giving her a curious glance as he turned away. There was no mistaking it, he *had* looked at her—this time.

That made her feel a bit better somehow. That he'd noticed her at all.

Of course, any stranger in Stoney Creek would stand out to a local. Even on a busy weekend like this, with the town full of hunters and basketball players.

"I've known you all these years, Mr. Furtz, and I never knew your name was Raoul," she said, smiling, when the customer had gone. "Was your mother Spanish or Italian?"

"Oh, no! Austrian, from the Tyrol, like my dad." Mr. Furtz's blue eyes twinkled. "But she was a *romantic* woman, my mama. You know what I mean? Very, very *romantic!*"

POOR MR. FURTZ! Zoey thought now, looking around at the crowded arena. She wondered if he was here.

The entire town and surrounding district of Stoney Creek seemed to have put in an appearance at the volunteer firefighters' dance, which was being held at the curling arena, with sheets of plywood laid out over the ice. She had no idea what his story was. As far as she knew, he'd never married. No wife, no children. But Zoey was sure she knew exactly what he meant when he'd said his mother was *romantic* and she suspected that Mr. Furtz was a romantic at heart, too.

She wasn't particularly romantic herself. She'd always viewed herself as sensible and clearheaded. A smart woman who knew what she wanted and knew how to get it. A risk-taker, but sensible. Impulsive? Sometimes. Adventurous? Always. Romantic? No, that was for teenagers and sentimental old women.

There was a five-dollar "donation" to get into the dance, and a band was tuning up on the makeshift stage when they arrived. She needn't have worried about how she was dressed. Her slim charcoal slacks with the matching jacket and the ivory silk short-sleeved sweater under it were businesslike, yes, but she preferred businesslike to the elaborate confections of skirts and crinolines some women wore. Others had on plain jeans and cowboy boots and, among the younger set, bare tummies and low-rider pants were in evidence, complete with tattoos and body piercings.

Arthur led the way and found a table near the bandstand.

"Drinks?" he mouthed, over the noise, and then disappeared to the refreshment concession. All proceeds—drinks, donations at the door, silent auction items ranged on tables around the rink—went to the local Boys and Girls Club, which was in the process, Elizabeth had told her, of raising funds for a building of its own.

Zoey spotted a dark-haired woman on the other side of the room smiling and madly waving so she waved back.

"Who's that, Lizzie?" she muttered, leaning across Becky. "Over there in the pink shirt?"

"That's Sherry Porter, used to be Rempel—you know her! She was one of the cheerleaders for the basketball team. We never made the squad." Elizabeth laughed and waved, too. Zoey felt pleased that some-one had remembered her. The shoemaker yesterday and now this Sherry Porter, who, she was sorry to say, she could barely recall.

The lights dimmed and the crowd immediately quieted. Zoey noticed Arthur on his way back to their table, balancing a tray filled with glasses.

A man dressed in a white shirt and tie and a rumpled sports jacket had mounted the stage and stood by the microphone.

"Just before the music starts, I want to remind all you folks that every cent raised this evening goes to the Boys and Girls Club." He pushed his glasses higher on his nose.

"The mayor," Elizabeth whispered, leaning toward her. "Herb Trennant, did you know him?"

Zoey shook her head.

"I think he was in Arthur's class," Elizabeth continued and her husband raised a finger to his mouth to shush her. She made an impatient gesture back and returned her attention to the stage.

"I recall moving to Stoney Creek when I was ten and didn't know a soul," the mayor said. "A Boys and Girls Club back then would have made things a little easier," he went on. "Moving to a new town can be a mighty lonely experience. Our own young people who grow up here could use a place like this, too, so be generous, folks! It's for a good cause."

The crowd clapped and the band struck up a Shania Twain tune, "Whose Bed Have Your Boots Been Under?" and people began to take to the dance floor. The mayor's words had struck a deep chord in Zoey. She remembered so well the feeling of being alone and new at school, a stranger in town. It had happened so many times. Youth could be highly overrated; she wouldn't be fifteen again for anything.

"Dance, Lizzie?" Arthur bent gallantly over his wife's hand. "You're next, Becky," he addressed his daughter with a grin and she giggled. "You, too, Zoey. You can get in line."

At that moment, Zoey spotted Ryan Donnelly pushing through the crowd, headed toward their table. Her heart lodged in her throat. She'd just been thinking she wouldn't be a teenager again—and here, standing practically in front of her, was one of the reasons.

"Lizzie!"

Elizabeth turned, still holding her husband's hand.

"Yes? Oh, Ryan, I didn't see you here." Elizabeth shot a triumphant glance Zoey's way.

Up close, Ryan was even handsomer than he was from a distance. His eyes, blue as the summer sky, were vivid and expressive. His hair, a rich tawny color, was neatly trimmed. He had on a dark blue shirt and black jeans, cowboy style.

"Hey, listen," he said, with a warm glance at Zoey. "I saw you in the hotel." He grinned, still the grin that could melt a girl's bones. "Who's your friend, Lizzie? Introduce me."

Zoey wanted to sink into one of the cracks in the ancient wooden fold-up she was sitting on. Ryan Donnelly hadn't recognized her in the restaurant! Had she changed *that* much? Or had she meant so little that he'd completely forgotten her in the ten years she'd been gone?

"*Friend?* You're kidding, right?"

Ryan shook his head. He looked truly mystified. Arthur was grinning.

"For Pete's sake, Ryan, that's Zoey Phillips—don't you remember Joey *Phillips?* You went out with her!"

## CHAPTER TWO

RYAN STARED at Zoey. Her face, then the rest of her. Zoey felt her cheeks burn all the way down to her toes.

Then, with a shout of laughter, he pulled her into his arms. "So it is! Well, well. Man alive, little Joey Phillips!" And he kissed her—right on the mouth! Zoey nearly fell over, she was so surprised. "Welcome home, Joey. Welcome back to Stoney Creek. You stickin' around for a while? I sure hope so. Man, have you turned into some kinda babe!"

"About a month," Zoey said, her face still burning. *Babe!* "If I can find a place to stay, that is. They're kicking me out of the hotel on Friday. By the way, I changed my name. Decided Zoey was a little more grown-up." She knew she was babbling. Ryan's greeting had totally unnerved her.

"No kidding!" Ryan's gaze hadn't shifted. He was giving her a look of admiration she'd rarely seen from him before. Certainly not directed at *her*. "Zoey. *Zoey* Phillips."

He glanced around. Zoey noticed that the man and child who'd been with Ryan in the hotel restaurant had followed him to the table. "Hey! This is my brother's little girl, Melissa. Lissy, we call her." He patted the child on her head. "And this is my brother, Cameron. Cam? You remember the Phillips girls? Bunch of good-lookin' redheads? Maybe you knew some of Zoey's older sisters?"

The man she'd seen at the shoemaker's nodded. He seemed a little out of sorts. Annoyed. The little girl with them immediately began chattering to the two Nugent girls.

"Hey, these seats taken?" Ryan addressed Arthur, who shrugged.

"Go ahead, Ry. Sit down. I was just going to dance with my wife. Give you and Zoey a chance to get reaquainted." He winked at her. Honestly! He was as bad as Lizzie.

Ryan's brother frowned. "I'll go get us some drinks if we're going to be parking ourselves here." He didn't exactly sound enthusiastic.

"Sure, sure!" Ryan pulled out a chair and sat down, reaching across the table to clasp Zoey's hands, his blue gaze riveted on her. He was a toucher, all right. She remembered that from ten years ago. A very physical guy. She was still stunned, her heart beating a mile a minute. He hadn't forgotten her; it was just that she'd changed so much—looked so *good*—he hadn't recognized her.

Not in her wildest dreams had she—

"I can't believe it! And now I hear Mary Ellen's coming to town to spend some time with Edith." Edith Owen was Mary Ellen's stepmother, who was marrying her neighbor after many years as a widow.

"Yes. She'll be here this week. I can hardly wait.

Mary Ellen asked me to help with Edith's wedding. That's why I'm here, really.''

''You two used to be good friends, right?'' He was so close Zoey could smell the warm, manly scent of his aftershave, faintly woodsy, faintly citrus, could see the tanned crinkles around his eyes. Ryan Donnelly had always smiled a lot. If anything, ten years suited him. He was definitely handsomer than she'd remembered. To think that she'd once dated him! Well...sort of.

''Best friends,'' Zoey said, then added loyally, ''Elizabeth, too. But Mary Ellen was the first person I met when we moved to Stoney Creek.''

''Well, son of a gun.'' Ryan grinned. ''We'll have to get together, the three of us. We had some good times back then, didn't we, babe?'' Was he thinking of the kisses in the Rialto, as she was? Zoey nodded mutely, feeling every bit the gauche teenager she'd once been.

''Listen.'' He squeezed her hand. ''We'll have to have a few dances, for old times' sake, huh? I promised Lissy I'd dance with her first.'' He glanced at the little blond girl with the china-blue eyes who was standing at the table, sharing a drink with Tessa. Arthur had brought lemonades for the children. Lissy's father hadn't returned yet. ''Okay, honey?''

The ''honey'' was for his niece, Zoey realized after a split second. Then she was sitting alone at the table, with the two Nugent girls. Arthur and Elizabeth were dancing—somewhere, Zoey couldn't see them on the crowded dance floor. Ryan had whirled off dramatically, his niece clinging to his neck, her short blond hair flying. The girl seemed to be about Tessa's age, four or five.

"You okay here?" Ryan's brother—what was his name again?—appeared at the table and put down two paper cups of beer and a can of Pepsi. This time he was accompanied by the blond woman who'd been at the Gold Dust Café earlier. He didn't introduce her. Zoey nodded automatically, a little confused, and he headed immediately for the dance floor, hand-in-hand with the blonde. The band had segued into an old Hank Williams tune, a two-step.

Zoey watched Ryan's brother put his arms around his partner, smile at her and start moving to the music. He was a decent dancer. Most cowboys were. He glanced back briefly and Zoey stared at the wall, avoiding eye contact. The wife? Must be. A nice-looking woman, wearing a green print dress. The type men usually went for—lots of hair and big boobs.

Zoey studied the pair from the corner of her eye as they moved away. He was about the same height as Ryan, maybe an inch taller. A little heavier build, broader shoulders. He was obviously older if he'd known her sisters. She hadn't met any of Ryan's family; their pretend romance hadn't gotten that far.

Imagine! The customer she'd seen in Mr. Furtz's shoe repair shop, the man who'd ignored her—although she'd been pretty sure she felt some interest there for a second or two, which was weird, considering he was obviously married—turning out to be Ryan's brother.

Wait until she told Charlotte and Lydia. Small town life was just *too* full of coincidences!

RYAN RETURNED to the table with his giggling niece. He took Zoey's hand and bowed low over it. The other two girls were jumping up and down. "My turn!" Tessa yelled.

"Zoey first and then you, Tess," he said firmly. "Then Becky."

"Oh, no!" Zoey said, coloring. "I couldn't leave the girls here all alone."

"Why not?" Ryan shrugged. "They're fine. There's plenty of neighbors around. Hell, here's Cam, he'll sit with the kids."

As he led her onto the floor, he said something to his brother. Cameron looked at her, over Ryan's shoulder, and Zoey got the funniest sensation. That he didn't approve? What possible business was it of his, if Ryan danced with her?

Just then Elizabeth and Arthur came back and Becky launched herself at her father. "My turn, Daddy! My turn!"

Elizabeth fanned her flushed face and waved gaily at Zoey as she sat down. Zoey knew exactly what her friend was thinking. That she and Ryan had hit it off. That there was suddenly the excitement of romance in the crisp, cold air of the Fullerton Valley. That Zoey, unmarried at twenty-eight and probably, in Elizabeth's view, pretty near over the hill, could do a heck of a lot worse. That it was no coincidence that Zoey's old heartthrob was unmarried and very, very eligible. That, indeed, this was not only serendipity—it could even be fate.

Ryan was a good dancer, just as Zoey remembered. He held her close and her head swam. Everything about him was so familiar and yet so very, very strange.

"Where are you living these days, Zoey?"

"Toronto."

He whistled. "The big city, huh?"

She didn't say anything. She was normally an excellent dancer but for some reason she was having trouble keeping in step with him. Nerves?

"Hey! Remember the time we drove out to Varley's old barn and had a picnic, you and me and Adele and that guy she was going with—what the hell was his name?"

Zoey nodded. "Burke Goodall, wasn't it?"

"That's it! Burke the Jerk, I always thought of him." She felt his right arm tighten around her shoulders. "I was always crazy about Adele, remember that?"

Did she! "Whatever happened? You two ever get together?" Zoey hoped her question sounded nonchalant. It was a question she'd agonized about for a long time, even after she'd left Stoney Creek.

Ryan's face clouded, and he sighed. "No. Just one of those things, I guess. For a while there—" He shrugged, then went on. "Hell, it wasn't meant to be, I guess. Enough about me. What about you—married?"

"No."

"Boyfriend?"

"No."

"What? Good-looking lady like you?" He hugged her and Zoey thought she'd burst with pleasure and pride. He meant it, he actually meant it!

"Not that I believe you for a minute, but—"

"Hey, believe it. You were always a pretty little thing, but, damn, you're gorgeous now."

*Pretty little thing?* No way! Zoey didn't think she could stand much more of this. She was glad when the dance ended and Becky materialized beside them, tugging at Ryan's shirt. "My turn now!"

Elizabeth wanted to leave after the next dance. Tessa had obviously been crying; Zoey had no idea what *that* was about, either. Kids! At one time, she might've been annoyed that they had to go but tonight she welcomed the opportunity. Her head was spinning—worse than before.

"I'm just going to check out the silent auction, okay?" She might as well drop some more money while she was here. It was all for a good cause, as the mayor had reminded them.

"Sure. Fifteen minutes?" Elizabeth glanced at her watch.

"Fine."

Zoey moved along the line of products and services displayed on the paper-covered tables at the back of the room, pausing occasionally to mark down her bid, leaving Elizabeth's phone number for a contact since she didn't know where she'd be when the hotel threw her out. Looking for another place was next on her to-do list. She'd been invited to stay at the Nugents', but Elizabeth's offer, while kind, was impossible. She needed peace and quiet.

Okay. Twenty bucks for a manicure. That was a deal. Fifteen for a string of Christmas lights—she'd give those to Elizabeth if she won. Twenty-seven dol-

lars for a sack of premium dog food. Elizabeth and
Arthur had a big black Labrador that probably ate
them out of house and home.

"Ma'am?"

"Yes?" To her shock, it was Ryan's brother, hovering behind her right shoulder.

"Care to dance?"

# CHAPTER THREE

ZOEY SCRIBBLED on a piece of notepaper she'd found inside the desk in her room.

Greetings from the Fullerton Valley!
Lydia: You'll *never* guess. I ran into my first love—remember I told you about Ryan Donnelly, the great-looking rancher?—yesterday. Already! He was at a dance I went to with Elizabeth and her family. Here's the best news—he's single and he thinks I'm gorgeous! Nice change, huh? Oh, I also met his brother (didn't know he had one) plus a niece. The hotel is chucking me out this week and I might have to stay with Elizabeth until I can find something else. When you hear from Charlotte, pass on my news. Wonder if she's met *her* first love yet? Bet I got you both beat! I'll keep you posted.

Luv, Zoey

P.S. Haven't even had time to look at the manuscript—too much going on!

MARY ELLEN ARRIVED Monday night, and Elizabeth and Zoey met her for lunch the next day at the trendy—for Stoney Creek—Martha's Grainery, a fern-draped, health-menu establishment at the corner of Tremont and Main Street.

Mary Ellen, who'd worked for a travel agency for six years and had recently left it to open her own business, a bed-and-breakfast inn on Vancouver Island, was the same shy, warmhearted girl she'd always been. The Osprey's Nest—so-named, she told them, because it perched all alone on a hilltop overlooking Georgia Strait—was closed for the winter season, just like Zoey's hotel.

With no makeup and dressed in sneakers, jeans and a red silk shirt, Mary Ellen didn't look much older than she had in high school.

"So, any news on the man front?" Zoey thought they ought to get straight down to business. "Not you, Elizabeth, you're married—unless you've got some suggestions for us."

Elizabeth laughed, but Zoey thought she sounded pleased. Marriage, husband, children. In Elizabeth's eyes, she had it all. And Zoey had to agree; if you were going to live in a small town like Stoney Creek, you might as well be married. What was there to do for singles?

"No," Mary Ellen said, with a small shrug. She picked up one half of the shrimp-and-cheese-stuffed croissant she'd ordered. "Too busy these days. You?"

"Same." Zoey attacked her vegetarian burger, wishing she'd ordered some fries. Elizabeth looked content with her huge Caesar salad and grilled chicken breast.

"Speaking of men, you'll never guess who we ran into on Saturday?"

"We?" Mary Ellen raised her eyebrow, mouth full.

"Lizzie and me." She leaned forward. "Ryan Donnelly! Remember him?"

Zoey thought Mary Ellen seemed a little flustered, but maybe that was just because she was swallowing. "Of course I remember Ryan," she said. "Didn't you spill several buckets of tears over him, mostly on my shoulder?"

"Yeah." Zoey was perfectly aware that her friend was teasing. Mary Ellen knew as well as Zoey did that Ryan had never had any real interest in her, only as a stooge to make Adele Martinez jealous. "Did you know he almost married Adele? That's what Lizzie says. She ran off before the wedding. Jilted him."

"No!" Mary Ellen looked genuinely shocked. "That poor man!"

"Yes. And of course Lizzie—" they both turned to their good friend, Zoey with a grin and Mary Ellen with an expression of dismay "—knows *everything*."

It was true. Elizabeth knew who was in town and who wasn't and why they'd left and when they'd be back, if ever. She knew the price of beef and how much a new teacher made in the Stoney Creek district and that washing soda was a perfectly good substitute for detergent in the laundry. She bottled and preserved and made her own Christmas presents and sewed all her girls' clothing, as well as running a busy seasonal craft business specializing in candles and fridge magnets.

She was Fullerton Valley's own blend of Ann Landers and Martha Stewart.

Zoey had realized right away that Elizabeth was a wealth of local information and could steer her clear of any *faux pas* she might otherwise make in this small community. If the mayor's wife was sleeping with the fire chief, Zoey wanted to know.

"Yep." Zoey loaded her fork with alfalfa and black radish sprouts. They were dressed with a raspberry vinaigrette, quite tasty. "Ryan was with his brother and niece. Say, what's with the brother?" She turned from one to the other. "Weird. He asked me to dance and then never said a word the whole time we were dancing. Except once. I asked what his wife's name was and he said he didn't have a wife. End of conversation. He has the most darling little girl, though. He's your basic tall, dark and handsome type, but nowhere near as handsome as Ryan. You ever meet him?"

Mary Ellen shook her head. "I don't think so. Never mind him, what happened with Ryan and Adele?"

"They went out for a while right after high school and Ryan wanted to marry her. They were too young, of course. I don't think Ryan was twenty-one." Elizabeth set down her wineglass. "Anyway, the wedding was all planned and everything and then, bingo, she dumped him. Left him high and dry—"

*"No!"*

"Yes. It was quite a scandal around here. No one ever thought anything like that would happen to Ryan Donnelly. But, to tell you the truth, I don't believe she was ever in love with him. She'd been seeing some older guy, a married man, before she changed her mind and said yes to Ryan."

Mary Ellen's eyes were huge. "What happened?"

"Don't know. She never showed up for the wedding. Took off for Vancouver. I heard she had a baby seven months later." Elizabeth gave Mary Ellen a penetrating look, as though daring her to add it up. "A little boy."

"Oh, Elizabeth! Maybe it was Ryan's," Mary Ellen said in a stricken voice. Zoey glanced over her shoulder. She hoped no one was listening in on their conversation.

"You really think so?" Elizabeth gave them both an "oh, don't be dumb" look. "If so, why did loverboy leave his wife and run off to Vancouver to join the new mom and baby? Maybe he couldn't count, either. Anyway, it was a big fuss and I don't think Ryan's parents ever really recovered but—" Elizabeth took a sip from her water glass "—what did they expect?"

Zoey leaned across the table, desperately curious. "What do you mean?"

"The Donnellys are not lucky in love," Elizabeth said darkly. "They never have been. Ryan *or* his brother. Or most of the cousins, for that matter."

"So, what happened to *him?* Ryan's brother?'' Not that she cared much. He'd been an old stick when they danced and after the initial surprise, she had the feeling he was checking her over on behalf of his brother. Like some piece of ranch machinery they were considering putting a bid on! Ryan was the one she felt sorry for. Left at the altar, just like in a bad novel.

"Same thing. Although in his case they were actually married and had a baby. That's Lissy, of course. His wife wasn't from around here,'' Elizabeth said, as if that explained a lot. "I heard he met her in a bar. She took off with the baby, then came back two years ago and dumped her in Cameron's lap. He's not much for women anymore although quite a few have tried to change his mind, including, lately, one of the new teachers in town.''

"The blonde they were with on Saturday?'' Zoey was itching with curiosity. Who said nothing ever happened in small towns!

"That's the one. Sara Rundle. Cameron generally leaves the lady stuff to his brother. Ryan's never changed. He likes women. Arthur told me Cam's hauled him out of quite a few scrapes over the past few years. Of course, Arthur wouldn't tell me what *kind* of scrapes but I can guess.''

"Funny neither of them left the valley, considering their experiences here,'' Mary Ellen murmured. "Started over somewhere new.''

"Not everyone wants to leave the Cariboo, you know.'' Elizabeth stared at her with something approaching disapproval. "You and Zoey did, but there's a lot of us who stuck around." Zoey thought she sounded a little defensive.

"Are they on the Donnelly place?"

"No. Family ranch was sold when the folks retired a few years back and moved to Kelowna. Leave it to his boys? Old Man Donnelly didn't have any soft spots and if he did, no one ever found 'em, that's what Arthur says." Elizabeth laughed and shook her head. "What a bunch! No, they're west of town, paying down a brand-new mortgage. At least, Cam is. Ryan works for him, and their aunt, Marty Hainsworth, lives with them, kind of takes care of the little girl. Hey, is this too complicated for you?"

Mary Ellen smiled and shook her head and reached for the menu. Zoey had been thinking of the crème caramel. She hoped it wasn't made with soy milk. "Edith's told me bits and pieces over the years," Mary Ellen said. "She never mentioned the Ryan and Adele thing. What happened to her? Anyone ever hear?"

"The unnamed married man went back to his wife and family. They moved away. Some say Adele's a high-class call girl now, but I don't believe it. Small-minded people with not much imagination say *that*," Elizabeth sniffed. "Someone told me she was a model. Makes sense. All she ever cared about was clothes and hair." They all smiled, remembering.

"Hey, good for her. Looks don't last." Elizabeth sat back and rested her fork and knife diagonally across her plate. "Use 'em while you got 'em, that's what Mum always said."

"I feel sorry for Ryan," Mary Ellen said softly. That was one of the things Zoey loved about her friend—she was so loyal. So caring, so sensitive.

Zoey examined her own feelings for Ryan. She'd been thrilled when they'd met, no question. Even after ten years, her pulse had ricocheted all over the place. *He'd called her gorgeous!* Of course, he'd always been a flirt. Still, maybe now that Adele was definitely out of the picture...

Zoey was happy with her situation but she wanted a partner in life, children one day. Back when she was twenty, she used to tell Charlotte and Lydia that if she hadn't met anyone she felt strongly about by the time she was twenty-eight, she'd start looking. Well, she was *nearly* twenty-eight....

"Forget the Donnellys! Let's talk about Edith and the wedding," Zoey said suddenly, picking up the menu Mary Ellen had put down. "You're right, Lizzie, this place sounds more complicated than a soap opera."

"It can be," Elizabeth said serenely. "If you believe half of what you hear, and I do. Just 'cause we're small town doesn't mean we're boring. Hand over that menu, Zoe. You two feel like dessert?"

TWO DAYS LATER, Zoey was sitting at the beat-up fake mahogany desk beside the window in her hotel room, trying to decipher a particularly bad patch of her author's handwriting. Despite making a ton of money,

Jamie Chinchilla was cheap and persisted on writing down the margins of her badly typed manuscript and occasionally on both sides of the paper. Sometimes Zoey wanted to scream. She was glad she was paid top dollar to wrestle each manuscript into shape before it went to New York.

The hotel had told her she'd have to be out the following afternoon. She'd given up trying to find a decent place on such short notice and had reluctantly decided she'd have to accept Elizabeth's offer of her guest room, for now. Edith and Mary Ellen had no extra room and the two motels in town were totally unsuitable. Arthur had said he'd put out the word with his business associates. Someone was bound to know of a cottage or a short-term apartment rental. Four weeks, that was all she needed until the wedding.

A rap at the door had her sitting up straight. She wasn't expecting anyone. She waited until the polite rap sounded a second time, then put down her pen.

"Hello?"

Cameron Donnelly stood in the hall, a look of unease on his face, his hat in his hand. "Hello, ma'am. I'd like to see you for a few moments. May I come in?"

"Come in?" Zoey echoed like a speech-impaired parrot. She opened the door a bit wider. "Why, certainly. Come in and sit down." She hoped she sounded gracious. What she felt was surprised. Cameron Donnelly stepped forward and she shut the door behind him.

Omigod, the place was a disaster. For company, anyway. She'd made the bed, in a fashion, but she had the manuscript spread all over the bedspread and desk, damp panty hose hanging from the old-fashioned radiator by the other window, a half-eaten bag of Fritos open by the phone and she was dressed—just barely— in her favorite working costume of tights and a Toronto Maple Leafs jersey. Her hair was a mess.

"I won't take up much of your time, Miss Phillips."

He was so proper and old-fashioned it hurt. "Please call me Zoey," she invited. "It's my name."

He cracked a smile. "Zoey, ma'am. I won't stay long but I do have something I'd like to put to you."

"Sit down, please!" She cleared a cardigan sweater off the back of the loveseat that, together with the upholstered chair and low scratched coffee table, formed the sitting area to one side of the room. Nothing disguised the size of the bed, though, or the mirror on the ceiling.

He sat down on the loveseat. She whipped a magazine off the seat of the chair opposite him and sat down, too. What in the world could this be about? She'd met him once, danced with him for one short dance and they'd exchanged about seven words.

He looked around the room silently for what seemed like ages. "So this is the honeymoon suite."

"Yes. It's all they had available." She cleared her throat.

"I see." Cameron looked around again, and this time Zoey noted that he'd spotted the mirror on the ceiling. He studied it, then glanced at her. She felt the heat rise in her face. "I, uh, I've never been in one quite like this," he said finally.

"Me, neither!" It was an icebreaker. "In fact, I've never been in one at all." Time to change the subject. "How are things at the ranch?"

"Fine."

"Your daughter? Melissa? She's all right?"

"Oh, yes. She's in kindergarten this year." He nodded slowly, the proud daddy trying not to show any emotion. Zoey felt her heart squeeze. She was dying to ask about Melissa's mother but didn't dare; she was hardly on personal enquiry terms with him.

"Ryan?"

"He's okay." Cameron met her eyes and took a deep breath. "I, uh, wondered if you'd had any luck finding a place to stay? Arthur mentioned that you're looking."

Zoey felt a surge of relief. *That* was all! "Well, no, I haven't. I checked out a couple of bungalow rentals, but they were quite dreadful. The motel at the edge of town has a room, but I can't say I'm crazy about it, either. The ceiling has cracks and there were bugs in the bathroom. The other motel was—yuck!"

She shuddered dramatically, remembering the horror of finding half a dozen beetles scrabbling about the corners of the shower stall.

He looked skeptical. "That bad?"

"Really!" She paused, then added, "I might stay

with the Nugents for a few days until something turns up.''

''I see,'' Cameron said thoughtfully.

''I'm just wondering why—you know, why you ask?'' Zoey said, leaning forward. Did he know of a rental? If he did, couldn't he simply come to the point?

''I can suggest a place,'' he said, appearing more ill at ease than ever.

''*You* can? Why—why, that's wonderful! I'd be prepared to pay any—''

''Never mind rent,'' he said gruffly. ''This is free, if you want it—''

''Oh, I couldn't!''

''Wait until you hear what I have to say. You might not be so interested.''

Zoey stared at the man sitting across from her. He was certainly attractive, in a rough, outdoorsy kind of way. It was just that next to his brother he'd seemed rather...ordinary. Unexeptional. He had nice eyes, a sort of warm hazel, and thick, dark hair. Good teeth.

Zoey slapped herself mentally for letting her attention wander. ''Do go on. Tell me what this is about.''

''Well, we have a little apartment at the ranch, self-contained, that we built over the garage when Marty—that's our aunt—first moved out here. Then Ryan joined us. He'd had, well—well, he'd had some bad luck and needed a place to live.''

''You mean after his marriage fell through?'' She couldn't help it; she took some satisfaction in meeting the situation head-on. She hated beating around the bush, although she suspected Cameron Donnelly preferred it. Did he think he was sparing her feelings? Was he even aware that she and Ryan had had some history, pathetic though it was?

He frowned at her for a second or two. "Well, no. It was quite a few years after that."

When he said nothing more on the topic of his brother's aborted marriage, Zoey muttered, rather sheepishly, "Elizabeth told me about it."

"I see." He paused and gave her a stare that clearly said: women talk too much. "Ryan went to Alberta after the wedding fell through. He worked on the rigs and did some cowboying south of Calgary before he came back here." He shrugged. "Ryan never moved into the apartment. Nor did Marty. The place is empty."

He glanced at the mirrored ceiling again. It was like a two-ton elephant in the room; it couldn't be ignored. Zoey bit her tongue, knowing he'd eventually continue.

"If you're interested..."

"Oh, definitely!" Zoey blushed. What luck. Peace and quiet and nothing much to do out there in the country. The more she'd thought about it since she'd arrived in Stoney Creek, the more she wondered if there might not be some real basis to the feelings between her and Ryan all those years ago. Perhaps with Adele Martinez muddying the waters, that attraction—if any—had never had a chance to flourish.

"I, uh—" he shot a worried glance at her "—I

wouldn't feel right if I didn't tell you the whole truth. I've got another reason for offering you the apartment. It's to do with you and my brother.''

Zoey sat straight up in her chair. ''And that is?''

''I know he used to see a fair bit of you in high school. Now you're back and—well, I don't need to tell you you're a very beautiful woman. Very, uh, impressive. My brother, I believe, is still sweet on you…'' He paused, studying her as though to see how she'd taken his information.

*Impressive!* She was glad he'd noticed, but couldn't help thinking he was describing her more the way he would a new crescent wrench or a reliable snowblower than a woman.

And trying to match her up with Ryan—she was so embarrassed! *Sweet* on her? Ryan, obviously, had never told his brother that he'd used Zoey as a pawn in a ploy to snag another girl. ''D-do you really think so?''

''I do.'' Cameron Donnelly nodded. ''In fact, I *know* he's interested in you. He as much as told me so. He's talked about you nonstop since the dance, you and this Mary Ellen. And I was thinking, well, if the interest ran both ways, it might be handier for the two of you if you were right there, on the spot, so—''

''So we could—what, fool around?'' She'd realized what he was proposing. He had no inkling, of course, that *she'd* been thinking along the same lines. Somehow it seemed a lot worse when it came from him.

Cameron had a strange look on his face. ''I didn't

mean that, ma'am. Not at all. 'Course you *are* adults. No one would care much." He shrugged broad shoulders. "I just figured, well, maybe you still liked him, and things might work out this time."

"'Work out.' You mean, as in…forever? Love? Marriage? Kids? The whole nine yards?" Zoey couldn't believe she was having this conversation. If Charlotte and Lydia could see her now. If Elizabeth could see her!

"That's jumping ahead some, but as a matter of fact, yes, that's *exactly* what I'm hoping. Ryan's been at loose ends. He doesn't have his heart in ranching, although he pulls his share. I'm not complaining. He's got a good head for numbers. I believe he's ready to settle down, maybe go into business on his own."

"Move out?"

"Yeah. Get married, move out, start a family. He's pushing thirty. He's not a kid anymore. He sees a lot of women but nothing ever seems to come of it. Marty would like to move on, too. She feels kind of responsible for Ryan, though, and until something happens with him—" Cameron shook his head. "She's always talking about going off and traveling with her sister."

This was a very long speech for Cameron Donnelly, Zoey guessed.

"Sounds like you're the one who needs the wife!" she quipped.

He flushed darkly and, remembering what Elizabeth had told her about his marriage, Zoey wished she'd kept her big mouth shut.

"No," he said softly, looking away from her, toward the window. "I'd hire someone to help me with my little girl, if necessary. That's not the problem."

Zoey felt like a heel. She took a deep breath and pasted a bright smile on her face. "So you're thinking I might be a good prospect for your brother?" It was crazy even talking like this!

"You'd be a good prospect for any man," he said seriously. *Politely.* "Definitely for my brother. It's just an idea I had, ma'am—"

"Zoey."

"Zoey." He grinned, and suddenly Zoey had a completely different impression of him. Maybe he had a sense of humor. He was attractive when he smiled. Handsome, even. Well, after all, he was a Donnelly.

He put on his hat and stood. "You think it over and let me know."

Zoey stood, too. "I have to be honest, Cameron, and tell you that your idea is quite far-fetched. I have a good life in Toronto. I'm here temporarily. Contrary to what you probably think, I'm not exactly desperate to find a man and get married…although, of course, I have an open mind."

"Okay, forget the romance. Maybe it's a dumb idea. The place is available, though, and Marty would appreciate the female company. If anything happens between you and my brother, well, it happens. Let's leave it at that."

"Fine," Zoey said and he met her eyes directly. She

had a strange sensation in her stomach, like she'd had when he'd laughed in Mr. Furtz's store.

"Fine?"

She smiled. "You've talked me into it. I'm intrigued. I admit I had a crush on your brother in high school, but, that was ten years ago. Things change, right?"

His glance drifted from her face to her breasts, the hem of her jersey and lower. He seemed about to say something, but didn't; instead, he opened the hall door. "Yeah, things change. What time shall I come for you?"

"Make it just after noon tomorrow. I'll be packed up and waiting."

"I'll be here." He put on his hat and nodded. He looked one hundred percent serious again. The steady older brother. "You can depend on me."

## CHAPTER FOUR

*YES*, ZOEY THOUGHT, leaning against the closed door after he'd gone. Yes, somehow she knew she *could* depend on Cameron Donnelly. Boring, steady, reliable. The kind of man you'd like on your side in a difficult situation.

Especially when you have something as difficult—ridiculous!—as rekindling a romance with his brother on your mind. Zoey moved, went to the window in time to see him cross the street and get into his truck. He didn't glance up.

His proposition to her was probably just one more entry to be crossed off on his list this morning. If she'd said no, he'd just have moved on to his next item of business. It wasn't as though he *really* thought she was perfect for Ryan, just that she was on the spot. An opportunity, that was all she was. A happy coincidence.

As she'd told the elder Mr. Donnelly, she was not on the hunt for a man to complete her life. But, on the other hand, she wasn't averse to it either. Maybe Cameron was right. Maybe something *could* happen between her and Ryan.

As Elizabeth had told her point-blank a few days ago, she could do worse. She *had* done worse. Visions of her last boyfriend—hogging the conversation at parties, glancing in the rearview mirror to check his hair before getting out of the car—came instantly to mind. The worst of it was, she'd actually been prepared to put up with his vanity…until the day she'd caught him *in flagrante delicto* on his office sofa.

What did that say about her?

Ryan had been different, even at eighteen. Warm, loving, friendly. Considerate. And if it hadn't been real love back then, it had sure *felt* like real love.

She remembered the agony when she'd first fallen for him, when he didn't even know she existed. Then the utter delight that he'd chosen her—*her!*—to make Adele jealous and the overwhelming despair when he stopped calling. Endless tearful sessions with Mary Ellen, the quiet soothing voice of her mother, telling her not to take on so, there were as many men as there were fish in the sea. She remembered screaming that she didn't *want* fish in the sea, she wanted Ryan Donnelly!

She'd never thought of looking him up again until that conversation at the Jasper Park Lodge last spring. But Mary Ellen's invitation to return to Stoney Creek meant their paths were bound to cross. Fate? Maybe. Stranger things had happened.

If there was still a romantic spark that could be fanned to life, as Ryan's brother seemed to think—who was she to take the high road?

They were all adults now, as Cameron had reminded her. Not teens anymore, wearing their hearts on their sleeves. Pursuing a flirtation with Ryan would be fun, she decided suddenly—fun and not terribly risky at all. Regardless of what came of it, no one would get hurt.

Either way, wouldn't it be a knock-out story to take back to the Jasper Park Lodge reunion next year?

WITH THE VISIT from Cameron Donnelly, plus her determination to get through the first chapter of the Chinchilla manuscript, Zoey missed lunch entirely. At two o'clock, she decided to take a break and drive out to Edith Owen's place, three miles outside town along the river. She grabbed a sandwich from a takeout deli and drove with the radio turned up full blast, singing along to Nellie Furtado as she drove.

Edith lived in a double-wide trailer on a big open lot. There used to be a small three-room log house in that location, long since demolished, where Mary Ellen had lived as a child. Widowed twelve years earlier, Edith Owen was remarrying, a surprise romance with her neighbor, a retired army man, according to Mary Ellen, a tireless fisherman and a lifelong bachelor.

Edith wanted a quiet civil ceremony and had no idea that Mary Ellen was planning a big party for the whole town. Zoey was going to help with the planning and, most importantly, bake the wedding cake. Call-a-Girl had catered a number of small weddings, and Zoey had helped Lydia with the cakes many times. She'd never made one entirely on her own, and was a little nervous at the prospect.

Zoey was dying to meet Tom Bennett, Edith's fiancé. He must be quite a man, Zoey thought, knowing how madly in love Edith had been with Mary Ellen's father. And what had entered a long-term bachelor's mind to change his circumstances at this time in life? she wondered. Mary Ellen's stepmother was in her mid-fifties, and Zoey guessed Tom Bennett must be of a similar age. Plus, Edith was wheelchair-bound most of the time these days, suffering from spinal stenosis, a crippling long-term spinal condition.

*True love.* Must be. You never knew where it would show up, she thought, signaling for the turnoff that led to the Owens' place. Tom and Edith or—look at her. Who'd have guessed she'd even contemplate blowing on the embers of her long-ago romance with Ryan Donnelly?

Edith's yard was tidy but plain, no flower beds or any kind of landscaping that took extra attention. At this time of year, the grass was brown, with occasional patches of snow under the trees and in dips and hollows, all that remained after the last snowfall, a week ago, Elizabeth had told her. The trees were bare.

Because of her condition, Edith relied on her neighbors for help. Tom Bennett, who lived in a small house nearby, had kept her lawns mowed and her table supplied with trout, as well as vegetables from his small garden. In the fall, Mary Ellen said, he brought her fresh game for her freezer.

"Hi!" Zoey got out of the car and locked it. Mary Ellen was standing by the frame porch, holding an armload of firewood.

"This is a nice surprise!" Mary Ellen called.

"Come in. Edith just put on the kettle for a pot of tea. She'll be delighted to see you."

Zoey followed her. The porch door opened directly onto the kitchen, a warm and welcoming room, with two cats sleeping in a tumble on an upholstered rocker. The furnishings were simple and the tiled floor was spotlessly clean.

"Zoey!" Edith held up both arms and Zoey hugged her. Zoey thought she'd lost quite a lot of weight since she'd seen her last, which had to be when she and Mary Ellen were still in high school.

"How lovely to see you, Edith!"

"Sit down. Have a cup of tea."

Zoey sat as Edith busied herself in the kitchen, pouring the tea and getting milk out of the refrigerator. She was very adept at moving her chair around. Zoey noted the collection of framed photographs on the wall—landscapes and family pictures, including the wedding photo of Edith and Morris Owen, Mary Ellen's father. Edith had always been an avid amateur photographer when finances permitted.

"Congratulations on your engagement, Edith. I'm so pleased for you."

She blushed prettily. "Oh, some say I'm too old for this. But Tom and I will be very happy, I know. He's a very fine man."

Morris Owen had been killed in a logging accident. Zoey remembered the horrifying news as it spread through town, into the high school where a teacher had beckoned Mary Ellen from the cafeteria to the principal's office so he could break the news privately.

Mary Ellen had been devastated. Her father had raised her on his own until he'd met Edith Lowry, a thin, pale woman a little older than he was and originally from Vancouver, working in the Stoney Creek Rexall Drugs. They'd been happily married for four years, and all the while, Edith's condition had gradually sapped her strength. After her husband's death, Edith had eked out a living making and selling handicrafts, working for telemarketers from her home and spending her husband's Worker's Compensation settlement, penny by frugal penny. Somehow, she'd managed to finish raising his daughter, to arrange for Mary Ellen's education and to keep her house and property.

Mary Ellen loved Edith like the mother she couldn't remember. More than anything, Zoey knew, Mary Ellen wanted to give her stepmother a wonderful wedding.

"You find a place yet, Zoey?" Mary Ellen called from the living room, where she'd dumped her load of firewood by the fireplace. She joined them at the kitchen table.

"Well, sort of. You'll never guess who made me an offer I couldn't refuse." Zoey stirred her tea vigorously.

Mary Ellen shook her head. "No idea."

"Cameron Donnelly! He says they've got an apartment out there built over a garage or something, and I can stay in it while I'm here."

Mary Ellen had looked a little startled at her announcement. "You're going to take it?"

Zoey stared at her. "Of course I am!" She reached for a cookie on the plate that Edith had shoved across the table. "It's perfect. I can work on my book in peace and—" she winked at Mary Ellen "—who knows?" She hummed a few bars of "Young Love."

Mary Ellen didn't say anything. After a few seconds, she looked directly at Zoey. "You don't mean, you know—you and Ryan again?"

"Hey, I'm just joking. What's past is past and a good thing, too."

"Amen," Edith said quietly. "More tea?"

Zoey refused, and half an hour later, said goodbye. She'd wanted to see Edith and let Mary Ellen know where she'd be for the next little while, but she was anxious to return to the hotel and get herself organized for moving out to the Donnelly ranch. It wasn't as though she and Mary Ellen could toss around any ideas for the wedding, not while Edith was right there.

On the way back to town, Zoey pondered her friend's response to the news that she was going to be staying on the Donnelly ranch. Mary Ellen hadn't seemed too thrilled. The more she thought about it, though, the more she realized that Mary Ellen was only thinking of Zoey's welfare, worried she'd get upset about Ryan again. Zoey had been all primed to confess that she *did* have an ulterior motive in moving to the ranch. But, no, Elizabeth was the one to tell if Zoey really felt the need to confide. Elizabeth wouldn't take everything so seriously, the way Mary Ellen might.

Mary Ellen was too sweet and sensitive. Too soft-hearted. Zoey recalled how horrified she'd been at the story Elizabeth had told about Adele dumping Ryan at the altar and was doubly glad she hadn't spilled the beans about what she had in mind.

No, Mary Ellen would just worry and she had enough on her hands with Edith's wedding coming up.

ZOEY WAS PACKED and ready to leave by noon the next day. She went down to check out and retrieve a trolley for her bags. Cameron was in the lobby, reading a newspaper.

As dependable as he'd promised, she thought with a smile. She paid for her room and started back to the elevator with the trolley, assuming he hadn't seen her, when she heard a man clear his throat behind her. She half turned.

"Here. Let me take that." Cameron reached for the trolley.

"I'm fine! I can bring down my stuff," Zoey protested.

"I'll give you a hand." He strode down the hall beside her and they got into the elevator with the trolley. It made for close quarters. Frowning, he watched the lights on the ancient elevator as it laboriously ground its way up to the third floor.

Zoey eyed him sideways, wondering if she was making the right decision. Several weeks on a remote ranch with a high-school crush who hadn't even remembered her at first, a surly brother with matchmaking on his mind, a widowed aunt who was probably going to talk her ear off and a kid she knew nothing about.

She must be insane.

She unlocked the door to her room, relieved that Cameron didn't try to take the key and open it for her. On the third try, it meshed.

"That's all you have?" Cameron surveyed the room quickly. She had the distinct impression that he was trying very hard not to glance at the fly-spotted mirror on the ceiling. So was she.

"Yes. I travel light." She reached for the blue case that held the Chinchilla manuscript and her laptop. She'd carry that herself.

Cameron loaded her three bags onto the trolley, and as soon as they arrived back in the lobby, he strode ahead of her to the hotel doors. He hadn't said a word in the elevator. Yesterday must have been a real stretch for him, convincing her to cooperate with his plan.

Maybe his talents—like hers, she sometimes thought—ran more to scheming than talking.

Well, how could she help it? Much of her working life was spent trying to figure out plot twists and tangles in Jamie Chinchilla mystery-thrillers. So far, she'd never thought of this as a particular talent that she could apply to life, but this Romancing Ryan plot of Cameron's had definitely fired her imagination.

"Cameron?" she called when they reached the parking lot.

"Yes?" He was about to toss her bags into the back of his dark green pickup.

"I've got my own car," she reminded him, indicating the white rental Toyota sedan a few spaces away from his truck. "I'll follow you, okay?"

He nodded and carried her bags to the car and stood patiently while she fiddled with her keys, trying to open the trunk. Eventually it sprang open and he loaded her bags.

She closed the trunk, then turned to him. "Look, is there something I should know?"

He seemed startled. "Like what?"

"Well, you're awfully quiet today. I get the impression you're not as happy about this plan today as you were yesterday but you're too polite to say so. Don't feel obliged. We can drop the whole thing if you like—"

"Is that what you want to do?"

Did she? She dug in her handbag for her sunglasses, mulling over the difficulties of going to the Nugents for a few days and still having to look for a more suitable place. "No, I'm game. I've got quite a bit of work and I need a place to do it in."

"Let's go then."

Cameron started his engine and immediately reversed. Zoey started the Toyota and decided to give it a minute or two to warm up. She never drove in Toronto, although she'd maintained her driver's license over the years, and couldn't remember if you were supposed to warm up a car or not. It couldn't hurt. Plus, it wouldn't kill Cameron Donnelly to wait.

Which he did. He was waiting for her at the entrance to the parking lot. She rigorously observed the speed limit as they set out in tandem. When she dropped behind, he slowed. Zoey suspected he'd prefer to go faster. But that was okay, too, she told herself, smiling just a little.

It was clear that Cameron Donnelly was used to taking charge. He ran his ranch and organized his own life and his child's life and probably Marty's life. Now he was shopping for a romance for his brother. Well, he couldn't find out any earlier that she wasn't all that manageable. In fact, she knew she could be ornery as hell at times, something she wasn't exactly proud of.

But she *was* her own woman, with her own ideas and her own agenda. If she hadn't been, she wouldn't have gotten as far as she had in life.

And *that* she was proud of.

# CHAPTER FIVE

THE TRIPLE OARLOCK was about fifteen miles west of town, not far as distances went in this country. It was snugged up against the rolling hills of the Fullerton Range. A rambling one-story ranch house, seventies style, was nestled against a windbreak of trees to the west, and the ranch buildings, most of them, were to the south and southwest. The sturdy pole fences weren't painted and had weathered to a soft silver. The barns and outbuildings had been painted a traditional barn red; the lawns were tidy, the bare hedges clipped. Everything looked in good repair.

The apartment she was to occupy over the three-car garage stood about seventy-five feet southwest of the house. There was another parking spot, an open carport, attached to the house, probably a more convenient location for unloading groceries and passengers in inclement weather.

They parked by the garage and Cameron took Zoey straight up to the ranch house to meet his aunt.

"Marty? This is Zoey Phillips, you remember Harvey Phillips, used to be at the cement plant? This is his daughter." He turned to Zoey. "My aunt, Marty Hainsworth."

"How do you do?" Zoey said formally, extending

her hand. The older woman she'd glimpsed at the fire-fighters' dance shook it briefly, her grip firm and hard as a man's. She was slight, thin-lipped, and had a pink chiffon scarf tied over her head. Zoey spotted old-fashioned hair rollers under the scarf.

"How d'ye do? I'm glad to meet you. Cameron's been telling me about you."

"He has?" She glanced at Cameron with a smile. He seemed faintly embarrassed.

"Oh, yes, and all of it favorable." The aunt, who looked to be in her mid-sixties, put her hands on narrow, jean-clad hips. A toothpick bobbed in one side of her mouth. "Ryan, too. Matter of fact, he's talked nonstop since Sunday about you and Mary Ellen Owen being back in town. You want a cup of tea or anything? You *sure* you want to stay out in that drafty old suite? I don't like the idea. We got plenty of room up here in the house."

"No to the tea, thank you very much. And, yes, I prefer to stay in the apartment by myself. I'm not a guest, you know, Mrs. Hainsworth—"

"Just call me Marty."

"Marty." Zoey smiled. She had decided that she was going to get along very well with the Donnellys' aunt. "I have lots to do over the next few weeks—"

"What kind of work d'ye do, if you don't mind me askin'?" Marty's bright blue eyes, which reminded Zoey of Ryan's, were curious.

"I edit books. Mainly, I edit Jamie Chinchilla's novels and—"

"Oh, my! He's one of my favorites. My sister

Robin in Kelowna always sends me his books, when she's finished with 'em. Or is this Chinchilla a she?''

The reading public had never seen a picture of the author, nor did most people know whether Jamie Chinchilla was male or female. For purposes of publicity, the author and publisher had decided to maintain the mystery.

"I've never met the author," Zoey said truthfully. All her contact had been over the telephone. But she knew very well that Jamie Chinchilla was an elderly widow named Ruth Ohlmstad, who lived in Lunenburg, Nova Scotia, and who had never been farther away from home than Halifax and St. Andrews-by-the-Sea, New Brunswick. Well, she'd been to Boston once, when she was twenty, she'd told Zoey. But that was it. Unlike her characters, Ruth Ohlmstad had never had a hair-raising adventure in her life. Her stories were complete products of an amazingly fertile and inventive imagination. Even her neighbors thought she was just good old Ruthie, stalwart of the Women's League, co-president of the Lunenburg Historical Society and envied grower of prize-winning sweet peas.

"Well, ain't that something! You settle in and let me know if there's anything you need. We can supply most everything from brooms to biscuits. And you'll be eatin' with us, won't you?''

Zoey shook her head. "Oh, no. I can manage quite nicely on my own, thanks anyway.''

Marty Hainsworth shot a quick, questioning look at her nephew. "Well, you'll be havin' Sunday dinner over here at the house, that's for sure,'' the woman said decisively. "Roast beef and all the trimmin's, six sharp. I won't hear of you eatin' all by yourself on a Sunday. It ain't right.''

"Thank you," Zoey said, smiling. "That would be lovely. This Sunday, though, I'm having dinner with the Nugents. They've already invited me.''

"Well, all right. Just this once." Marty cracked a smile. She seemed as dour as her eldest nephew, but Zoey liked her immediately.

Cameron turned to Zoey, one eyebrow raised. "Okay?"

She followed him back to the garage. Where was his daughter? Mind you, it was Friday. She was probably at school.

The entrance to the apartment was up an outdoor staircase with a landing midway. It wouldn't be very convenient in deepest winter but she'd be going home before Christmas. "Cameron?''

Cameron was getting her bags out of the Toyota's trunk. "Yes?''

"Um. Ryan *does* know about this, doesn't he?'' She'd received the distinct impression from the aunt that this was something dreamed up by Cameron and, possibly, Marty herself.

He straightened and appeared to think deeply about her question. "Well, no. He doesn't actually *know* about it, not about you moving in here today—''

"That's ridiculous! Why haven't you told him?'' Zoey panicked. She wanted to order Cameron to put her bags back in her car, wanted to return immediately to Stoney Creek. She'd stay with the Nugents. Or in the motel with the cockroaches, if she had to.

"It was his suggestion," he said, regarding her carefully. "When he heard you were looking for a place, he mentioned the apartment to me as a possibility."

"I see." Although she didn't really. "Well, if he doesn't like this idea, I'm moving right back to town!" Zoey picked up the case that contained the manuscript. "This is downright underhanded. I don't like it. It makes everything seem…cheap. Like—like I'm actually part of this stupid romance plan of yours." Which she was…sort of.

Cameron Donnelly had the grace to color slightly. "Believe me, it was his idea," he repeated stubbornly.

Zoey sighed. She gave up. First things, first: move in and get to work.

BY LATE AFTERNOON, after a trip back to town to buy groceries, Zoey had settled in. She hung her clothes in the wardrobe in the tiny bedroom, furnished sparsely but comfortably with a double bed, a carpet on the floor and bright chintz curtains at the window, which looked over the mountains to the west.

The combination kitchen-living room was small but efficient, with a sofa, several lamps and a coffee table. There was also a table by the window; it was covered with plants, which Marty must have brought in recently and which Zoey would remove as she needed the table for eating. The bathroom had a shower and a tiny tub, trailer-size, and just off the kitchen was a little sunroom. Zoey decided she'd use it as a dining nook. She moved the small white-painted wooden table and two chairs from the kitchen to the sunporch, then dragged a rocking chair from the cramped living room into the space she'd freed up. An aging fridge, humming happily now and full of provisions, completed the kitchen equipment, along with a narrow three-burner electric stove.

Now, to let Lydia know… She found a blank card and envelope in her briefcase.

Dear Lydia,
Just a quick note to tell you where I'm living—
at Ryan's ranch! No kidding. His brother suggested a little apartment over their garage as a place to stay—

Zoey decided not to mention the bit about Cameron's proposition. There *was* something sneaky and unsavory about the whole thing.

—and it's going to be ideal for my purposes. Work *plus* getting to know a certain somebody again! I rearranged some furniture, got in some food and will be using my cell. You've got my number, right? Anyway, goodbye for now and send Charlotte's address when she has one.

Luv,
Zoey

Zoey sealed the envelope, pasted a stamp on and looked around the little apartment again. It would do. In fact, considering her purposes, it was ideal. She needed quiet, freedom from ringing telephones and interruptions, and she'd certainly get that here. There wasn't a sound to be heard beyond the whisper of the wind in the trees and the far-off bawl of a calf or the occasional bark of a dog.

She shivered, looking out the sunroom window at the long stretch of frozen pasture to the east and south. Way in the distance, she could see reddish brown dots. Cattle, probably. This was rural! The snow dumped so far hadn't stayed, and the weather had been glorious— crisp, cold and sunny.

Zoey had a peanut-butter-and-cucumber sandwich on rye for her supper and settled down to work. She heard a vehicle drive past about half past nine as she sat at the table in the living room, trying to make sense of the first chapter of this book, which was about danger on the high seas, Caribbean skullduggery, kidnapping, murder, an impossibly rich and beautiful heiress and an ancient Egyptian curse. She'd read this chapter, such as it was, several times already. Chinchilla might be one of the world's most wonderful storytellers, but she didn't know diddly about spelling or grammar or syntax.

Ryan?

She peeked out the curtains, staring into the darkness. There were lots of lights on up at the house; perhaps Melissa wasn't in bed yet. She'd seen the child when Cameron had brought her home that afternoon, skipping and chattering beside him, going directly into the house without even a curious glance toward the apartment. Had they told her about the stranger living over the garage?

Zoey felt like a peeper. Or a mad relative hidden away from the neighbors. She had to fight the urge to look out the window every time she heard a sound. A dog. A car door. An airplane overhead. It was so quiet here that any noise seemed not only more noticeable than in her downtown Toronto apartment, but more significant. Zoey sighed. Maybe she'd get used to it. The main thing was to focus, concentrate on her work. All this other stuff was only a distraction. Interesting, but still a distraction.

She'd just returned to her desk with a cup of hot milk, thinking about packing it in and going to bed, when she heard footsteps coming up the stairs outside. Footsteps in twos and threes. There was a bang on her door.

"Zoey!"

She peered out the small glass square in the door, then unlocked and opened it.

"Zo-ey, ba-by!" Ryan was grinning as he stepped into the apartment, swept her into his arms and hugged her tightly. "Man, this is terrific news! Cam just told me. I don't know why he didn't say something earlier, the old son-of-a-gun. Thought he'd surprise me, I guess." He held her away from him, his eyes devouring her hungrily. Then he looked around the room. "Everything okay? Can I get you anything? Warm enough?"

He stepped away from her and bent to check the thermostat on the electric baseboard heaters that ran around the room. "I see they're working fine. Good!"

He glanced at her cup, and she suddenly remembered her manners. "Would you like something to drink?"

"What are you having?"

"Hot milk."

"Hot milk!" He laughed and shook his head. "No thanks. Now if that was a glass of brandy, maybe. Hell, I just wanted to come over tonight and welcome you to the ranch. Cam's a terrific guy, eh? Doesn't say much," he said, winking at her, "but he's got his head screwed on straight."

"I'm glad to be here," Zoey said simply. Obviously, Ryan didn't have a clue as to the original reason Cameron had invited her. "It's perfect for me."

"Perfect for me, too. I like the idea of you being nearby where I can keep an eye on you." Ryan moved toward her and kissed her mouth softly. "Sweet dreams, Zoey. See you in the morning."

And with that he was gone, clattering back down the stairs. Zoey touched her lips gingerly, stunned. *He'd kissed her again!*

Sweet dreams, indeed.

RYAN HAMMERED on her door again before she was dressed the next morning. She'd just settled down in the sunroom in her bathrobe and slippers with a bowl of Froot-Loops when she heard the same thump-thump up the stairs outside.

She let him in, feeling a little grumpy. She hadn't even brushed her hair yet. He *could* have waited. It was barely nine o'clock.

"'Morning, sunshine," he said, with his trademark grin, and thrust a handful of frostbitten flowers at her. Asters, chrysanthemums, a few straggling marigolds—they must've come from the Triple Oarlock flower beds.

"Thank you." She took them from him. How

thoughtful! They might be considerably past their prime, but you couldn't fault a man who brought flowers.

"A welcome bouquet." Ryan scanned the room. "They're not the greatest but this place could stand some livening up, don't you think?"

He walked into the kitchen area and picked up the coffeepot, reaching into the cupboard for a mug. A devious thought struck her—was this his little love nest? He seemed to know his way around. Cameron had said he saw a lot of women.

He was her guest now. This was her place. She needed to make that clear. She stuffed the flowers into a pitcher and went to the refrigerator. "Cream? Sugar?" she asked.

"A little cream. No sugar," he said, then flashed her his easy grin. "I'm sweet enough as it is." Zoey had the impression he'd used that worn-out line many times before.

"Would you like a piece of cake?" she asked. "I've got some frozen Sara Lee."

"Just coffee." He strolled toward the paned windows in the sunroom. "I like what you've done in here, moving things around. Makes it homey."

"I hope you won't mind if I finish my breakfast," she said, somewhat stiffly. He was overwhelming her with his big, handsome and very physical presence. She needed perspective. Romantic potential was one thing, but bursting in at the crack of dawn and taking over her life was another. "I'm a bit of a late riser," she added lamely, wishing it sounded less like an apology.

"No problem." Ryan studied the apartment again. "What about the phone? You got it hooked up yet?"

"I've got my cell," Zoey said.

"No big deal to hook this up. I'll call the company on Monday."

"Oh." Zoey took another bite of her cereal, feeling a little uneasy. He was definitely taking over. "No, I think I'll just use the cell."

She stared at his back. He stood at the window, gazing to the east, sipping his coffee. Jeans, flannel work shirt, sheepskin vest, gray woolly work socks—he'd left his boots at the door, which she felt was quite thoughtful of him. Typical Cariboo-Chilcotin guy gear. "Mary Ellen know you're living here now?" he asked suddenly, turning around.

"Yes," Zoey said. "I saw her two days ago. This has all been...rather a rush."

"Yeah." He grinned. "I know Cam. He decides, he acts. Bam!" He snapped his fingers. "Mary Ellen like the idea?"

Zoey frowned and swallowed a mouthful of cereal. "What idea?"

"You livin' out here?"

Zoey shrugged. "She seemed fine with it. Why?"

"We'll have to do some stuff together, you and me and her." Ryan rubbed his hands together briskly. "What do you say? Just like old times."

Zoey was glad he was including them both. It could be lonely for Mary Ellen if she was stuck out there with only her stepmother for company until the wedding.

She felt a tiny cold shock. *Does that sound like a*

*man ready to revive a romantic relationship?* With *one* woman—*her?*

*Oh, who cares!* She spooned up the last Froot-Loop sticking to the side of the bowl. She was reading far too much into everything. Cameron's idea had sent her rushing headlong down what could very well be a dead-end trail. Sure, she might be interested in re-establishing a relationship with Ryan—well, maybe. She hadn't decided a hundred percent yet. But she had to be careful to read the signs from him, too. He was a flirt; he was exuberant. Maybe he hugged and kissed every woman he met.

"Why don't we do something this afternoon? Drive around." He put his empty mug down on the table and thrust his hands in the pockets of his jeans. "How about it? You and me and Mary Ellen?"

"Sounds great."

"Okay." Ryan ruffled her sleep-mussed hair as he walked by, the way an adult did with a child, and opened the door. "Two o'clock? We can go for a drive up the valley or go to Pete's for ice cream. Cam's got me busy around here all morning, so I can't leave any earlier. You want to call Mary Ellen?" His eyes settled on her. "Or you want me to?"

"I'll call her," Zoey said, gathering up her bowl and spoon and Ryan's mug. "Two o'clock. See you then. Why don't we take Lissy with us if she's home?"

"Good idea."

Things were moving faster than she'd thought possible. Zoey didn't know whether to be pleased or not. Ryan was showing some interest, as Cameron had maintained he would. But was it *romantic* interest?

## CHAPTER SIX

WHEN THEY ARRIVED at the Owen place, Mary Ellen was covering some flower beds with straw at the foot of a tall willow growing on the margin of the creek. Ryan insisted they stop by, even though Zoey hadn't been able to get through on the phone.

"Hi!" Mary Ellen said, carrying her rake and approaching the window of Ryan's Blazer.

"You're finished here. Come with us," Ryan invited, leaning over Zoey to speak out the open passenger window. "We're just going to Pete's for an ice cream—" he nodded significantly toward the back seat "—and then we're going for a little drive. Lissy and I'll show you two the valley, the new ball park, how things have changed around here. Just in case you want to move back someday."

"Oh, I don't know if I should leave." Mary Ellen glanced worriedly toward the house. "Edith's napping. I'd better stay—"

"Get in," Ryan ordered, in a mock growl and with the smile that no woman—including Zoey—had ever been able to resist. "Edith's fine for an hour or two. What do you think she does when you're not here?"

Mary Ellen bit her lip. "Okay. I'll leave a note." She disappeared into the double-wide and emerged a few minutes later with a fleecy jacket slung over her shoulder.

She got into the back with Lissy and Zoey noticed that the child warmed to her almost immediately. Maybe it was the fact that Mary Ellen had pulled a roll of Lifesavers out of her pocket. Or that she took off one of her rings and let Lissy play with it. Or maybe Mary Ellen just knew what to do around kids. Zoey didn't. So far, Lissy had been polite but had basically ignored her.

"My mom was a dancer," Lissy announced loudly, holding up her hand to show off the ring on her middle finger. "She's in-fam-ous. Aunt Marty said so."

"Oh? Well, that's just great!" Mary Ellen said. Zoey wondered at the pronunciation—famous or *in*-famous? She glanced at Ryan, whose hands had tightened on the steering wheel.

"Never mind all that, Lissy. We're nearly at Pete's. What kind of ice cream do you want?"

Lissy ignored her uncle. "My mom was the prettiest thing ever, that's what my dad says." She glared defiantly at Zoey when Zoey turned her head to look back at her. "You have to be really, really pretty to be a dancer, you know."

"I know that, Lissy," Mary Ellen murmured, tousling the child's hair. "Almost as pretty as you."

Lissy giggled, pulling off the ring.

"Here." Mary Ellen stuck out her finger and Lissy carefully slipped the ring back on.

"Is that a ring for getting married?" the girl asked, eyes wide and serious.

"No, it's not," Mary Ellen said, flexing her hand

and smiling down at the turquoise stone. "I got it from someone special, though."

"A man friend?" Ryan asked from the front seat.

"You could say that," Mary Ellen replied. "My dad. No, honey," she added, speaking directly to the girl, "I've never been married."

"Hoo!" Lissy said, making a funny face. "And you're so *old,* too!" The adults laughed and Zoey thought Ryan seemed relieved that the subject had veered to a lighter one. Obviously, talk about Lissy's mother was not welcome. Why?

"Are you going to marry my dad now?" the child asked innocently. Zoey hardly dared to meet Mary Ellen's amused eyes.

"I'm not marrying anybody. Not just yet. Even though I *am* so old."

"What about *her?*" Lissy pointed at Zoey.

"Marrying your dad? Nope." Mary Ellen shook her head. "Nobody's gettin' married to nobody," she said, ungrammatically and with emphasis. "We're all just friends here."

"How about him?" The girl pointed at the back of Ryan's head. "My uncle. Is she gonna marry *him?*"

Zoey felt her face flush. Normally she'd just laugh off a question like that, especially from a kid. But considering the scheme she'd discussed with Cameron...

Mary Ellen made a big production out of whispering loudly, so that Zoey and Ryan could hear. "Maybe we'd better ask them. What do you think?"

Lissy giggled and gripped her toy cat more tightly. "Guess so!" she whispered back.

''Pete's place comin' up on the left!'' Ryan boomed out, and the little girl laughed as they turned the last corner. Zoey felt the tension slip away. Between the girl's embarrassing questions about who was going to marry whom and the topic of her absent mother—a dancer, no less!—the atmosphere had been thick enough to cut for a few moments there. Zoey wondered what kind of dancer the child's mother was. She could guess. Elizabeth had said Cameron had met her in a bar.

The adults had sundaes and Lissy ordered a double-decker banana and bubble-gum cone, chocolate-dipped. When they'd finished, Ryan drove out into the country north of Stoney Creek. The trees were bare, but there were patches of green from the spruce and pine trees and the occasional ragged flash of red from a mountain ash, still loaded with scarlet berries.

The mountains looked so close and yet so distant. The air was clear and clean. And cold. The mountains were brilliant with fresh snow, snow that hadn't reached the valley yet.

Mmm. Zoey breathed deeply, letting her hair blow in the wind from the partly opened window. This was heaven.

THE FOLLOWING WEEK, Zoey turned down two invitations from Ryan. One was to a movie, which she didn't mind missing at all. She had painful memories of that old Rialto Theater, most of which involved Ryan holding her hand and whispering in her ear while Adele Martinez looked on from a few rows behind.

The other invitation was to accompany him to a

neighboring ranch to load a bull that the Triple Oarlock was borrowing. That was even easier to decline.
Later, Zoey was surprised to hear that Mary Ellen had
gone with him, but then she remembered that she'd
lived around Stoney Creek a lot longer than Zoey had
and knew a lot more people. One of their classmates,
Patricia Somebody-or-Other, was married to the
rancher who owned the bull.

Zoey had to keep her mind on business. It was all
very well to pretend that this was a lark, that she was
out to "snag" the high-school heartthrob all over
again, but the fact was, she had a living to earn. And
a wedding cake to produce. She'd meant to ask Elizabeth about recipes on Sunday when she'd had dinner
with the Nugents. She'd also meant to have a heart-
to-heart about Ryan Donnelly and get Elizabeth's advice. With Arthur or one of the girls around every
single second of her visit, Zoey hadn't been able to
raise either subject.

The manuscript was painfully slow going. Zoey
spent four straight days and evenings working on the
first three chapters, with one short trip to town to buy
milk, eggs and some fast food. From experience, Zoey
knew that after a solid week of intensive work on a
Chinchilla manuscript, things tended to fall into place.
She hoped this one would follow the same pattern.

On Wednesday evening, after a quick meal of oven-
heated leftover pizza, a glass of milk and a handful of
raisins and raw carrots, Zoey slipped outdoors for a
walk to clear her head. She had a little route worked
out—down to the mailbox at the end of the lane, a
good half mile or so, past a line of tall trees, leafless

at this time of year, past some frozen pasture and across a Texas gate, which kept livestock on the ranch proper, then back again. The cold air was invigorating. When she returned in the thickening dusk forty-five minutes later, chilled and ready for a hot drink, some-one was sitting at the top of the stairs to her apartment.

Her heart leaped, then she recognized a familiar sil-houette as he stood.

"Surprised to see me?"

"I am," she said. She'd seen very little of Ryan's brother since she'd moved in. He always seemed to be busy somewhere on the ranch or in town or working in his office. She trudged to the top of the stairs, then fumbled for her key in her jacket pocket. "I don't get many visitors."

"We don't lock our doors around here," he said, waiting for her to use the key.

"Well, I do." He followed her inside and she flicked on several lights. Her apartment, she thought proudly, was looking quite homey. The fresh flowers she'd bought in town the day before glowed on the nondescript coffee table and the radio she kept on low for company was—unfortunately—oozing some schmaltzy instrumental. Sexy and intimate. His eyes met hers. "Expecting someone?"

Zoey couldn't read his expression. Was he serious? Joking? Expecting to find some strange suitor hiding in a corner somewhere?

"No, not expecting anyone," she said, snapping on two more lamps to dispel the dim, almost expectant atmosphere. "Sit down. Can I get you some coffee?

Herbal tea? I've got chamomile and peppermint.'' One to perk her up, one to put her to sleep.

"Coffee sounds good. Thanks.''

He took the upholstered chair, which left the sofa for her. She moved toward the tiny kitchen area, conscious that he was watching her.

"Milk and sugar?''

"Both.''

She reached for a mug, trying to think of a possible reason for this visit. "I suppose Marty's angry with me.''

"Angry?''

"For missing dinner last night?'' She looked at him quickly, then poured the coffee she'd perked and put in the vacuum jug much earlier, around four o'clock. "I did apologize this morning, but...'' She let her words trail off.

"No idea.'' He accepted the evil-looking brew, only faintly lightened by a good dollop of coffee cream. Zoey wished now that she'd made a fresh pot, but he wouldn't be staying long. Surely.

"She asked me to join your family for dinner, which was extremely kind of her. A sort of getting-to-know-you thing, I guess,'' Zoey said and shrugged. "I was working and I totally forgot the time—'' She held her breath as he took a sip. He frowned and peered into the mug.

"This is terrible coffee,'' he said.

"I know.'' Zoey wasn't sure what else to say. "I should've made fresh. Would you rather have tea?''

"No.'' He took another swallow and this time didn't make a face. Maybe he was getting used to it.

His gaze wandered into the kitchen again, and Zoey cringed. Her plate and glass were on the sideboard and the cardboard pizza box was still sitting on the counter, next to the stove. She'd stored the half she hadn't eaten the day before in the refrigerator. Front and center on the countertop was the brand-new mini-microwave she'd bought at the co-op in town. She'd stocked up on frozen dinners and intended to donate the microwave to the local hospital auxiliary thrift store when she left.

"Not much for cooking, are you?"

Zoey bristled. "I'm a very good cook, as a matter of fact. It's just that I don't enjoy fixing meals for one and when I'm working, I don't mind what I eat. I basically stick to healthy stuff and—"

He glanced pointedly into his mug.

Well, with the exception of that. "Was there something you wanted to talk to me about?" she asked, deciding it was time they got to the point of this visit.

"Yes." She wished he wouldn't study her like that. His level, faintly curious gaze made her feel like a little kid who'd been caught doing something she shouldn't. "As a matter of fact, I was wondering how things were going between you and my brother."

Oh, that! "Fine." She leaned forward, hands on the sofa cushion on either side of her, knees together, and nodded. "Everything's going just fine. Why do you ask?"

"It's been two weeks. I understand he's asked you out a few times?"

"Yes." She nodded again. "He has."

"I see he took Mary Ellen over to the Nagles' to

pick up that bull the other day. Would've been a good chance to show you a little ordinary ranch life.''

*Your point, Cameron Donnelly?* Zoey realized she was starting to simmer. ''Uh-huh,'' she said evenly. ''Actually, he did ask but I turned him down. Visiting a bull isn't my idea of a really good—''

''I can understand that,'' he broke in. ''But is anything happening? Anything *romantic?*'' He looked at her earnestly, his coffee cup abandoned on the low table in front of him.

Zoey deliberately reined in her irritation. ''Do *you* think anything romantic is 'happening,' as you put it?''

Cameron shrugged and frowned. He actually seemed to be considering her question! ''I know he's tough to pin down. A lot of women have tried, believe me.''

''And you don't think I could do it,'' she said flatly.

''I just wondered, that's all.'' He had the grace to look somewhat uncomfortable. ''I'm hoping with you out here he'll have a good chance to appreciate your, uh, womanly qualities.''

Zoey stared at him for a full count of ten. ''Don't worry, Cameron,'' she said finally, proud of the way she managed to control her voice, ''you'll be the first to know if anything develops.''

''Don't get mad—''

''I'm not mad, dammit!''

''I just thought I'd see if I was right about Ryan being sweet on you....''

''And if it turns out he isn't—as you so quaintly put it—*sweet* on me, do I have to move out?''

"Of course not."

"That's good," she snapped, "because you are aware, I'm sure, that my work is my first priority. I have also given my word that I will provide a wedding cake for a friend's mother's wedding and help her in any way I can. Which I will do." Would a lousy cook have been asked to take *that* on for a friend? "Believe it or not, my first thought when I wake up each morning is *not* romancing your brother."

"Fine," he said, shaking his head a little. "I knew it would be a long shot. Well…" He stood. "I'd better be on my way."

*Yeah, you'd better be,* Zoey thought. A long shot? Her romancing his brother? She followed him to the landing outside the door. "Cameron?"

"Yes?" He was one step down already, which put him almost directly level with her. She swore he was trying not to smile. The very thought made her even madder. What did he find so amusing about Zoey Phillips?

"It's probably a good idea to keep things clear between us, don't you think? After all, this matchmaking idea of yours is pretty dumb." Obviously she wasn't going to mention that she'd had exactly the same idea herself. "And it has nothing to do with the fact that he plays hard to get."

"Right." Cameron put his hat on slowly. "I'm aware it's, uh, fairly unlikely."

"Okay. Just so long as you understand that no matter what we talked about in town, my primary reason for being here is *not* to seduce your brother."

This time she did see a flicker of a smile. "Hell,

no. I wouldn't expect you to go that far. Besides, I believe he's generally the one who does the seducing."

"Although," she went on as if he hadn't spoken, "I think you should know that I could if I wanted to." She'd show him—or anybody else—*womanly qualities.* Whatever they were. "I'm perfectly capable, if I set my mind to it."

"Of what—seducing someone?"

"Exactly!"

"Uh-huh." He nodded and started down the stairs. At the landing he turned to look up at her. "I imagine if you set your mind to it, you could do almost anything."

Not for the first time, she had a nagging suspicion that she wasn't being taken seriously. It was the old Harvey Phillips story. Dreamer. Loser. *Fool.* No one in Stoney Creek had ever taken the Phillips family seriously.

Now Cameron Donnelly was saying that her chances of "romancing" his brother were remote. *A long shot.* As if he, personally, hadn't had quite a lot to do with getting her out here to attempt that very thing.

Zoey waved rather stiffly in response when he touched his hat in a polite gesture of farewell. She walked, ramrod straight, back into her apartment. She began to close the door, then at the last second, changed her mind and slammed it.

Sunday family dinners! She shuddered. A home-cooked meal—she'd bet on roast beef and mashed potatoes—sounded appealing enough. But could she deal with two Donnellys at a sit-down dinner? Three, counting the aunt. No, four—how could she have forgotten Lissy?

## CHAPTER SEVEN

ROAST BEEF TURNED OUT to be a good guess. Marty served Yorkshire pudding as well as mashed potatoes and her pumpkin cheesecake was *incredible*.

Ryan welcomed her at the door. She hadn't known what sort of dress was expected at this obviously important weekly event, so she'd gone middle-of-the-road with a trim cardigan set and dress slacks. Hoop earrings. Flat shoes. Ryan was wearing a pale-blue shirt, his hair was freshly combed and he looked like he'd just shaved. He greeted her with a big hug and a kiss. He felt solid and warm. His aftershave smelled of citrus and something woodsy.

"Come on in, Zoey," Marty called from the kitchen. "Don't be shy, make yourself t' home." She wore a frilly apron over the pencil-thin GWG jeans she favored, with the cuffs rolled halfway up her skinny calves, showing their plaid flannel lining and giving the denims an unexpectedly fashionable Capri-pant look. She had on a striped cotton blouse and her hair had been released from the curlers she usually wore under a headscarf during the week. It turned out to be a frizzy salt-and-pepper mix, well-permed. The ever-present toothpick in the older woman's mouth was missing, no doubt an acknowledgement of the solemnity of the day.

Cameron was nowhere in sight, and Lissy was playing quietly with a couple of Barbie dolls in the family room, which adjoined the kitchen. The child glanced swiftly at Zoey as she entered the room, then returned her full attention to the dolls.

The dining room, already set for six places—*six?*—was off to the right.

"Can I help you, Marty?" Zoey knew her cheeks were still flushed from Ryan's enthusiastic welcome. She wished she'd brought some flowers, but where did one get flowers out here in the middle of the Cariboo Chilcotin at the end of November? If she'd been in town, she could have stopped at the florist's, where she'd bought hers last week, except it probably wasn't open on Sunday. Besides, she knew rural hospitality didn't run to hostess gifts, anyway. A good appetite and a smile were all that was needed.

"No, dear. I don't share my kitchen," Marty said, shifting her weight as she adeptly took the lid off a huge pot of potatoes, sending steam rising to the kitchen fan. "I know what I'm doing and I hate other folks gettin' under my feet. Cam will hammer these spuds into shape for me like he always does. Ryan! Where the heck's your brother? He ain't still at church with that Sara Rundle, is he? The woman's positively shameless!"

"No idea, Marty." Ryan shrugged. He looked handsome and fit and tanned. Zoey felt some of the old excitement zip through her veins. His welcome kiss hadn't hurt; in fact, it had knocked her pulse up a notch. "Wouldn't be surprised. Cam's a softie, especially for a pretty woman." He winked at Zoey, as though to say *who wouldn't be?* "How about a drink before dinner, Zoey?"

Zoey became instantly aware of Marty's eagle eye on her. She got the impression Marty didn't approve. Maybe because it was Sunday, maybe as a general principle.

"I'll pass, thanks, Ryan," she answered lightly and noticed Ryan shooting a glance at his aunt. Marty said nothing, simply strode over to the refrigerator and pulled out a carton of cereal cream.

Ryan went to a tall cupboard in the dining room and returned with a crystal glass in his hand, an old-fashioned. "I'm going to pour me a splash of rye," he said cheerfully, with a definite nod in Marty's direction. "That is if nobody around here *minds*." His aunt gave him a thunderous look.

Zoey decided it was time to extricate herself from the situation developing between aunt and nephew. She walked into the family room wondering what "shameless" meant in Stoney Creek, as applied to someone like Sara Rundle. Elizabeth had told her she was a teacher, not a profession typically classified as "shameless."

Ryan entered the room carrying a glass that was more than half-full of a golden liquid and sloshing with ice. He put his arm around her and pulled her close. "So, how's it going out there? Everything working out?"

"You mean the apartment?" She noticed that even though Lissy appeared to be playing with her dolls, she kept a careful eye on the two adults.

"The apartment, yeah. Any trouble with the lights?"

"No, why?"

"We get plenty of power outages up here. The electricity was off for a couple of hours on Friday."

"Was it?" Zoey gave him a puzzled frown. "I went to town for part of the afternoon." She and Mary Ellen had discussed wedding plans and booked the United Church hall, next door to the church, for the occasion.

"You'll notice it. That apartment doesn't have insulation and the baseboard heat is electric. There's a drawerful of candles in the kitchen somewhere. Anytime you get real cold, though, you come on up to the house and sleep here." He winked at her and glanced toward the kitchen. "There's always plenty of room in my—"

*"Ry-an!"* came the holler from the kitchen. "You watch your mouth! There's little pitchers with big ears! Mind your manners!"

"It's down the hall, second from the end," he whispered loudly, winking again. It seemed to Zoey that he and his aunt actually got along very well but he couldn't resist teasing her.

"How about some music?" He sauntered over to the side of the room and began fiddling with dials on the sound system.

"Nothin' too loud! And come in here and mash

these spuds, will you, please, since Cam ain't showin' up?''

Marty didn't miss much, Zoey thought, smiling. Did Ryan find living with his brother and aunt restrictive? If so, he could've lived on his own somewhere. She wondered why he didn't. Of course, it wasn't uncommon for grown siblings to live in the family ranch house, especially if they worked together and were single.

Zoey sat down on the beige upholstered sofa in front of the television set and the fireplace. What she'd seen of the place was furnished in a vague, offhand manner, as though little thought had gone into colors or furnishings. The curtains were old, a tired leafy pattern that she was sure hadn't been popular since the seventies, and the carpet—a sort of shaggy burnt orange—was way out of date, although in good condition and clean. Cameron had probably bought the place decorated like this.

''Sorry I'm late.'' Speak of the devil!

Cameron appeared in the doorway just as Ryan returned from mashing the potatoes and sat down beside her, once again pulling her close with his left arm draped over her shoulders. Cameron, freshly showered and fastening the buttons on his cuffs, eyed the group in the living room.

Zoey snuggled a little closer. She glanced toward the doorway in time to see Cameron's small smile and narrowed eyes. He'd gotten the message. Good. You want a little *romance*, Mr. Donnelly? She was still annoyed about his fact-finding visit to her apartment on Wednesday.

"Lissy?" He turned to his daughter. "Ready to help Marty put the pickles out?"

Lissy tore off toward the kitchen, whooping.

"It's a little tradition they have. Marty lets her put the pickles on the pickle dish for Sunday dinner. A little fun for her, I guess." Cameron looked embarrassed to be making the explanation. He remained standing by the fireplace. An odd uneasiness hung in the room. There was something so...maternal about the image of Marty helping her grandniece learn some little cooking rituals. The kind of thing a mother usually did.

"Drink, Cam?" Ryan asked suddenly, jingling the ice in his glass.

Cameron shook his head.

"Man! What would we do without her?" Ryan said, raising his glass toward the kitchen. "Here's to Saint Marty." Ryan smiled and shook his head. "My big brother, Mr. Hundred-and-Ten Percent Rancher, trying to raise a kid on his own. A girl, yet. Now, a boy—" His tone grew serious. "A boy might be another story. Fishin', huntin', driving tractor. But who knows spit about girls? Not *little* girls," he added with a meaningful smile at her.

"Never mind, Ry." Cameron gave his brother a grim look, almost a warning, Zoey thought. "She's *my* responsibility, not yours or Marty's."

Zoey wondered if they knew spit about raising boys,

either, but there was no time to contemplate. Marty was calling them to the dining room.

Just as they were about to sit down, Zoey heard a knock at the door and Ryan ushered in a shifty-looking man in fairly clean jeans, a wrinkled shirt of uncertain color, and a big felt hat. His dark eyes were everywhere.

"Come in, Gabe, sit yourself down," ordered the hostess and the old cowboy—as Zoey discovered he was—instantly obeyed. The mystery of the extra setting at the table was cleared up.

Even with the silent and unsociable cowhand, who was a full-time ranch employee, the meal was a zany kind of success. Zoey sat across from Ryan, who was beside the cowhand. Cameron sat at one end of the table, with Lissy to his right, beside Zoey. Marty took the other end, nearest the kitchen.

The food was superb, especially welcome after all the warm-up and microwave meals she'd fixed for herself recently. Zoey complimented Marty on her culinary skills and the little woman blushed to the roots of her wiry hair.

"I've fed plenty in my day and ain't had too many complaints," she admitted grudgingly, relieving her agitation by frowning severely at the gravy boat. "I don't know *what* in the world is wrong with that gravy today, it ain't what it usually is."

"It's excellent gravy, Marty," Cameron said looking across the table at his aunt. "You know it is." He slid his glance sideways to Zoey, and she smiled slightly before focussing on her plate again. Cameron didn't tease his aunt the way Ryan did. He appeared to have a genuine and deeply felt respect for her. Of course, he relied on Marty to help raise his daughter. He couldn't afford to offend her, could he?

Marty grunted some sort of response, but Zoey was more interested in the rather pointed questions Ryan was sending toward the head of the table, trying to find out what his brother and Sara Rundle had been up to all afternoon.

"Just helping her set up for the concert tonight. No harm in that," Cameron said quietly. He seemed unperturbed by Ryan's third-degree. Apparently, a wind quartet from Kamloops was using the church basement for a presentation of Christmas music that evening.

"Nope. No harm in that," Ryan said with a big grin on his handsome face. "Nice to see you holdin' your own with her, Cam. She's got a lot of fellows chasing her. You notice she didn't ask *me* to stay and help her after church."

"Well, you're pretty occupied with Zoey here, aren't you?" It was a terribly ham-handed attempt at splicing the two of them together and Zoey blushed furiously. "Aren't you two sweethearts from a long time back? High school?" As if he didn't know!

"That's right," Ryan answered gallantly, his eyes warm. "We saw quite a bit of each other in high school, didn't we, Zoey? Had a lot of fun together. You bet I've got my hands full." He leaned toward his brother again. "Listen here. You keep your eyes open with the widow Rundle, Cam. I got money on you. Fifty bucks says—"

"Oh, stop teasing Cam!" snapped his aunt. "Sara Rundle's too fashionable and fine to wear rubber boots in a pigpen, if you ask me." Marty scoffed. "Quartet! Fiddle and accordion's always been good enough for folks up here. She's not the woman for any sensible rancher. City gal through and through!"

"Oh, give her a chance, Marty," Cameron put in mildly. "She can't help it if she's from Vancouver. You can't hold that against her."

Suddenly Zoey realized she'd been siding with Marty all along. Quartet, indeed!

"My mommy and me lived in a city once," Lissy announced proudly. "A bi-ig city." She spread her arms wide. "My mommy and daddy got dee-vorced when I was little," she whispered, turning toward Zoey. "Dee-vorced means people don't live together and sleep in the same bed like Becky's mom and dad do. Then my mommy got lots and lots of boyfriends when we moved to the city. *Lots!*"

Her big blue eyes met Zoey's in bewilderment. Zoey put her hand over the child's on the tablecloth and squeezed it gently. "Cities are fine places, honey," she said lamely, contrary to Marty's opinion, apparently, but totally at a loss for any other comment after Lissy's outburst. "Why, I come from a city myself." She felt a sudden and surprising need to reassure the child, who, until now, had not even addressed her directly.

"Eat your peas," Marty ordered the girl, with a black look across the table at her father.

Why was Cameron's ex a forbidden subject? She

was Lissy's mother, after all. Zoey couldn't figure out the undertones in the room. It was easier to concentrate on the inscrutable cowpoke across the table, who'd said nothing during the meal, not one word, probably because his mouth was always full. Gabe definitely appreciated Marty's home cooking, judging by the quantity he stuffed into his creased and whiskered face. Was he a regular fixture at the family's Sunday dinner? If so, Zoey guessed he probably didn't eat much on Friday or Saturday, priming himself for the big event.

"Say, anyone goin' to the Winter Fair next Friday?" Ryan asked, with a smile for Zoey. "I thought I'd take Zoey here and introduce her to one of the high points of the Christmas season. Maybe take Mary Ellen, too. And Lissy, if she wants to go."

Ryan ran his hand amiably over his close-shaven jaw and shot a glance at his brother. "Say, pass those spuds over here, will you, Gabe? Before you eat 'em all up."

LISSY WAS HOME from school by noon on Friday, in time to join Zoey and Ryan for their planned trip to the Stoney Creek Christmas Fair. Zoey watched her get out of Ryan's Blazer at one o'clock, after he'd picked her up at the bus stop, a tiny blond waif dressed in a red winter coat, clutching her limp Pokémon book bag and lunch box. She was a sweet, sober child with big blue eyes and a chin-length cut with straight bangs. *She must look like her mother.*

At the last minute, Zoey learned that Cameron in-

tended to join them. After Lissy had changed her
school clothes and they'd all gathered at Ryan's vehicle, Zoey saw her whisper in her father's ear. He
looked at Zoey, then said the child wanted the back
seat so she could sit with Mary Ellen who was joining
them en route. Cameron suggested Ryan get in the
back, too, so that Zoey would have a better view of
the country. She was the visitor, after all. Which meant
Zoey was stuck in the front passenger seat beside
Cameron, who was driving.

She didn't have to worry about making conversation. He didn't say anything most of the way, except
for the occasional comment tossed to the back seat, to
his daughter or, later, to Mary Ellen. Zoey hid behind
her sunglasses and stared out her window. She had an
unpleasant feeling in her stomach. Had Lissy told her
father she disliked Zoey and didn't want to sit by her?
Zoey knew she wasn't good with kids, but it hurt to
think the child had made her preferences clear and her
father, in turn, had made sure that the people who sat
with his daughter were her uncle and Mary Ellen, not
the strange new lady who lived above their garage.

Cameron drove fast. Zoey was about to spout some
remark about either his silence or his driving but before she'd quite screwed up the courage, they arrived
at the Stoney Creek Community Center, where the annual Christmas craft fair was held. The open space
outside the center had a play area for children, plus
what looked like a petting zoo under temporary shel-
ter. Out behind, a small-time carnival company had

set up a few rides, mostly designed for very young children.

Lissy, who clung to Mary Ellen's hand, begged to visit the petting zoo first. "Uncle Ry, you'll take me, won't you?" Zoey had noticed before that Ryan and his niece seemed to have a good relationship, while her own father seemed a little distant, even stiff with her.

"Zoey, too? Your dad?" Mary Ellen called to the child, but Melissa shook her head. With an apologetic look at her and Cameron, Mary Ellen hurried off with Ryan and the little girl.

# CHAPTER EIGHT

"RELIEVED?" Cameron murmured, over the top of Zoey's head as he scanned the busy parking lot, hands in his pockets.

"I'm not sure what you mean," Zoey said. "Shall we go in?" She walked straight ahead and rummaged in her purse for her wallet so she could pay the entrance fee.

Before she could come up with the three dollars, Cameron had stepped ahead and paid for them all. "That'll be Mary Ellen Owen and Ryan and my little girl coming in later, Marge," he said to the iron-haired ticket-taker. She nodded and beamed at them. Zoey thrust her wallet back into her purse with a frown, muttering to herself about take-charge men.

Cameron leaned toward her as they walked into the building. "What did you say?"

"Oh, nothing." Zoey spotted some stained glass ornaments at a table near the door. They'd look great on her living room windows.

She loved Christmas. Now that she rarely joined her sisters and parents for the holiday, she tended to go all out with decorating and baking and entertaining for her own friends. So far, she hadn't spent a Christmas alone. Sometimes she went away, took a holiday trip to the sun with a girlfriend. This year? No plans. After the wedding, she was flying home to an empty apartment.

Cameron followed her to the table. "What I mean is," he said, continuing the conversation he'd started outside, "I get the impression you're not too crazy about my daughter."

She took a deep breath and bit her lower lip. "I don't think she likes me," Zoey confessed. It was the truth, and it felt good to finally admit her suspicions. "It's my fault. I'm not good with kids. I never have been."

Her voice faltered, and Cameron put his hand on her elbow. They stopped in the aisle, facing each other. Several shoppers bumped into them, with cheerful apologies.

"I just don't know what to say to them," she finished. "They just seem so—so *strange* to me. One of those things, I guess." She dug through her wallet to see how much cash she had, since none of these craft booths took debit cards. It was a good excuse not to look at him.

"Listen." Cameron thrust out one hand again, as though to touch her shoulder, then seemed to think better of it. "Don't worry about it. I never thought I'd be any good as a dad myself until Lissy came to live with me. Believe me, kids grow on you." He smiled, his eyes distant, as though he was thinking of his small daughter as a tiny, blond baby. Or her beautiful, absent mother who, according to Lissy, was a dancer, although Elizabeth said she'd been a drunk. Maybe both.

"You're good at being a dad?" she teased.

"I'm okay." He shrugged, smiling.

He should smile more often, she thought. When he did, he was a very attractive man. What with running the ranch, arranging Ryan's love life, raising a child on his own, she supposed he didn't have much time or inclination to smile.

"You might be right." She sighed.

Anyway, it didn't matter about Lissy. It wasn't as if she was *Ryan's* child—he was the Donnelly she was interested in. She turned to survey the exhibits that lined the north wall of the community center. It was a large building, and there were booths and tables everywhere. "I'm going to look around. Shall I meet you somewhere?" He might as well know she was perfectly capable of strolling around on her own. These Western guys could be a little too protective of their womenfolk sometimes.

*Womenfolk!* Was that what she'd become now that she was back in Stoney Creek? Talk about cornball western!

"Nope. I'll stick close to you, if you don't mind," he said, taking her elbow as they turned to go down another aisle. He smiled at a familiar-looking blond woman coming from the other direction. "Sara," he acknowledged, nodding and raising one hand in a casual salute.

The woman glanced quizzically at Zoey, then suddenly reached toward him. "Oh, Cam—"

Cameron stopped and Zoey quickly moved ahead, relieved and yet annoyed at the interruption. That, of course, was the ''shameless'' Sara. She was very pretty.

Zoey inspected some hand-quilted Christmas ornaments on a table. She wished Elizabeth had a booth but she'd told Zoey that she'd booked into another event before the date for the Stoney Creek Craft Fair was settled. A few minutes later he was at her elbow again.

''Cameron, you don't need to follow me around. Really. Go along with your friend, if you'd like. I won't get lost, I promise!''

''I know you won't.'' He picked up a glittery object, turned it over, then set it down again. The delicate Christmas ornament looked unutterably fragile in his large, work-hardened hand. The contrast grabbed at something in Zoey's heart. It was thinking about Christmas, she told herself; that was all.

''It's *not* necessary,'' she murmured stubbornly.

''I know.'' He was as stubborn as she was.

''I'm sure you're not interested in crafts! Quilts? Candles? Table runners? Tree decorations?''

''Maybe they're like kids—they can grow on you. Some kids, anyway.''

Zoey laughed. She bent to examine the stained glass Christmas ornaments at the next table. She felt a bit better. It helped to laugh. Even though they were worlds apart, she and Cameron obviously had a few things in common. Ryan, for one. And he seemed to have a sense of humor, if you dug deep enough. If she ever ended up in a relationship with Ryan—a big if!—

it was important to get along with the whole family. Including Cameron and Lissy.

Zoey held up a flat circular glass pendant with three colorful rabbits. It was meant as a sort of sun-catcher or window ornament. "Think Lissy would like this?"

"Bribe?"

"Incentive," Zoey replied with a smile. "Kids enjoy getting presents, right? I always did, although," she mused, hunting through her wallet for a twenty, "I never got many."

"No?"

"Too many little Phillipses in the family, I guess," she said as she handed over the money. "Too little cash." She grimaced quickly. "Dad was always getting fired and we'd move, and then there were six of us girls to feed. I'm sure they were trying for a boy, don't you think? With names like Thomasina Henrietta for my oldest sister and Josephetta Antonia for me? They gave up after Stephie."

"Josephetta?" He frowned, and Zoey wished she hadn't blurted out the dreaded name.

"Dad was an inventor," she said, hurrying on. "An original thinker. He made up everything, including names."

"I didn't know him," Cameron said. "I believe I met one or two of your older sisters, though. I may have gone to school with them."

"How old are you?" Zoey asked baldly.

"Thirty-four," he said, with a glimmer of amusement in his eyes, which were an interesting compromise between green and brown. "Why?"

"No reason. Just wondered if any of my sisters were your age. Frederica's thirty-two and Tiggy's thirty-five. They're both married, with kids."

"And you?"

"Married?" She shook her head. "No. But of course you knew that. I'm twenty-eight and I have a sister, Teddy, who's twenty-nine. Her real name is Frances Theodora—can you imagine naming a baby that? She's not married, either. Stephie is, she's twenty-six. Roberta is in between Frederica and Tiggy. Anything else?" She was babbling. She had no idea why. Why did she keep getting into these ridiculous conversations with Ryan's brother? First food and cooking, back at the apartment, now age and weird names. Next they'd be exchanging zodiac signs.

"Nope."

Maybe he was checking her out for his brother. Cameron was the careful type. He'd want to know what the family might be getting into.

Maybe she was just growing cynical in her old age. Zoey gathered up her bag with the ornaments and the gift for Lissy carefully wrapped in tissue paper. "Look at that—baking. Mmm. I could use some." She headed across the aisle to a table that was groaning with cakes and pies and rolls—the finest the good ladies of Stoney Creek and District had to offer.

Cameron bought a lemon meringue pie while Zoey studied some mincemeat tarts and warm cinnamon buns.

"My favorite," he said sheepishly. "Marty can't

make pastry worth a damn. But don't tell her I said
that.''

Zoey felt a warm glow. She liked secrets. She'd
helped Lydia with all the baking on the catering jobs
for Call-a-Girl and had learned the finer points of the
art from Corinne Phillips, her mother, who'd baked
and cooked for the entire family of eight, mostly to
save money. Zoey remembered dying for a slice of
white store-bought bread when she was a kid, usually
getting it in the form of a peanut butter sandwich at
Mary Ellen's house. Edith Owen didn't bake twelve
loaves every Saturday the way Zoey's mother did.

''Half an hour!'' She glanced at her watch. ''How
long does it take to pet a goat?''

Just then, as though on cue, she spotted Ryan and
Mary Ellen. Then the little girl emerged from the
crowd and Zoey could see why they were walking so
slowly.

A kitten!

Ryan had a rather pained look on his handsome
face, Mary Ellen was smiling and Melissa was beaming. ''Look, Daddy! Look what Uncle Ryan bought
me—a kitty!''

She gazed lovingly down at the tiny orange ball of
fluff in her arms, then up at her father. ''Can I keep
it? Please, Daddy?''

Cameron was definitely in the family hot seat. He
scowled at his brother. ''I thought it was a *petting*
zoo.''

Ryan gave him a half-embarrassed grin. ''Well, it
is. Mostly. A kid had a box of kittens, though, and

Lissy really wanted one. Mary Ellen, too. I couldn't handle the two of them whining for that damn kitten. I *had* to give in."

Ryan smiled at Mary Ellen. Her cheeks were pink and she seemed almost as excited as Lissy was.

"Oh, he's beautiful, honey," Zoey breathed, reaching down to stroke the tiny head. "What are you going to call him? If—" she shot a severe look at Cameron "—your daddy lets you keep him."

"Or her. We don't know if it's a him or a her, do we, Mary Ellen?" Melissa said importantly. She was including Zoey in the conversation, which was an improvement. "I'm going to call him or her Kitty for now. Daddy, pleeeease?"

The little girl was adorable. How could Cameron refuse her anything? "Okay, sweetie. You'll have to take care of it. You can't expect Aunt Marty to look after it when the novelty wears off."

"Oh, thank you, thank you—*ouch!*" Lissy was jumping up and down in her enthusiasm and the terrified kitten had dug its claws into her arm. "Oh! Kitty, don't *do* that!"

"That's a good name," Zoey said, smiling. "Kitty. Suits a him or a her. Right, Mary Ellen?"

Mary Ellen's eyes were alight. Zoey wondered if she was the one who'd *really* wanted the kitten. "Let's take him back to his mama now that you've had a chance to show him to your dad and Zoey," Mary Ellen suggested. "We'll pick him up when we're ready to go home."

"Or her," the little girl interjected seriously.

"Or her," Mary Ellen agreed.

The two of them retreated the way they'd come, Lissy chatting happily to Mary Ellen as they walked.

Ryan put his free arm around Zoey's neck suddenly and pulled her against him. "Mmm, you look good enough to eat today, Zoe. Doesn't she, Cam?" He kissed the side of her face several times, making appreciative little growling noises. "Smell good, too." Zoey was horribly aware of Cameron's presence nearby.

"Probably the cinnamon buns I bought," she murmured, trying for a laugh and adjusting the packages in her arms so her baked goods didn't get squashed. Kissing her in public? This was totally new!

"Can you believe it?" Ryan asked, turning to his brother, yet keeping her in the awkward embrace. "My good old double-date pal from high school? Look at this!" He grinned proudly at her. "Back home and all grown up and gorgeous. I can't get over you and Mary Ellen being in town. Seeing you both again after *ten* years. It's fantastic!"

He turned back to his brother, who was frowning. "Look, Cam, I'm sorry about the cat. I know I should've checked with you first, but Mary Ellen and Lissy were crazy about that damn animal—"

"Oh, hell," Cameron said quietly, sounding irritated. "Forget it. Still, I'd have thought we had enough cats living in the barn."

"Those are barn cats. Mary Ellen says it's not the same." Ryan's face was a little flushed. "I'm the kid's uncle, aren't I? Gotta do something nice once in a while. And she's worn out that stuffed toy cat of hers, dragging it around." He tightened his arm around Zoey's shoulders. "Maybe I should get busy looking for an aunt for her, huh, Zoey?" He winked at his brother. "What do you think, Cam?"

Cameron nodded, and Zoey took the opportunity to slip out from under Ryan's arm. The blatant possessiveness of his gesture surprised her. He was sweet, he liked to flirt and tease and hold hands, but so far he hadn't put his arms around her publicly. Or kissed her so brazenly, almost as a statement, a badge of ownership. Zoey felt confused. What happened to being "old friends" all of a sudden?

"Sounds like a good idea, Ry," she heard Cameron say.

Zoey avoided Cameron's eye. He'd be pleased at these latest developments. She knew her face must be as red as Ryan's shirt. Naturally, Cameron would see this incident as more evidence of his brother's being "sweet" on her, whatever that meant, fanning the old high-school flames.

"I'm going back to the car for a minute," she said, taking the dinner rolls Cameron had carried for her. "I'll dump these packages in the trunk. Want me to take your stuff, too?"

"Sure." Cameron handed her the string-tied cardboard box containing the pie. "Thanks."

She started toward the exit, grateful for the opportunity to be alone for a few moments. She felt hot and her heart was still pounding wildly.

"Zoey?"

She turned. Cameron dangled the car keys, one eyebrow raised. ''Need these?'' There was no doubting the challenge in his eyes, directed solely at her. He hadn't missed a thing. Not the kiss, not the hug, not the male swagger that had accompanied them. Definitely not the reference to Ryan snagging an *aunt* to go along with Lissy's *uncle*.

''Thank you.'' She grabbed the keychain with a mutinous expression and headed toward the exit again, squelching her impulse to look back.

She knew Ryan was grinning. She couldn't bear it if they both were.

# CHAPTER NINE

ZOEY STOOD with Ryan and Mary Ellen at the railing, watching Cameron and his daughter on the midway's tiny tot bumper cars. An elderly couple had just walked by, arm in arm, smiles on their faces, and Mary Ellen murmured "ah." You could tell, just tell, that the old people were crazy about each other—after how many years?

She glanced sideways at her friend, then sent a skeptical eye toward the bumper cars. Hmm. Mary Ellen and Cameron Donnelly—were *they* a possibility? Tall, dark and sometimes handsome meets short, sweet and totally adorable? One a brokenhearted single dad, the other a softhearted travel agent-turned-inn operator who had a knack with kids? Mentally, she kicked herself. *Get a grip, Zoey Phillips!* A matchmaker she wasn't. She couldn't even conduct her own love life—or lack of it.

She'd had boyfriends, lovers. Several. One or two had even said they were in love with her. She couldn't say she'd ever returned the feeling, at least not a feeling like that long-ago desperate crush on Ryan Donnelly. Maybe love at sixteen or seventeen was special; maybe you never felt the same way again. Unfortunately, many of the men in her life had been the caliber of her most recent ex.

True, she often yearned for the solid security of a relationship like Elizabeth and Arthur's. A rock-solid partnership. Marriage. Respect. A man you could love with all your heart, who loved you. A man you could count on. Then she thought about her mother, dragging after her dad all over the country, pregnant every two or three years, raising children, baking bread, having to support the family, too. Now in his sixties, her father was finally earning a decent living, about to retire, and her mother was all worn out. What kind of Happily Ever After was that?

So far, Zoey had made every single decision that affected her adult life. Her future was hers. Any mistakes were her own. Any triumphs? Well, she could take the credit for them, too. She had friends, an interesting career, a respectable bank account. She was independent, free to travel when she wanted and where she wanted.

She had a life. A *good* life. But she wanted more. She wanted love. Real, true, knock-your-socks-off love.

"Uncle Ryan! Did you see me bump Daddy's car? I smashed right into him."

The girl's face was flushed, her fair hair flying. "Come with me to the Haunted House now, Uncle Ry!"

"No way!" Ryan laughed and made a face at the child. He shuddered unconvincingly. "Too scary for me, honey."

"Daddy?" Lissy looked up at her father.

Cameron settled his hat back on his head. He took her hand. "You mind, Ry? We won't be long."

"Take your time. We've got nowhere to go this afternoon." He slung his arm around Mary Ellen's shoulders. "I'm too old for this stuff, anyway. How about you meet us inside when you're through? Brrr." He shivered. "It's colder than a witch's—"

"Ry," Cameron broke in with a warning look and a glance at his daughter.

"A witch's toenail," Ryan said innocently. "What did you think I was going to say?"

Lissy giggled. "*I* know, Uncle Ry. C'mon, Dad."

"Okay."

Zoey watched father and daughter walk toward the series of joined trailers that formed the Haunted House exhibit. Zoey could just imagine how frightening it was. Spider webs and wiggly mirrors. Creaky doors and scratchily taped groans. It bothered her a little that Ryan had thrown his arm around her friend, the way he so often did with her.

"Zoey!" She heard her name just as she'd turned with Ryan and Mary Ellen to go back to the community center. Sounds of a few guitars and a fiddle came faintly through the hot dog-and-onion-scented air. Zoey looked over her shoulder.

Melissa was waving frantically. "Come with us!"

Zoey pointed to herself in a questioning gesture. "Me?" The little girl nodded and waved with her free hand. The other was firmly attached to her father's.

"Go on, Zoey," Ryan said, giving her shoulder a quick squeeze. "We'll meet up with you and Cam later."

Zoey walked around to the entrance and dug in her pocket for change to buy her ticket, aware of the warm buzz of pleasure she felt. *They'd included her.* Maybe she'd been mistaken, thinking Melissa didn't like her.

Cameron had an odd look on his face. Zoey suddenly wondered if he'd been the source of the last-minute invitation. But why would he do that?

"Cotton candy for everyone?" She'd noticed a stand selling spun sugar just beside the ticket booth. Lissy clasped her hands together and smiled endearingly up at Zoey.

"Oh, please, please, *please!*"

Cameron turned down her offer. No surprise there.

Zoey came back with two cones, jumbo-size, and handed the pink one to Lissy who whispered "thank you," eyes huge. Zoey stepped into line with Cameron.

"Incentive?" he murmured, one eyebrow arched.

Zoey shrugged. "Bribe."

"I see." They waited in line for their turn to enter the Haunted House. "Scared?" he asked.

"What do you think?" she said, smiling as she dipped into her cotton candy and tore off a chunk. Purple.

"I think you are," he said, peering over her head at various passersby.

Zoey didn't answer. He was teasing her; it was a refreshing change to see him relaxed like this. The cotton candy brought back lots of happy memories. She was enjoying the long-forgotten taste and texture of the spun sugar—more like sweet sand after it disintegrated in your mouth.

Why did kids like this stuff so much? "Want some?" she asked Cameron.

"No, thanks."

"How about some pink, Daddy? It's yummy." Lissy held up her cotton candy, shreds of pink fluff sticking to her face.

"No, thanks, honey."

"We-ell," Zoey began, with a wide-eyed look at Lissy, "I guess your dad just doesn't know what's good, does he?"

Lissy shook her head and shrugged her small shoulders. "Guess not." Cameron's daughter seemed to have warmed toward her considerably. That was terrific news. So what if it took a little bribe? Wait until she presented the sun-catcher....

"All right. Next, next, next...one more." The ticket-taker ushered them inside the enclosure and fastened the gate after the couple standing behind them. Lissy darted ahead.

The Haunted House was really quite pathetic. A lot less scary than Zoey remembered as a ten-year-old. The cobwebs weren't very well-done, just tatty fishnet draped here and there from the ceiling. The wobbly floor wasn't very wobbly, the floorboard squeak clearly came from a tape machine secreted somewhere, the skeletons hanging in the corner looked more sad and in need of dusting than scary.

"It's not even that dark in here," Zoey whispered to Cameron, feeling a little outraged that childhood memories were made of so little.

"You're not a kid," he reminded her, his hand on

her elbow as they went through a corridor between one trailer and the next. Lissy was somewhere ahead.

They heard a scream and came around the corner to see Lissy covering her eyes and stamping her feet in fright. Her cotton candy, Zoey noticed, was still clutched in one sticky hand. "A *monster,* Dad!"

Cam growled and grabbed Lissy's waist from behind and the girl shrieked again and broke away. Zoey could hear the delight in her voice. Other children were screaming all around them in the semi-dark. Adults were smiling indulgently. The "monster" was nothing more than a crude robot-like face, probably made out of papier-mâché, with plenty of painted-on scars and bandages, set in a shadow box lit by flickering purple and green Christmas lights.

Honestly!

The next room contained trick mirrors. Lissy giggled at one that made her appear ten feet tall, while her father, in the mirror beside her, looked like a dwarf. Zoey had to admit that a six-foot-plus man looked pretty ridiculous with a hat wider than his height, a huge belly and ten-inch legs. Optics. Things weren't what they seemed.

In mirrors—and sometimes in life, she thought. Wasn't that true? Chad Renwick, Jr., or so she'd assumed, was a thirty-something good-looking young realty executive focussed on a serious relationship with her. Turned out he was Mr. Uncommitted and Sneaky, getting it on with just about any like-minded female, including his brand-new receptionist. She'd blissfully believed *she* was the love of his life! Perhaps she was, but he'd had an awful lot of love to share.

Luckily, dumping him hadn't hurt too much. Zoey was just glad she'd found out when she had. Did big-city things like that happen in Stoney Creek? According to Elizabeth, they did. People were the same, no matter where they lived.

Chad wasn't the only man in her life who'd revealed himself to be a jerk. Just the last in a fairly long line. She'd always thought she just had bad luck, but it had recently crossed her mind that maybe she just didn't know how to pick men.

Concentrating on Ryan Donnelly was more and more appealing all the time. He still cared for her, if his attention meant anything, and she'd been head-over-heels in love with him once, even if she *had* been an impressionable teen. She'd always wondered *what if*.... Wasn't this a chance to find out?

Years ago she'd dreamed of her and Ryan together. In bed, on the beach, dancing, sharing breakfast. Adele Martinez had always loomed large in those scenarios, but Adele was out of the picture now. If she didn't give Cameron's matchmaking set-up an honest try, she'd never know for sure, would she?

If things didn't work out, she'd be flying back East soon, no one any the wiser. Except her. But what if true love really did exist, buried, a dormant spark, ready to be coaxed into full flame now that they were adults?

Anything could happen, her mother had always said. *You never know until you try*. The biggest risk was not taking any, her father had said, not that she put much stock in *that* advice, judging by Harvey Phillips's success in life. Ryan was an extremely handsome, generous—well, free-spending, anyway—man. Most women would find it thrilling just to look at him. He was employed, owned property, paid taxes. He wasn't as involved with the ranching business as his brother would like him to be, Cameron had hinted, but marriage to the right woman could change a lot of things about a man. And if he didn't like ranching, well, he could do something else. She didn't care. He could move to Toronto.

The possibilities were definitely something to think about, Zoey thought. She had to make up her mind. Either she'd go after him in a serious way or not. She couldn't keep wavering about it.

"Zoey!" Melissa called back to her as they entered the last compartment, a fake jungle set with corpses and skeletons and skulls everywhere and a rickety rope bridge to traverse to the exit door. "Come on with me. I'm sc-a-a-a-red," she said, shivering dramatically.

Zoey laughed, absurdly pleased that the child had asked her. "Okay. You go on first and I'll be right behind you."

"Whoa!" A huge rubber spider suddenly dangled in front of Zoey's face. Lissy screamed and Zoey realized she'd nearly screamed, too. She felt ridiculous. She heard a growl from behind and then suddenly someone grabbed her. This time she did scream—as loudly as Lissy had. The spider bobbed back up into the recesses of the plastic foliage overhead and a rubber snake dropped down. Shivers ran up and down her spine.

"Cam!" She giggled then, sagging back against him, relishing the solid feel of his chest behind her and his arms around her. Her heart was still rocketing all over the place.

"Omigosh!" She stepped forward, away from him. The spider was quite realistic-looking—at first, anyway.

"So, said you weren't scared, huh?" He looked mightily pleased with himself.

"Well, okay. Maybe a bit." She placed both hands on the wooden railing and inched her way to the exit door. Lissy was five or six feet ahead of her, shrieking in fine form at every wobble, at every fake insect or creepy-crawly that pulsated or wiggled.

They emerged into the sunlight, blinking and giddy. Lissy staggered this way and that, eyes shut, arms outstretched, pretending to be something, Zoey wasn't sure what. Cam was the only one who looked fairly normal.

"Okay," Zoey said, deciding it was time to act like a grown-up. "Come on, Lissy. Let's go find your uncle."

"And Mary Ellen," she reminded her soberly, as though Zoey had really forgotten.

"And Mary Ellen."

"We have to go get Kitty, too!"

Lissy took each of their hands in hers and marched between them. Zoey looked over at Cameron, ready to catch his indulgent smile, but he wasn't paying attention. He stared straight ahead. Even frowned a little.

What a strange man. What had turned his mood sour? She'd thought they were having great fun, all of them. Zoey swung Lissy's hand and listened to her

patter as they worked their way toward the beer garden
tent inside the community center.

He ought to be pleased. Why wasn't he? The day
was going very well. He was spending quality time
with his daughter and, if he only knew, she'd almost
made up her mind to enter wholeheartedly into his
matchmaking scheme.

They had lunch at one of the hot dog stands and on
the drive home, Lissy said her stomach hurt. Cameron
slammed on the brakes and the little girl lurched out
of the Blazer to throw up. Luckily, Mary Ellen had
damp wipes in her handbag. Lissy looked ghastly. Too
much excitement, Zoey murmured. Too much sugar,
Cameron said grimly, with a glance at her.

The cotton candy! *Oh, no.* She couldn't do anything
right....

Then the little kitten, which had been forgotten in
the ruckus of stopping the vehicle and letting Lissy
out, disappeared and was finally found hiding under
the front passenger seat. Ryan cursed. Cameron told
him to shut up. Lissy started to cry. Mary Ellen put
her arms around the child and soothed her, but it was
Zoey who managed to stick her hand in under the seat
and grab the kitten, getting severely scratched in the
process. Lissy gave her a weak smile and whispered
thanks.

*Reprieve.* Okay, so she didn't carry damp wipes in
her purse, but she was a woman of action. She could
get a cat out of a tight spot, if required. You never
knew when a talent like that might come in handy.

"*OF COURSE* YOU'RE PERFECT for him!" Elizabeth
leaned forward over the table at the Stoney Creek Golf

Club. The Nugents were members. "I've *always* thought so, ever since high school. I never could figure out why he didn't have the sense to see through that Adele Martinez. Just think! You could've been living here in Stoney Creek all along!"

Zoey wasn't sure she really regretted leaving town. Stoney Creek was a lot more interesting than she remembered. But she was almost twenty-eight now. At seventeen, fresh out of high school, the prospect of staying had felt like a prison sentence.

"Well, it's just a thought," she said, not quite as enthusiastic now she'd confided in Elizabeth that she still had feelings for Ryan Donnelly. Lizzie was the type to get involved. Luckily, she was busy with her family and her craft business, getting ready for the Christmas fairs coming up. Otherwise, Zoey knew she'd take a prime role in rearranging Zoey's love life.

Love life? She kept forgetting—she didn't have one!

"How's the book coming?" Elizabeth had been thrilled to find out that Zoey edited Jamie Chinchilla. It seemed as though, even in Stoney Creek, everyone read Chinchilla. No wonder the big bucks kept rolling in for author and publisher.

Zoey nodded, licking the last bit of chocolate mousse off her spoon. "Quite well. I'm pleasantly surprised." She grinned. "I can almost follow the plot on this one, which isn't always the case. Although," she added, in response to Elizabeth's shocked expression, "I don't suppose that's something the average Chinchilla fan would want to know. Sorry." She'd found that people generally had no idea how a book was written, edited or published.

"Definitely not!" She leaned forward, eyes alight. "Hey! Why don't I throw a party? Arthur and I? Christmas is always a good reason to have a party. We can invite a bunch of people, including you and Ryan, of course. That's the whole point. The mayor and his wife—you remember Allie Trennant?"

Zoey shook her head; she didn't.

"Anyway, Arthur golfs with the mayor. You know, we'll invite enough people so it doesn't look too much like a set-up and—"

"Elizabeth!" Zoey laughed. "I'm living right out there on the darn ranch. Why would you think I need a set-up?"

"So we can all get dressed up! I bet Ryan's never seen you in anything sexy. Mary Ellen and her stepmother and that fiancé of hers—Bob?"

"Tom," Zoey said.

"Oh, yes, Tom Bennett. Arthur says he used to be in the army, which means he can probably dance. I think they make them do that in basic training. Or at least they used to. Not that it'll do poor Edith any good."

Zoey collected her handbag and the few items she'd purchased in town. "Well, I've got to run, Lizzie. I have a couple more errands and then it's back to the grindstone." She made a face. "Sunday dinner with the Donnellys tomorrow. If Ryan proposes over the mashed potatoes, I'll let you know right away so you can call off the party."

Elizabeth laughed and they both rose from the table.

Zoey watched her as she rummaged in her purse for change for a tip. Elizabeth looked pleased. Zoey got a clear picture of Elizabeth's role in Stoney Creek society. The gracious hostess. The magnificent cook. The pillar of country club hospitality.

Ah, well. Let her take charge, as Zoey knew she would anyway. Besides, Zoey was getting sick of jeans and sweaters. She liked the idea of Ryan seeing her in something sexy. She liked the idea of the entire town seeing her as a sophisticated woman. Might as well put all the old ideas about little Josephetta Antonia Phillips, tomboy, to rest.

# CHAPTER TEN

DINNER THE NEXT DAY was probably going to be a lot like the Sunday before, although Zoey felt that at least she and Lissy had the beginnings of some kind of relationship since the fair.

She arrived at about ten minutes to six and Marty answered the door, waving a spatula. She shooed Zoey into the family room, muttering that she was just about to finish the sauce for the green beans and if the men didn't get here soon, they'd start without 'em.

Lissy and her kitten were playing in front of the fireplace. Zoey noticed the Barbie dolls had been dressed and set to one side, propped up as if they were spectators at a circus. The kitten, puffy and orange and certainly larger than it had been a few days before— to Zoey's eyes—wrestled with a soft ball Lissy rolled on the floor, growling and sinking tiny fangs into the fabric and shaking it wildly, which caused the hidden bell to rattle. "Hi, Lissy! How's the kitten? Change his name yet?"

"No, 'cause we still don't know for sure if he's a boy or a girl," the little girl returned seriously. "I'm going to keep calling him Kitty. *I* think he's a he, but Aunt Marty says nobody but the Lord knows yet, she's never seen a smaller—"

"Lissy!" Marty shouted from the kitchen. "That's *enough!* We got company. And I never said that, your Uncle Ry did."

Zoey stifled a giggle.

"You want to hold him?" The little girl, looking perfectly angelic in a blue velvet dress with a big white collar, held up the animal. "My dad says he likes ladies."

*Like all the Donnellys.* Or Ryan, anyway. Zoey took the kitten. He sniffed her hand and wrist and his soft pink nose tickled her skin. He was orange all over, except for one white paw, and he had big blue-green eyes. The kitten started to purr loudly, a surprisingly big sound coming from such a small creature.

"He *does* like you!" Lissy announced happily.

Zoey handed him back. "I hope so. He's gorgeous, no matter what. Does he sleep on your bed?"

Lissy absently brushed cat hairs from the fabric of her skirt. "I wish he could. Aunt Marty says he has to stay in his basket in the kitchen until he learns to use his litterbox." Lissy giggled behind her hand, then whispered, "He goes to the bathroom on the *floor* sometimes."

Zoey heard the sound of a door opening in the back entry area, and a minute later both Cameron and Ryan stepped into the room, dressed in work clothes. Ryan blew her a kiss and winked. Then he disappeared down the hallway, toward the bedrooms and bathroom.

Cameron looked tired. He made a slight gesture to catch her attention.

"Can you tell Marty we'll be right in?" he asked her. "Just give us a chance to wash up and change."

"Problems?"

"A few." He shrugged, then disappeared in the same direction his brother had gone.

Zoey passed on the message and helped Lissy set the table and by the time they'd finished, the two men were back, cleaned up and wearing fresh shirts and jeans. Cameron went to the door, although Zoey hadn't heard anyone knock, and Gabe, the hired man, entered, his eyes darting everywhere but at her. Maybe he didn't like women. Maybe he was shy.

His routine was exactly the same as it had been the previous Sunday. He sat down, dished up and ate, repeating the last two actions several times. Then he muttered something to Marty, presumably thanks, and bolted from the table, pulling his hat down over his ears as he rose, while the rest were still finishing their blueberry cobbler. Marty might not be much of a pastry chef, according to Cameron, but she sure hadn't missed out on any other culinary skills.

No one seemed to find Gabe's behavior at all odd. The routine was probably repeated at the Donnelly Sunday table fifty-two times a year.

"Corky gonna be okay?" Marty asked when she'd said grace. Zoey raised her eyebrows and Marty added, in an aside to her, "Corky's a horse."

"I think so," Cameron said. He frowned and reached for the bowl of green beans that Ryan passed him. "He's tough."

"What happened to Corky?" Zoey asked, ladling gravy onto her mashed potatoes. Much more of

Marty's home cooking and she'd be busting out of her jeans.

"Run-in with barbed wire." Cameron shook his head. "Some damn fool left a gate down and Corky got tore up in it."

"Torn up in a *gate?*"

"It's a wire fence," Cameron explained. "Barbed wire tacked onto posts. Horses don't handle junk on the ground very well—brush, wire, that kind of thing. Gets tangled up with their legs."

"I figure it's gotta be four-wheelers, don't you, Cam?" Ryan glanced up at his brother. "Huh? All-terrain vehicles," he explained, looking at Zoey. "We got a lot of recreational users around here. They can be careless with gates."

Cameron didn't say anything. Zoey could tell he was preoccupied. Poor horse! She wondered how badly injured it was.

Ryan changed the subject and managed to get in a few digs about Sara Rundle before dessert was served, which made Zoey wonder how long this ragging of Cameron had gone on. Maybe it was a regular Sunday topic. Another routine. Just how long had the teacher been in the picture?

Was Cameron serious about her? He acted as though he wasn't. Did it matter? If a relationship between Zoey and Ryan took root, it mattered. If Cameron married Sara, she'd be Lissy's stepmother. If *she* married Ryan, then she and Sara would be related. Sort of. If Cameron had romance on his own mind, that could account for some of his interest in getting his brother married off and moved out.

She decided to do a little prying of her own an hour later, when Cameron accompanied her back to the garage apartment. Fair was fair. He'd stuck his nose in her business when he'd come over to her place specifically to ask if she was getting anywhere with his brother.

It was pitch dark at nine o'clock, with only the cold unnatural glow from the yard lights. Ryan had asked her to stay and watch a video with him and Lissy after supper, and she'd agreed. At least Ryan clearly enjoyed the child's company, which was more than could be said for Cameron, who always seemed stiff around her. Careful. As though she'd break if he bounced her on his knee.

Zoey had helped Marty with the dishes while Ryan gave Lissy a ride on his back in the living room, complete with "gee haws" and "yahoos," to the girl's delight. Then she half dozed through *Lady and the Tramp*. Zoey had always regarded Lady as such a wussy little dog, not nearly good enough for the exuberant Tramp. Cameron had disappeared shortly after the meal and reappeared just as the credits were rolling on the small screen, wearing a canvas winter jacket and gloves.

"Ry, you go ahead and run Lissy's bath and I'll walk Zoey down the hill, seeing as I'm dressed for it."

Zoey had protested that she was perfectly capable of going back to the apartment herself, but neither man would hear of it. In a way, she was surprised Ryan didn't offer to escort her. But it did seem silly when Cameron already had his coat and boots on.

"How's Corky?" she asked when they got outside. She presumed he'd been with the horse since supper, although there must be all kinds of chores to do on a ranch like this. *Brrr!* She thrust her hands deep in her pockets. The forecast she'd heard on the radio before leaving the apartment had mentioned snow flurries.

"Holding his own. The vet's coming out to check him again later."

"Pretty bad, huh?"

"Couple dozen stitches. Maybe a tendon damaged, we don't know yet."

"Oh." They walked another few steps and then Zoey decided to broach the subject she'd had on her mind all evening. "I was just wondering. Are you really serious about this Sara Rundle or is Ryan teasing you?"

He stopped and stared at her for a full three or four seconds, then started walking again. "Why?"

"Oh, no reason. I was just curious." She was glad the dark masked her expression somewhat. She hoped he recalled that he'd grilled her about Ryan not a week before.

He stopped again and Zoey nearly bumped into him. "I'm not serious, okay? But I *might* be interested. That satisfy you?" He turned and kept walking, not waiting for an answer.

"She's a teacher, right?"

He made an impatient sound. "You met her—she's the one who talked to me at the craft fair, in the aisle."

Well, she knew that. "The blonde."

"That's her."

"She seems like a very nice person," Zoey rattled on. How would she know? She hadn't even met her.

He didn't say anything. Zoey trudged on, taking three steps to his two. "Listen. I thought I should tell you, I've made up my mind about Ryan. I think you're right. I think he likes me. There was definitely something between us ten years ago, at least from my point of view, so I've decided, why not go for it now?" She felt embarrassed to have to put it into words like that. It sounded so...so naive. So afternoon *TV*-ish. And who was she trying to convince with her definitely-something-between-us argument?

"I'm glad to hear it," he said. He didn't *sound* that glad.

He strode on. Zoey shivered, thankful she'd worn her down jacket. Okay, just one more question. Why not get everything out at once? "I, uh, actually, I do have something else I'd like to ask you."

"Now, why doesn't that surprise me?" he murmured ironically, with a quick glance her way. She slipped on the icy ground and his hand shot out to grab her elbow briefly. "Steady."

"Why doesn't anyone at your place ever talk about your ex? Marty even shushed Lissy last week, and it's her own mother."

She held her breath for a few seconds, certain she'd gone too far this time. They were at the foot of the stairs that led to her apartment before he answered. And when he did, his voice held a note that gave her shivers.

"Why, exactly, do you want to know?"

He didn't mean it. He wasn't really asking her a

question, she realized. He was saying: *none of your damn business.* She *had* gone too far. *Zoey Phillips, have you ever heard of privacy?* Of a person's right to his own secrets? She was a stranger here; she had no right to pry into this man's life.

She took a deep, shaky, breath. "I'm sorry. Forget I asked. None of my business anyway. Well!" she said brightly, as though the set of stairs was a brand-new structure she'd never noticed before. "Here we are! Thanks for walking me home."

He stood in front of her at the bottom of the steps, the light on the landing above and behind him, so that his face was in shadow. He kept looking at her. She couldn't quite make out his expression and managed to resist the urge to hum nervously as she fished in her pocket for her key. Big-city habits—and she was a big-city girl, like Sara Rundle—died hard.

"My ex is never discussed in this house, on my orders. Lissy's mother abandoned her two years ago," he said flatly, ignoring her suggestion to forget it. "Now she's *dead* and—"

Zoey gasped and put her gloved hand to her mouth. Elizabeth hadn't told her! "Oh, I'm so sorry—"

"—there's no rewriting history. The faster Lissy forgets about her, the better, in my view."

She was shocked at the harshness of his tone, aghast that she'd touched such a raw nerve in this difficult, contradictory man. "I'm so sorry for bringing it up. That's so awful—you must have loved her very much," she whispered. What else could account for the household silence? The pain in his voice now?

"I never loved her. She never loved me. She was a

drunk. A sad, pathetic woman I happened to marry one day. But that is none of your concern, either. Our mutual interest is my brother's love life, not mine. Right?''

''Yes—yes, of course.'' She'd found her key and began to climb the stairs.

''Careful,'' he said stonily, as she grabbed the banister. ''Watch the ice.''

''I will.'' She didn't see any ice on the steps. She didn't see anything. Her vision was blurry with tears, tears of embarrassment.

She jammed the key into the Yale lock and pushed open the door. Omigod! She closed the door, leaned against it and dug through her pocket for a clean tissue. She blew her nose.

Why, oh, why had she said anything? She'd upset him badly, regardless of what he said. She could tell. His marriage, his love life, his past—all totally none of her business!

And she *still* had no idea what this Sara Rundle's role was—not that it mattered now, in view of the revelation about Cameron's ex, which was vastly more interesting. He'd never loved his wife! She'd never loved him!

THE NEXT MORNING Zoey awoke to an unusual brightness in her bedroom. She'd worked until well after midnight on the Chinchilla manuscript, jotting down a detailed list of questions to ask the author next time she spoke to her. Anything to take her mind off Cameron Donnelly.

*I never loved her.* He pretended it didn't matter, but

Zoey knew it did, knew it mattered terribly. He'd said his wife was a drunk, a sad, pathetic creature, but Zoey wanted to believe that he *had* loved her. Of course he'd loved her! Cameron Donnelly wasn't a man to take that sort of thing lightly. Marriage. Children.

The Fullerton Valley was in the Pacific time zone, and Chinchilla was on the other side of the continent, which meant telephone calls had to be carefully scheduled. Zoey planned to call her author at noon. She yawned, stretched and got up. It was already nearly ten o'clock. She pulled on a robe and yanked open the curtains.

The entire world was white. Snow still drifted lazily from a gunsmoke sky. At least three inches of fresh snow covered the ground, the fence posts, the trees, the corrals and barns, the vehicles, the ranch house roof with its homey-looking tendril of wood smoke from one chimney.

*Winter!* She dressed quickly, and headed outside, wearing her good leather gloves when she couldn't locate any mittens.

''Whee!'' She scooped up some snow and lobbed it at Ryan, who'd just come out of the house and was about to get into his pickup.

''Hcy!'' She missed, but he saw her, of course, and tore in her direction, yelling. Zoey turned and ran, glancing once over her shoulder. Two farm dogs barked at Ryan's heels, chasing them both. Zoey shrieked as her foot slipped and before she knew it, she'd fallen and Ryan had jumped on her. He rolled her over and rubbed a handful of snow in her face. She screamed.

The dogs went frantic, barking and wagging their plumed tails, at a distance of about ten feet from where the two of them lay, half-buried in soft, granular snow.

"No!" Zoey twisted her head, grabbed up a handful and tried desperately to stuff it down his shirt collar, with little success. She was laughing and panting at the same time.

"Aha! Oh, no, you don't," he growled, pinning her right hand to the ground. His eyes were brilliant and blue and his cheeks were ruddy from the cold.

"Sez you and whose army?" she taunted, with a long-forgotten childish refrain that had popped instantly into her head.

"Oh, baby," he said, and then he lowered his head and kissed her. Zoey kissed him back, with every ounce of feeling she had, but it didn't last. She was winded from the snow fight and had to break contact to breathe. His arms felt so good, so tight around her. She waited for some kind of *feeling* to grab at her, but other than a pleasant, friendly warmth, there wasn't much. Maybe she was out of practice. It'd been months since she'd been with a guy—a guy she knew well enough to kiss, at any rate.

"'Mornin', Zoe," he said with a smile. His eyes were twinkling. "Remember smooching in the old Rialto?"

She nodded. "You taught me how. I don't think I'd really kissed anyone before."

"I did?" He kissed her again briefly. "Remember that time we dropped water balloons on the grad parade from the top of Lowry's store?"

Zoey remembered. One of the balloons had knocked

the town cop's hat off his bald head and he'd been
furious. Ryan's shot, she recalled. They'd both run like
weasels, down the fire escape at the back of the old
store and up the alley. "Seems like a long time ago,
doesn't it?" Grade eight.

"A million years," he replied, then rubbed noses
with her before standing up and offering a hand to
help her to her feet. He bent to brush the snow off her
jacket and jeans. "I gotta go pronto, before the boss
catches me fooling around. Cam wants me to pick up
some stuff in town. Hold this thought—" He tweaked
her nose and she squealed. "I'll be back after lunch
and when Lissy gets home from school, we'll make a
snowman."

What a sweet idea. Zoey watched as he got into his
pickup, revved the engine and then slammed out of
the yard, the back end of his truck yawing dangerously
on the snowy road, clearly for her benefit. He waved
cheerfully out the open window.

*What a kid.* Zoey's blood was still hammering in
her ears and her nose felt pleasantly tingly in the cold
air. She was a bit disappointed. She wanted to play in
the snow, anything to put off having to go in, get some
breakfast and phone her author.

A movement near the barns caught her eye and she
turned to see Cameron standing in the distance, by one
of the corrals. Oops. Did the boss approve of Ryan's
driving? Had he seen the two of them wrestling in the
snow? Kissing?

She hoped so. She lifted her gloved hand and he
waved back after a second or two. Had last night been
forgiven? His plan to settle his brother down with a

good woman—as he'd put it—might be crazy, but she *did* believe she was really, truly onto something with Ryan—if his actions since she'd arrived were anything to go by.

He seemed willing, even eager, to take up where they'd left off ten years ago. Well, not exactly "left off"—Zoey never forgot for a second that all his attentions back then had been designed to make another girl jealous. But that was then and this was now. If today's kisses didn't inflame her the way they once had, well, she *was* nearly twenty-eight. A woman of some experience, not a girl of seventeen who'd never been kissed.

She just wished he'd quit calling her "kid." She wasn't a kid anymore and she was tired of anyone in the town—especially Ryan—still thinking she was just "that little Phillips girl." It bothered her that no one, not even Elizabeth, seemed all that interested in who she was today, where she lived, what kind of friends she had. Sure, they were all excited when they heard she edited a famous writer, but Zoey didn't get any pleasure out of riding on someone else's coattails. She wanted to be appreciated for who she was, the person she'd become—competent, successful editor in a tough business, a savvy woman with a good life. Well, a pretty good life.

Maybe that was just small towns. Everybody was caught up in their own lives, which revolved around the town and the people who lived there. That made sense.

She saw Marty come onto the back steps to shake

out a broom. Marty waved at her, calling out, "Come on over for coffee—I just made a crumb cake!"

Zoey yelled back that she would and when she climbed up the stairs to her apartment, she felt better.

Marty seemed to take her seriously. So did Cameron, really. Lissy had thawed considerably. And Elizabeth—well, Elizabeth had even sounded a little envious when Zoey had described her apartment in Toronto and mentioned that she had a cleaning lady once a week. Lizzie had called her a "high-powered career girl," which had sounded awfully old-fashioned, but now that she thought about it, maybe it wasn't.

That left Ryan. But he'd take her seriously, too. It was a question of time and circumstance. She just had to convince him that she was no longer seventeen, that she was all grown up and—how did that song go?—"ready for love."

## CHAPTER ELEVEN

DESPITE THE LURE of the fresh snow, which was followed by another big dump the next afternoon, Zoey put in two long hard days on the Chinchilla manuscript and then drove to Mary Ellen's on Wednesday to help with the final fitting for Edith's dress.

At least that was the plan. When she got there, Edith told her the dressmaker had come out the previous day—hadn't Mary Ellen called?—and in fact, Mary Ellen wasn't even home, she'd gone to Prince George with Ryan to do some Christmas shopping.

That was a surprise. But, then, maybe it wasn't. Mary Ellen had told her on the phone the morning of the first snowstorm that she wasn't keen on driving in the icy conditions. Ryan must have offered to chauffeur her. And, as for letting Zoey know, she'd had her phone turned off for the past two days while she worked on the manuscript.

Zoey drove home slowly. Home! She was starting to think of the cramped apartment over the garage at the Triple Oarlock as home. The roads had been plowed and sanded and she felt quite confident, even though it had been years since she'd driven in winter.

Wasn't it just like Ryan to help a friend out? Mary Ellen probably wanted to pick up some things for the wedding party without Edith's knowledge. Who better to take her than Ryan? He always seemed generous with his time, always prepared for an adventure.

However, Zoey was beginning to wonder how much actual work he did for Cameron. Two days before, when the snow first arrived, he'd met Lissy's school bus at the ranch road, as promised, and brought her back just after one o'clock. Someone always had to meet Lissy at the road, a distance of over half a mile. It was a long walk for a kindergarten girl burdened down with book bag and lunch box, especially in winter.

Zoey had finished her call to the East coast and she'd been ready to play again. Lissy was as delighted with the new snow as Zoey and Ryan. They'd spent a hilarious afternoon, trying to build a snowman out of the few inches that had fallen. They'd finally given up, just shoveling a big pile—Ryan's idea—into one place and burying the little girl in it, with her arms and head sticking out. Afterward, Marty called them in for hot chocolate and the rest of the crumb cake. More than once, Zoey had wondered where Cameron was—shouldn't he be out here enjoying this experience with his daughter?

Perhaps he wasn't home. Or maybe he was in the barn nursing the injured Corky. Zoey decided she had to give him the benefit of the doubt. After all, distant and reserved or not, he *was* Lissy's father. The child was just lucky that she had a doting great-aunt and such an outgoing, fun-loving uncle.

Zoey hadn't felt comfortable since their discussion when Cameron had walked her home three nights before. It had occurred to her that maybe he felt the same way and was avoiding her. She'd pried into his affairs, but he wasn't the sort of man to tell her flat-out to mind her own business. He was an expert at avoidance. After all, wasn't he the man who'd said the sooner his daughter forgot about her own mother, the better? As if that was going to happen!

When Zoey finally drove into the yard, safe and sound, she'd made up her mind. She'd track Cameron down, wherever he was, and apologize. Take the blame and clear the air. Promise to mind her own business in the future. Whatever it took.

She found him in the barn. He and Gabe were applying a poultice to the injured gelding's shoulder when she located them in a dimly lighted box stall on the far side of the big, dark building. It was a creepy place, with black cobwebby corners and ropes hanging from nails and the smell of straw and hay and horses everywhere. She spotted several barn cats dozing on bales of hay and was quite sure she'd seen something skedaddle into a corner. A rat? She shuddered.

The instant Gabe spotted her, he mumbled something to Cameron and disappeared.

She attempted a laugh. "I get the feeling he doesn't like me!"

"Not you." Cameron glanced her way, but she could tell he did not welcome the interruption. "Any woman. They scare him." He poured a pail of steaming water into the gutter that ran in front of the box stall.

"Oh?" Zoey waited, but no elaboration was forthcoming.

"What can I do for you?" Cameron leaned against the animal's rump and tilted his hat down a little over his eyes, so she couldn't see his expression clearly. He wasn't making this easy.

"H-how's the horse?" Zoey said breathlessly. Actually, that wasn't what she'd planned to ask at all, but now that she saw the animal covered with bandages on his belly and legs, she felt sorry for him.

"Oh, pretty well, considering," Cameron answered, slapping the horse's rump lightly, causing him to swing his big head around with questioning eyes, his mouth full of hay wisps. "He'll pull through. No tendon damage, from what we can tell. Poultices are keeping the swelling down."

"That's good." Zoey shifted her weight from one foot to the other and reminded herself why she was here. She took a deep breath. "I feel you've been avoiding me the past couple of days."

"Avoiding you? Well, maybe I am," he said slowly, frowning.

She kept her eyes on the horse's ears. "I think I know why. I want to apologize for the other night—"

"The other night?" He looked genuinely perplexed.

"You know, bringing up that stuff about your ex-wife and Lissy and asking you about Sara and all that. It was none of my business. I apologize for poking my nose into your affairs. I don't know why I did. I won't do it again."

He laughed.

Zoey was stunned. *Laugh?!* That was the last thing she expected.

"You asked because you're a woman. Because you

wanted to know." He gave a good-natured shrug. "Hey, I'll bet you're even *more* curious than you were before. You've probably got half a dozen other questions you're dying to ask me."

She *did* have a dozen more questions, maybe two dozen, but she wasn't telling him that! "Believe what you like," she said stiffly, "but I am sincere. I shouldn't have asked about Lissy's mother. It must be a sensitive subject for you. Or about Sara Rundle. As I said, it's none of my business."

Cameron's expression darkened and he unsnapped the rope that was attached to the horse's halter. "There's no need to apologize, but if you feel better apologizing, fine. I accept."

He kneeled down and began to run his hands gently down the horse's left rear leg, paying careful attention to the area above the hoof. The horse flicked his tail nervously.

"Don't you want to know how things are going with me and Ryan?" She wanted to make it clear that it was okay with her if *he* asked questions. She owed him.

"No," he said, turning his head to look directly at her. "I don't."

"I thought you'd be interested," she said, taken aback. He'd wanted her to establish a relationship with his brother; that was his whole reason for offering the garage apartment in the first place.

"I'm not."

Zoey couldn't think what to say after that, so she left, trying to walk down the exact middle of the wood corridor that separated the stalls, for fear of getting her boots in the icky stuff that ran in the gutters, or spotting another mouse or rat. Some rancher's wife she'd make!

She was also extremely aware that Cameron had straightened as she left and that his gaze followed her all the way out of the barn. She knew the horrible Gabe was lurking somewhere nearby, peeping.

Marty wasn't home and Zoey was in desperate need of female company. She wished Lydia and Charlotte were here. On impulse she dialed Lydia's number in Toronto. No answer. No sense calling Charlotte. She was off in the wilds of Prince Edward Island right now. Mary Ellen wasn't available, either, so she decided to drive back to town and see Elizabeth.

She'd kill two birds with one stone. Zoey and Mary Ellen had agreed that she should make a fairly plain wedding cake. Not too plain, Zoey hoped. That was half the fun of wedding cakes—going crazy with the decorating and presentation. Elizabeth would have some good ideas and, with any luck, Elizabeth would also know where she could rent pans.

The actual cake didn't worry Zoey; she'd baked enough of them when she and Charlotte and Lydia were doing Call-a-Girl. But she wasn't sure if she could get roll-out fondant topping out here in the sticks. The special fondant was critical to achieving a smooth, professional effect. Also, what about actual cake decorations? Candied or silk flowers? She'd ask Elizabeth.

Zoey waved to her friend through the kitchen window as she parked and by the time she'd entered the back door, depositing her snowy rubber boots just inside, Elizabeth had put the kettle on for tea.

"What's this?" Zoey waved toward the kitchen table, which was covered with Styrofoam balls, velvet ribbon, fake eyes and bits of silky fluff.

"The Santa fridge magnets sold so well at the Nimpkits Lake craft fair last week that I thought I'd make a bunch more for the one at the Anglican church here on Wednesday," Elizabeth explained. "I want to get everything finished before the party." She gave Zoey a knowing look. "How are things going?"

Zoey knew exactly what she meant. Ryan. "Oh, fine. We've been doing stuff together. Having fun. I just wish he'd quit calling me 'kid.'" She made a face at her friend.

"Wait until he sees you all gorgeous in a party dress," Elizabeth said with a laugh. "*Kid* will not even occur to him. Book going okay?"

"Great." Even when she'd been up to her eyebrows in the book for the past few days, she kept thinking of Cameron's grim admission that he'd never loved his wife. "Lizzie, did you know Cameron's ex?"

Elizabeth paused, holding the teakettle high as she began to pour it into the Brown Betty teapot. "Not really. Why?"

"It's so weird. I had dinner over there again on Sunday and it was like, I don't know—the twilight zone. As though she doesn't exist. No one's supposed to mention her apparently, not even Lissy."

Elizabeth sighed. "It's kind of sad," she said, bringing the teapot to the table and pushing her craft material to one side. "He met her in a bar, she got pregnant right away and he married her. End of story. She wasn't from around here, from up in the Bulkley Valley somewhere. They tried to make a go of it for a while, I guess. Then shortly after Lissy was born, she disappeared.''

Zoey stared at her friend. ''Disappeared?''

''Took off and took the baby with her. It nearly killed Cam.''

''How long has he had Lissy? I don't get it—did the mother bring Lissy here and just dump her?'' Zoey couldn't help the unexpected surge of sympathy she felt. No wonder he was so grim. No wonder he acted as though he didn't know how to raise his own daughter.

''Just over two years ago. She brought Lissy back because she was involved with some older man who didn't want kids around. Not someone else's kids, anyway. Imagine!'' Elizabeth frowned as she poured tea into two mugs. ''Actually, I kind of felt sorry for her, although I only met her a couple of times. She was a wreck. And then—'' Elizabeth shrugged helplessly. ''Did Cameron tell you that she and the new husband were both killed?''

''*Killed?* He just said she died.''

''A car accident. Somewhere in the mountains around Field, near the Alberta border. Wintertime. Drunk driver. Not them,'' Elizabeth added quickly, shaking her head. ''Ironic, isn't it? She was such a lush herself and then some strange drunk weaves over the center line, head-on, and it's game over.''

''How horrible.'' Zoey thought of the shy overtures Lissy had made to her lately, after being so reserved at first. The way she'd watched her and Ryan together that Sunday evening. Ryan had had a drink in his hand. Lissy probably had some bad memories of adults with drinks in their hands. Her mother *and* her mother's friends.

Zoey stared at her friend. "He told me the sooner Lissy forgot about her mother, the better."

"I hate to say it, but I don't think Cam's doing that little girl any good by not letting anyone talk about it. Maybe he thinks that's best, but I don't agree."

Zoey looked at her clasped hands, thinking of Lissy so proudly telling her that she and her mother had lived in a big city, far, far away. How her mother had lots and lots of boyfriends.

"Well, thank goodness for Marty and Ryan," Zoey said finally. "That's all I can say. Ry's really good with Lissy. Cameron is—well, he just doesn't seem that relaxed around her. It's hard to describe." She took a sip of the hot tea and reached for one of the sugar cookies Elizabeth had brought to the table. "Have you ever noticed."

"Everyone has." Elizabeth picked up her own mug and blew gently on the surface. "Still, you can't blame him. He's learning. Fathering doesn't exactly come naturally, you know?" She laughed at Zoey's expression. It didn't? Zoey hadn't had a clue. "Why are you so curious?"

"I—I don't know. I just wondered, that's all. Last Sunday he told me his ex wasn't to be discussed in his house. That's it, period." Zoey lightly bounced the flat of her hand against the tabletop. "I thought, what a pompous turkey. Then he said he hadn't loved his wife—imagine telling a stranger something like that! I still don't get it—if he didn't love her, why would he have married her?''

"Circumstances," Elizabeth said. "He's the type, don't you think? Old-fashioned. And she must have figured it was a good idea, too. Took her out of the bar life for a while. Maybe they both thought it could work. He's a decent guy. Actually, I think it would be great if he got married again." Elizabeth's eyes lit up. "Don't you? Apparently he's been seeing that new teacher in town, Sara Rundle, did Marty tell you?''

"Marty says she's shameless," Zoey muttered sourly. "Whatever that means.''

"Oh, gosh!" Elizabeth rolled her eyes. "Marty's a mother hen. Still thinks her nephews are little boys. Well, maybe Ryan acts like one sometimes, but they're hardly boys," she said, with an arch look at her friend.

"Yeah," Zoey said noncommittally. She'd definitely noticed that Ryan was no boy, as Elizabeth put it, and she'd also noticed that Cameron had a certain rough-edged appeal. Not that *she* was attracted to the type, but she could see that other women might be. She wondered what the ex, Lissy's mother, had looked like. Blond, no doubt, like Lissy. *And like Sara Rundle.* "Let's forget about the Donnellys for a while— can I do anything for the Christmas party?''

"Just show up looking sexy and glamorous. If you want, you can help with the kids' party I'm having earlier in the evening. It's Tessa's birthday and I always do a birthday-Christmas sleepover thing." Elizabeth grabbed a notebook and pen from among the craft supplies.

"Sure," Zoey said. "I'd be glad to. What else?"

"I'm inviting twenty-two people—"

"Twenty-two!"

"Mary Ellen is coming, of course, and so are Edith and Tom. Shall I invite Cameron?" Elizabeth was writing busily.

Zoey got a crumb of sugar cookie stuck in her throat and coughed. "Sure, why not?"

"The girls will want Lissy to come for the sleep-over. I'll invite Sara, too—"

"Why her?" Zoey broke in. "Are you two friends?"

Elizabeth glanced up, surprised. "Well, they're an item, aren't they?"

"Oh. If they are, I suppose he'd bring her as his date, wouldn't he, if you invited him?"

"Maybe." Elizabeth picked up her pencil and scratched out the last name she'd entered. "Better leave her off. After all," she said, laughing, "it's not as though we're trying to match *him* up with anybody. Just you and Ryan."

"Maybe," Zoey interrupted, reaching for another cookie. "These are great cookies, by the way."

"No 'maybe'—Ryan and you," Elizabeth said firmly. "Like those? I can give you the recipe."

ZOEY DROVE to Williams Lake Friday, to see if she could find a suitable dress for Elizabeth's party. It was all very well for Elizabeth to expect glamour and so-phistication, but Zoey hadn't exactly packed for that. She had the outfit she planned to wear to Edith's wedding, a pale lavender wool skirt and jacket, very classy that made her look terribly elegant—in her opinion—but it wouldn't do for the party. Party meant fun. Slinky. Sexy. Over-the-top drama.

She couldn't find anything she wanted in the stores that lined Main Street, or at the one mall she visited on the outskirts of town. Why not go to Vancouver for the weekend? she suddenly thought. It was only an hour and a half flight and she could park her car at the airport. If she could get a flight on such short notice, she'd do it.

Four hours later, Zoey was happily wandering down Vancouver's trendy Robson Street, loaded with bags and boxes. The Christmas lights were wonderful. The enormous decorated tree in Robson Square brought tears to her eyes. *Christmas!*

She'd checked into a small, upscale hotel in the West End and had a spa afternoon booked for the next day. A steam bath, a massage and a mud wrap with manicure and pedicure to follow. Then a nice meal out and maybe a play. She'd see what was on. Oh, to be pampered again!

Life in the city. Really, a girl had to be crazy to even consider living anywhere else.

## CHAPTER TWELVE

Hi, Lydia,
Here I am, in Vancouver! Flew in for the weekend to do some shopping, on the spur of the moment. Bought the cutest dress at a little shop on
Robson. Needed something sexy and new to im-
press my rancher at Lizzie's big party next week.
It's great to be back in the city again—makes
me wonder why I'm chasing Ryan down out
there in Stoney Creek! Called Lisa—remember
her? From Call-a-Girl, way back. Unfortunately
she couldn't meet me for drinks or dinner. It's a
busy life being a single mom.
The city's really crowded with Christmas shoppers—makes me feel a bit lonely. Everyone
seems to have someone—husband, sisters, kids,
lovers. Say hi to Charlotte when you talk to
her—when's that girl getting home, anyway?
                                        Luv, Zoey

ZOEY GLUED a stamp onto the oversize postcard she'd
picked up of Vancouver's Stanley Park in full summer
glory and took it down to the desk with her when she
went for breakfast.

It was true; she *was* feeling lonely.

She didn't know anyone in Vancouver. Lisa Hudson, who had worked with her, Lydia and Charlotte briefly at Call-a-Girl years ago, had recently moved to White Rock, south of Vancouver. Lisa would've loved to get together, but she was busy with her son, her new apartment and her new job and just couldn't squeeze it in on such short notice.

Zoey understood. Being a single mom was a job and a half. The luxury spa, the trendy shops, the exquisite dining were all very well, but everything would've been that much more fun if she'd been able to share it. Preferably with someone special.

Was Ryan determined to stay in Stoney Creek and make his living out in the back of beyond? Cameron had said Ryan had a head for business and accounting. If something happened between her and Ryan—well, that kind of aptitude for business could be exercised anywhere, couldn't it?

Even in a city?

Zoey realized she'd never really considered how her life might be affected if she fell in love with a rancher. Her work was portable, that was a plus, but would she want to live in a remote rural location again? Icy roads, bitter cold in winter, endless bugs and drought in summer. She'd been caught up in the notion of pursuing Ryan Donnelly and hadn't given the reality of ranch living much thought.

She had a late-afternoon flight back to Williams Lake. The pure white hills and fields once she got on Highway 97 North out of Williams Lake helped raise her spirits again. It might be lonely and remote, this country, but it was wild and beautiful just the same. The quiet, empty landscape held a spirituality all its own, a sense that spoke to something deep within her, something she'd cherished since she was a child growing up in one ragtag town after another throughout the B.C. interior, longing for a home.

The snow-capped Coast Mountains in the distance, their summits lost now in the rapidly thickening dusk, were eternal. The rolling hills, partly forested, partly open range, that tumbled at the foot of the mountains had a taciturn quality, as though they cradled secrets and treasures. The annual fall roundup was evidence of those secrets, as crews of cowboys teased reluctant cows and calves out of the coulees and ravines to be joined to the main herd and cajoled down to the lower levels where they could be fed and cared for over the bitter winter.

*That's what life here is all about.* Wrestling a living from the soil, caring for animals and the land, providing for your family, standing up for your neighbor and what you believed to be right. Simple, strong beliefs. Fleeting but deeply felt pleasures.

Savvy marketing and the Christmas glitter of "Robsonstrasse," as Vancouverites fondly called their trendiest street, was a long, long way from that life. Seeing her stolen big-city weekend from the perspective of these hills and mountains, it made the anonymous, mostly commercial, Christmas spectacle just that—a spectacle. Hired choirs. Designer trees. Fake snow. Piped-in carols. Everything phony. Created for only one reason—to sell stuff.

Zoey took her time driving, enjoying the sense of gradually re-entering the world of the Fullerton Valley, glad to be back. She stopped in town to pick up milk, fruit and salad ingredients from the IGA, then continued on to the ranch. It was dark by the time she'd unloaded her car—her sexy new purple velvet dress, her groceries and the Christmas gifts she'd bought for Elizabeth's children and Lissy, plus Marty and even, in the end, little items for Ryan and Cameron.

The lamps inside threw a warm amber glow that made the little apartment seem welcoming against the blackness of the bare windows, and she hummed Christmas carols while she changed into more comfortable jeans and a green sweater before putting on the kettle for tea. Philosophical thoughts aside, she was a sucker for Christmas, and she knew it. The apartment was chilly. She should turn up the thermostat when she—

All of a sudden, the cosy evening quiet was broken.

She heard heavy boots ascending the stairs outside and then a rapid hammering at her door. "Zoey? Is that you? Dammit—open up!"

Zoey ran to the door and unlocked it. Cameron burst in and slammed the door behind him, spraying snow from his boots and jacket all over her clean floor. Had something gone wrong? Ryan? Lissy?

"Where the *hell* have you been?"

Zoey was shocked. "Wh-what?" She took a step backward.

"You heard me."

"What do you mean—where the hell have *I* been?" she repeated, dazed.

He grabbed her by the shoulder, his expression furious. She wrenched herself free, her anger flaring to match his.

"I mean it. People have been going out of their minds wondering where you were. Wondering if you were—if you were all right. Dammit, don't you ever think of other people?"

People were *worried?* Confusion replaced her anger. "Other p-people? Worried about *me?*"

"Other people! Ryan was worried sick. So was Marty." He looked into her eyes, adding in a slightly softer tone, "So was I. We all were."

"But—" Zoey felt behind her for a chair—she'd backed all the way into the kitchen by now—and sank down into it. "I—I went to Vancouver. It was no big deal. I just decided on Friday that "

He swore and flung his hat down on the chair that stood by the door. She noted, in some distant part of her mind, that the hat actually bounced. "You just *decided* to go to Vancouver!" He snapped his fingers. "Just like that. It never crossed your mind to tell anyone. It never occurred to you that people might worry. That they might wonder if you'd—" he threw up his hands in a gesture of frustration "—been kidnapped by some creep you met in a bar somewhere and been raped and tossed in a gravel pit. Or driven off the road or—"

Zoey leaped to her feet. "Listen here, Cameron Donnelly! It's a free world and I'm a big girl. I can go where I want, when I want—"

"Not when other people are concerned about you, you can't. Not without having the decency to let them know. It's just common courtesy—or is that something big-city women like you don't bother with?''

Zoey was furious again. Just as furious as he was. No, it hadn't occurred to her that she should notify anyone. Going to Vancouver to buy a dress had been a spur-of-the-moment impulse, granted, but it was the kind of thing she did all the time. One lonely Christmas a few years ago, she'd called a travel agent on Christmas Eve and been jetting her way to the sunny Caribbean on Christmas Day, the entire airplane almost to herself, nursing a *cuba libre* while other people opened gifts, ate turkey and squabbled with their in-laws back home.

''Listen here,'' she said again. ''I take responsibility for myself, Cameron Donnelly. I always have. And I don't meet men in bars and go off with them, for your information. Maybe I—'' She felt awful, actually, that she'd caused anyone—especially Marty and Ryan—a moment's worry. ''Maybe I should've called, as you say, and I'm sorry about that, but you can climb off your high horse right now. I'm home, I'm safe, there's nothing more to worry about. So you can put your hat back on and go straight—''

The fridge motor whined, lurched, and then went off. So did the lights. It happened so quickly that Zoey didn't have a chance to make a dash for the drawer where Ryan had told her the candles were kept.

''Oh, *hell!*'' Just what she needed. She moved slowly toward the kitchen counter. She could hear Cameron swearing softly in the inky blackness behind her. She heard him open the door, then shut it again. Silence. Had he left? She wasn't quite sure. There was only the dimmest light coming from outside, reflected from the moon off the fresh snow.

She felt for the emergency candles and lit one with shaking fingers. It flared briefly, as the long end of the wick burned, then settled into a steady glow. She reached for a saucer from the cupboard and waited for some hot wax to drip onto it so she could affix the candle. There wasn't a sound behind her. It was as though he'd stolen silently away while she was busy with the candle, in complete contrast to the way he'd arrived. Maybe he'd realized he was completely out of line....

Finally, the candle and makeshift holder joined. Slowly, eyes on the wobbling flame, she retraced her steps. Cameron still stood in the tiny entrance to the apartment. She moved his hat aside, hanging it on the back of the chair, and set the candle carefully on the wooden seat.

He looked almost frightening, lit from below by the sputtering flame, like a villain in a scary, B movie. She couldn't see his eyes or his expression at all.

She brushed her hands together in an exaggerated gesture of readiness, took a deep breath, and said, "Okay, now, where were we?" then let out a yelp as he lowered one hand to douse the candle and with the other, pulled her toward him.

She lost her balance and fell against his chest, raising her hands automatically to protect herself. His canvas jacket was cold and snowy. His hands, rough and hard, were suddenly on her face, cupping it, and then, to her absolute horror, she felt his mouth on hers...

His mouth was cold at first, then warm. Zoey's

enormous surprise turned to something else that frightened her terribly.... *She liked it.* At least, she liked it a little. The tiniest bit. It was a completely visceral reaction, she told herself. Her own body working against her clear, sensible, rational mind. This wasn't right, no, definitely not, but she realized she was thrilled by the feel of his hard, man's body against hers, even the unyielding way he gripped her head, keeping her face tilted up so he could kiss her. *Forever.*

Then sanity prevailed and she began to struggle for her balance. "Let me go! Stop—!" She pushed against his chest, wishing she could see.

He released her abruptly. He swore and said something that buzzed in her ears. She heard the door open, a gasp of icy air on her face, and the sharp slam as it closed, followed by the delicate tinkle of glassware on the kitchen cupboard shelves.

He was gone. Twenty seconds since she'd lit the candle, maybe thirty, and it was over.

Zoey's heart was ready to jump out her throat. Her ears rang. She put one hand to her hot face, aghast. Where had *that* come from? And, worse, her reactions. She hadn't had a boyfriend since the Realtor, over five months ago. She hadn't felt a man's kisses in quite a long time. Well, that wasn't exactly true—Ryan had kissed her. But he'd been polite. Gentle. The way she expected a man to be.

Her temper started to flare again. How could she respond, actually *respond,* to a—an *attack* by someone like Cameron Donnelly? Someone who clearly despised her? Probably despised all women, considering what she'd heard about him. He never should have touched her in the first place. *What had possessed him?*

Zoey shivered and felt for the dead candle with shaking fingers, then carried it back to the kitchen counter, walking slowly and carefully so she didn't trip over anything. Her knees were weak. All she needed was to fall down and break a leg. Yeah, wouldn't that be great—having to depend on a man like Cameron Donnelly to come to her rescue? She could just imagine what his opinion of her would be then.

Where was Ryan, by the way? If he'd been so worried, she thought irritably, why hadn't *he* checked on her when she drove up?

She relit the candle and examined herself in the small round mirror hanging on the wall to one side of the tiny kitchen. Even in the candle's dim glow she could see that her hair was a mess, her eyes teary, and her mouth—well, it looked as though it had been kissed, all right. She wiped her lips with the back of her hand. Then scrubbed hard at them. Tears filled her eyes, making her image wobble.

Damn him! Damn Cameron Donnelly. She'd thought they were partners, united in their common goal to link her up with his younger brother. Ryan was starting to feel something for her; she was sure of it. Before long, he'd realize he had the same tender feelings for Zoey that she'd always had for him.

When he saw her in the sexy new dress she'd bought for Elizabeth's party, he'd forget she'd been a gawky, uncertain kid. So would everyone.

This—what Cameron had done just now—wasn't the action of a friend or a partner. This was the action of a man with an entirely different agenda. What agenda? She didn't know nor, she decided, did she want to find out.

She went to bed, only to fall into a fitful sleep that ended when the lights came back on two hours later. The whole apartment, well-chilled, blazed with light, and in her half-dazed state, she wondered for a moment why she'd gone to bed without turning off the lamps.

With the quilt wrapped around her, Zoey crept around shutting off lights and turning up the thermostat. Then she burrowed back into her warm bed, craving the oblivion of sleep.

What had he said at the end—when he left? "Witch," she'd thought. It could very well have been "bitch."

ZOEY WORKED on the Chinchilla manuscript the next day. She spent an hour and a half on the phone to the author, trying to convince her that the Caribbean island of Tortola was quite small, and if the drowned heiress's ex-husband, who was extraordinarily tall, was living there, someone would be sure to notice it.

It was a hard sell. The author had the idea that a six-foot-eight Caucasian ex-basketball player could blend easily into the weekly market crowd on a tiny Caribbean island. Zoey often wondered why Chinchilla's books were such an enormous success when the author's experience, particularly travel experience, was almost nonexistent. Anything the author couldn't look up, she just made up, relying on her editor—Zoey—to fix things. Her excuse was always that this was fiction. Fiction, she'd tell Zoey, meant "made up."

If the average reader only realized, Zoey often thought, how much an editor had to do with the success of a book... Well, maybe not its commercial success—after all, Chinchilla was a fine storyteller—but its readability.

Ryan came over to see her at noon and she invited him to have dinner with her. Cameron's visit had really thrown her. She was feeling irritable and contrary and generally out of sorts. Just to be annoying, she made some lemon tarts, using fresh lemon juice, which were every bit as good—better, even—than the best lemon meringue pie she'd ever eaten, in the hope that Ryan would carry news about her cooking prowess back to a certain someone at the ranch house.

Lemon tarts for dessert, an easy-to-make but delicious pork fillet with white wine sauce, plus fresh broccoli—Stoney Creek's produce selection was pretty limited in the winter—with a tarragon cheese sauce and roasted potatoes. Ryan brought over some wine, which was a happy addition to the meal.

Zoey got a bit tipsy on her share and told Ryan all about her mad shopping trip to Vancouver. He seemed impressed that she'd done something so impulsive and, despite what Cameron had said, not worried in the least. He confided that he was itching to get started on a business venture of his own someday. When the time was right. Zoey was a little too muzzy by then to ask what he meant by the time being right.

At last Ryan kissed her lightly as he got up to leave and Zoey threw her arms around his neck and nestled against him, insisting on a more involved goodbye kiss. Ryan affably complied. She was pleased that he actually seemed complimented by her attentions—if perhaps a little unnerved—and did not refer to her as "kid" even once. He commented on the excellent meal a dozen times, which Zoey took to be a good sign that he'd talk her up with Marty and—especially—his skeptical and irritating brother. She hoped he mentioned the tarts.

Ryan finally seemed to realize that he had a warm, vibrant, sexy woman living right there on the ranch and that she was interested in him as more than an old pal from high school.

The party was next. And then Edith's wedding. By the time Christmas came around, Ryan was bound to see that Zoey Phillips was the woman for him. Who could tell? Maybe there'd be *two* weddings in the near future.

## CHAPTER THIRTEEN

ZOEY'S VISIT with Elizabeth before her Vancouver trip had yielded an interesting recipe for a "Prince of Wales" cake; she'd found a "Bride's Cake" in another cookbook. Both were plain, rich white cakes, but the "Prince of Wales" had a layer flavored with spices and dried fruit; that should make the presentation more interesting, Zoey thought. A white cake with white fondant icing might look dull. She liked the idea of the darker layer but she was afraid to commit herself without trying the recipe first. No way, though, was she going to make an eight-pound cake for a test.

Marty offered to let her use the kitchen on Wednesday while she was at choir practice, so Zoey decided to halve the recipe. Marty had said her crew would eat the resulting cake in a "jiffy." It was also a chance to try out the new pans she'd purchased in a wedding specialty shop on South Granville Street in Vancouver.

If the recipe was sound and the pan size worked, then everything depended on the oven. Not all ovens were created equal, she'd discovered; she'd made wedding cakes in ovens ranging from a high-tech Dacor to a decidedly low-tech wood and coal stove at a northern Ontario reception she and Charlotte and Lydia had catered for a mutual friend. Even run-of-the-mill electric or gas ovens often had hot spots that could jeopardize the final product.

Usually, in the general excitement of a wedding, no one cared much. But Zoey did. A perfect cake was a matter of pride. Double pride, now that a certain someone thought she was not only a rotten cook, but a careless person who gave little thought to concerns and worries others might have.

Interestingly, no one else had taken her to task for disappearing over the weekend. Elizabeth hadn't even mentioned it. Mind you, Elizabeth might not have realized she was gone, whereas everyone on the Triple Oarlock would have noticed that her rental car was gone for three days. Marty hadn't brought up the subject either, though.

No one, other than Cameron Donnelly, mentioned anything. The man was just too—too ridiculously serious! What gave him the right to take her to task for her decisions? You'd think he had enough to worry about, considering his plans to marry off his brother.

*With her help.*

But then Zoey wondered if Cameron was still part of the plan. If there *was* a plan. He'd been quite definite when she offered an update in the barn: he didn't want to know. That might mean he'd changed his mind about either his plan or her suitability.

Zoey dumped the butter called for in the recipe into a large mixing bowl. She tried hard not to think of what else had happened Sunday evening—The Big Bad Kiss. She'd decided it was just an act of primitive, feudal male frustration. What else could account for such rudeness? Grabbing a woman and kissing her!

Well, he'd certainly proved there were still men who
simply couldn't abide a strong woman standing up for
herself. Men who might even believe that kissing her
the way Cameron had would bring her right into line.
Show her who was boss. Show her what she was missing by being so ornery and independent. Yeah, right!

Falling into step, preferably behind *them*—that was
what some men liked in a woman. The feudal type.
They preferred their women modest and obedient.

Not her. De-fin-ite-ly not her!

Sugar. Two and a third cups. Zoey dumped it into
the bowl and began to cream the butter-sugar mixture
with an electric beater. The appliance moaned and
groaned, then began to zip along as the mixture soft-
ened. She stuck a finger into the pale yellow mixture
and tasted it. Mmm. Next, two cups of egg whites,
then vanilla, flour and baking powder.

Zoey couldn't find an egg separator, but she located
a small funnel and found that if she cracked the eggs
into it, the whites slipped through into her measuring
cup and the yolks stayed back. Wow, an invention!
Her dad would be pleased. She'd tell Marty about the
yolks, which she planned to leave in the fridge so she
could use them for pancakes or something.

The sun had been streaming in the windows of the
scrupulously clean, tidy kitchen for the past hour or
so, but now the world outside turned dim and white
as snow began to fall. Zoey put part of the batter into
one of the smaller pans and added spices and chopped
dates and raisins to the other portion. Then she poured
it into the second pan and stuck them both in the oven.
She hummed "It's Beginning to Look a Lot Like

Christmas'' as she washed up, getting more furious by the minute as she obsessed about Cameron's high-handed behavior.

One part of her wished she knew how to get back at him; the other part, the more grown-up sensible part, said *forget it*. Yes, unexpected, annoying and unwelcome but really…no harm done. She'd had her share of unwanted New Years' and mistletoe kisses; how was this much different?

"Surprise!" Zoey whirled at the sound and the feel of a hand across her eyes from behind—right into Ryan.

"Oh!" She giggled at the streak of creamy white left on his cheek by the spatula she held. He grinned and hugged her.

"Suits you," she teased, turning to the sink again to rinse the soapy bowls and utensils.

"Mmm." He drew one finger across the streak of batter and tasted it. "Hey, not bad. When does this stuff come out of the oven?"

"Not for another twenty minutes," she said, checking the timer. "Want some tea?"

How domestic. Making a pot of tea. The two of them sitting in the window seat, across the table from each other, talking. Ryan leafed through the local paper.

"Looking for something?"

"I'm trying to find a good second-hand snowmobile," he said.

"Oh?"

"Sure. Great winter fun if we get any more snow. I think Lissy will get a kick out of it, too."

"I thought you might be looking for a job," she said idly, glancing out the window at the falling snow.

He frowned at her. "Job? Now why would you say that?"

"Oh, I don't know. Elizabeth tells me you're quite a whiz with figures. I gather you've done some work for Arthur. I just wondered if ranching's what you really want to stay with. That's all," she said, smiling.

Ryan's expression of interest in her offhand remark changed as he looked behind her. Zoey half turned.

Cameron had entered the kitchen silently, on stocking feet. He'd placed one hand on the refrigerator handle. "Any more of those cinnamon rolls Marty made yesterday?"

How long had he been standing there? How much had he heard? Not that it mattered. They were hardly discussing how to make a pipe bomb.

"I think so, on the shelf at the back," Zoey said. She'd noticed the gooey-looking pecan-and-caramel rolls earlier and had been thinking she'd share one with Lissy once she got home from school.

Zoey watched as Cameron carried the pan of rolls to the counter, got out a cutting board, and cut off one section, on an absolute square. You'd think it was brain surgery, she thought with a grimace. Was this the way he did everything—so deliberately and precisely, as if the fate of the world depended on it?

"You finish up that statement for the bank, Ry?" he asked as he returned the rolls to the fridge.

Ryan sighed and closed the newspaper. "Not yet, Cam. You want me to go get Lissy?" Zoey looked quickly at the kitchen clock. It was nearly half past one, about the time the school bus arrived at the end of the lane.

Zoey got up. "I'll go get her today." She opened the oven door, gingerly tested the surface of the nearest cake with her index finger, then retrieved two pot holders and bent to lift out the pan. "These are ready to come out."

"Never mind, I'll get Lissy," Cameron said. He pushed a wire rack toward Zoey, positioning it on the counter so she could put down the cake. "Man, that smells good. What is it?"

"A cake!" she said, pushing a lock of hair back from her overheated face. He was acting as though nothing had happened, she thought crossly. "I'm testing the recipe I'm using for Edith and Tom's wedding."

"You're making the cake?" He couldn't have sounded more shocked. "A *wedding* cake?"

"Yes." She tested the cake with a toothpick, which came out clean, took out the other pan and set them both to cool. Then she untied her apron and hung it carefully on the peg behind the door. "Amazing, isn't it?"

He caught her triumphant glance. Zoey held his eyes boldly. She wasn't giving up anything with this man, not one miserable inch.

"Ain't that great, Cam? We get to eat this! After she's done fooling around with it, that is."

Cameron stepped toward the window and frowned at the swirling snow. "I'd better clear the road again before Marty comes back. Any gas in the Dodge?"

Zoey had seen both men clearing the lane with an older pickup equipped with a front-end snow blade.

"I think so, Cam. Listen, you want me to go for the kid? I can finish up those figures when I get back."

"No," Zoey said, stepping forward. "Let me— please." She reached for the fleece jacket that she'd hung over a kitchen chair earlier. "You both have work to do and I need to wait until the cakes cool, anyway. Lissy can help put the icing on. She'll like that."

She slipped into her jacket and took her mitts and toque out of one of the pockets. She'd bought new sage-green mittens and a knitted, Nordic-style hat in Vancouver.

Cameron still looked skeptical. "Maybe I'd better go for her...."

"It's no problem. Believe me." Zoey tucked her hair into her toque. "That rental car has snow tires, the works. It'll be a piece of cake." No one laughed, so she didn't either.

"Okay," Cameron said.

"Don't you trust me with your daughter?" she said, frustrated with his reluctance. "I've never had an accident, if you want to know. Well, one—" she might as well be completely honest "—but I was rear-ended. Not my fault."

Cameron gave her a long, hard look. "Of course I trust you. I—" He held up his hands in a gesture of helplessness. "Hell, what can I say? Go ahead and get her."

*Thanks would be nice,* she thought as she bent to pull on the long, leather boots she'd bought in Vancouver. They weren't the warmest or the most water-proof in this climate. Nor did the soles have much traction. But they looked good. She was tired of the fashion-challenged rubber clump-along boots she'd been using. And it wasn't as though she'd be spending the entire winter out here in the sticks where things like looks didn't matter.

The falling snow lent the world a mute, surreal aspect. Sound was deadened, but the crunch of snow under her boots seemed unusually loud. The whole ranch was quiet; she couldn't even hear an animal, a cow or calf, bawling anywhere. The dogs, appearing suddenly in the white swirling snow to yawn and whine at her feet, were the only source of movement and sound.

Glancing back, she saw that the ranch house looked cosy and warm. A refuge in this quiet, dead, white world. Zoey shivered and slid behind the wheel of the rental car, parked on the pavement strip beside the garage. To her relief, it started on the first try. She fastened her seat belt while the wipers took care of the two or three inches of soft snow that had settled on the windshield already.

Nothing to it, she thought, easing toward the lane that led to the public road, just over a kilometer away. As she'd said, piece of cake.

Speaking of which, the cakes had looked great coming out of the oven. Once she put the two of them together with apricot filling, completing her experiment, she'd let everyone else try a piece, too. Not until Lissy had helped her with the frosting, though.

Mary Ellen wanted everything to be perfect for her

stepmother. At least Zoey was confident now that her contribution would be. Or close, if she didn't mess up on decorating the cake.

Zoey drove slowly. Trees that lined the road on both sides waved in the sudden blasts of wind that blew loose snow across the road, momentarily reducing visibility to zero.

It was colder than it had been earlier, and the surface of the lane, frozen hard underneath the soft new snow, was slippery. The back end of the vehicle slid to the left once, and Zoey took her foot off the accelerator, instantly regaining control. Winter driving. She wasn't used to this anymore.

The school bus hadn't arrived when she got to the road, so she turned the vehicle and parked in the small lay-by. She yanked the heater to full blast and left the headlights and wipers on. Then she waited, her gloved hands gripping the wheel, while she searched for lights coming down the main road.

When she realized she was holding her breath, she let it out a snort of amusement, released the wheel and switched on the radio. Mall-music Christmas carols filled the small space. It was cheery company, at least. There was something about the blowing, swirling snow and the feeling that she was the only human being for miles around that gave her the creeps.

At last, she saw headlights approaching, and an instant later, there was the jolly orange school bus with the door opening wide. Zoey jumped out of the car and hurried toward the bus.

"You looking for Lissy?" the driver called, glancing back into the interior. He wore a Santa cap. "She's a-comin'. Lots of stuff to bring home from school today, eh, Lissy? Nice weather, ain't it?'' he asked, addressing Zoey. "Here she is.'' He winked and smiled again as the little girl appeared and made her way slowly down the big steps. The flashing red lights and the children's faces pressed against the foggy glass, watching, made everything seem normal for a minute or two.

Then the bus was gone in a roar of diesel fumes and a swirl of snow thrown up by the tires, and it was dim and very quiet again.

"You came to get me?'' Lissy said, as Zoey took her lunch box and backpack. "Where's my dad? Oh, boy! I get to ride in your car!'' She skipped through the heavy snow to the passenger side and clambered in when Zoey threw open the door.

"Buckle up!'' Zoey ordered when she'd settled herself in the driver's seat.

"Okay.'' Lissy fastened the seat belt around her, with Zoey's help, and clapped her snowboots together, leaving big clumps of fresh snow on the floor mats. "Here. This is some Christmas stuff we made today. It's for decorating.''

Zoey took the handful of creased artwork and an open envelope that held a length of paper chain in festive red and green construction paper. "Did you make these all by yourself?'' She laid everything carefully on the back seat.

Lissy nodded proudly. "Yep. And I even made my dad a surprise for Christmas.'' She leaned toward Zoey. "It's a decoration with my hand on it and we painted it and put sparkly stuff on and everything!''

"I see." Lissy must mean a drawing or one of those plaster of Paris creations using a mold of the child's hand. She could remember making them in school.

Zoey put the car into gear and gently pressed her foot on the accelerator. The back wheels slid sideways and the engine raced briefly. Zoey's stomach lurched. *This wasn't supposed to happen.*

"Whoa! That was fun," Lissy said, looking up at her with bright eyes.

"For you, maybe." Omigod. She'd been so adamant with Cameron about her driving skills. This new snow was treacherous. The tires spun and again Zoey recovered control. She'd have to drive at a snail's pace all the way back to the ranch. They'd wonder what was taking her so long. Well, better safe than sorry.

They inched along, Zoey praying silently that they wouldn't meet a vehicle coming in the other direction. Who would it be, though? If it was Ryan or Cameron, she'd gladly get either one of them to drive her vehicle, with her and Lissy as passengers. She wished now she'd let Ryan come to meet the school bus. Or Cameron.

The wind burst a dollop of snow over the windshield and for a few seconds, Zoey couldn't see a thing. Lissy seemed delighted. The strains of "We Three Kings" resounded through the darkened interior of the car. Although it was only ten to two, the storm had obliterated all daylight. Distances were impossible to gauge. Obviously the child had no idea of what could happen. Why would she? She was five years old. Adults looked after things in her world. Zoey was the adult on duty here, entrusted with the girl's safety.

They'd come to a complete stop while the wind
blew snow in front of them and now, gingerly, Zoey
pressed the accelerator again. The car began to spin
slowly and awkwardly. She tried to steer in the direction she wanted to go, as some long-ago driving school
lesson popped into her brain. They stopped sideways
on the road.

Even Lissy seemed a little overwhelmed by this latest movement. She stared questioningly at Zoey, as
though reconsidering the possibility that Zoey had
been putting on a show for her benefit.

"Never mind, honey. We'll just take it a little
slower. The road's pretty slippery."

"We can walk if we want to," Lissy said. "My dad
and I've walked before, lots of times."

"Not in this weather," Zoey muttered under her
breath. Or in her boots. She'd heard horror stories of
prairie folk who'd gone out to the barn to feed cattle
in a blizzard and been lost, frozen to death mere yards
from the barn or house. The rental car was warm and
it was full of gas. If they had to stop and wait out the
snow they would. They had a heater. Zoey even had
half a roll of Lifesavers in her handbag and a few linty
jujubes. They wouldn't starve.

Actually, the storm seemed to have abated slightly.
The road was clear in front of them now and the wind
had died down. Zoey pressed a little harder on the
accelerator. So far, so good. Perhaps that had been the
worst of it, back there, near the junction with the public road.

Gaining a little confidence, she sped up. She'd been

going at barely a walking pace. They'd take forever getting back at this rate.

The car responded smoothly and picked up speed. Then the sickening sensation of whirling, heaving all over the road, began again, and this time Zoey couldn't control the car's movements, no matter which way she turned the wheel. Lissy screamed. The car lurched toward the side of the narrow road. They ploughed through a soft snowbank and then Zoey felt a huge, ear-ringing bump as the car came to a stop at the bottom of the snow-filled ditch.

"Lissy! You all right?" There was no answer. *"Lissy!"*

## CHAPTER FOURTEEN

FRANTICALLY, ZOEY REACHED over to the passenger side and felt around for the girl. The headlights had been buried in a snowbank and, reflected back, gave a weird greenish glow to the interior. "Lissy!"

"I—I'm scared," came the tremulous reply. *Thank goodness the child was all right!* "I w-want my daddy." She began to cry.

"We'll be all right, honey, don't you worry. You're not hurt anywhere, are you?" Zoey wanted to ascertain that before anything else. Why hadn't she brought her cell phone? It was in her apartment and she'd come straight from the ranch house to pick up Lissy.

She gently squeezed the child's arms, probing for injuries, although she was sure Lissy was okay. The stop, while abrupt, had not been that violent and they were both securely strapped into their seat belts. "Anything broken? Anything broken off? Your hand? Your elbow? Tell Dr. Zoey!"

Lissy giggled through her tears. "That t-tickles."

"Okay, let's put on our thinking caps." Zoey rummaged around for her handbag, which had fallen, and found the half roll of Lifesavers. The car—and therefore the heater—was still running.

*Well-named candy.* "Here. Have one." She handed the child a piece and popped one into her own mouth.

"What kind is it?"

Zoey tucked the remainder of the roll back in her purse. "You tell me."

"Mmm." There were sucking noises. "Cherry!"

"Guess what mine is," Zoey said lamely.

"Orange!"

"Nope."

"Lemon."

Zoey rolled her candy around in her mouth, tasting. What flavor *was* it? Lime? "Guess again."

"Tutti-frutti!"

"Right!" Zoey had no idea what tutti-frutti tasted like, but it sounded okay. "So, what did you do in school today, Lissy? Besides make presents and decorations."

"We had a Christmas story about reindeers. We sang songs and—when's my daddy coming?" Lissy's voice trembled again.

"Never mind your dad," Zoey said briskly. "Let's see if we can get out of this little predicament by ourselves." She put the transmission into reverse and cautiously touched the accelerator. The car lurched a few inches, which was promising, then, with a grind of spinning wheels, settled deeper.

Forget that. She shifted into park, then began to think about carbon monoxide. Wasn't this how people died on lovers' lanes—keeping their engines running until they were overcome? Idly, she wondered why Jamie Chinchilla had never used carbon monoxide to kill any of her characters.

She turned off the ignition, just as a precaution. The interior of the car was quite warm. It wouldn't be long before someone, Ryan or Cameron, came looking for them. The radio went off, too, with the engine, so Zoey turned the ignition to battery so that they could at least have the radio. Running down the battery was the least of her problems right now.

The Christmas music was at least lively. She checked the luminous car clock dial—nearly half past two. They should've been back at the ranch by now.

"I'm cold," came Lissy's soft complaint from the darkness.

"Here—" Zoey took off her new Nordic toque. "Put your hands in that."

"My feet are cold, too."

Zoey reached down and felt Lissy's feet. Her boots were bulky and fit loosely over her leather shoes. "I'll tell you what, honey."

"What?"

Zoey fumbled on the seat beside her, looking for her new mitts. "Let's put these Santa socks over your feet, then stick them back in your boots and that ought to make everything toasty. What do you think?" She tugged her big woolly mitts over the child's tiny feet, shoes and all, then jammed her feet back into the fleece-lined winter boots. That should do it.

"How's that?"

Lissy giggled and swung her feet. "Good! Hey, you're funny!"

Zoey took that as a compliment. "Another candy?"

"Sure."

For a few seconds Zoey contemplated correcting the

girl, teaching her to say *please* and *thank you,* then discarded the notion. This wasn't the time or place for a manners lesson.

"Okay, now how about if we sing a Christmas song? Which ones have you learned?"

"'O, Christmas Tree' and 'Here Comes Santa Claus Right Down Santa Claus Lane.'"

Zoey smiled. "Let's start with the Christmas tree song."

By the time lights moved toward them from the direction of the ranch thirty minutes later, Zoey had learned a French verse to "O, Christmas Tree" and knew "Here Comes Santa Claus" by heart.

A truck stopped on the roadway, about level with Zoey's window.

Her door was wrenched open. A grim-faced Cameron stuck his head in, and Zoey was so happy to see him she could have kissed him.

Almost.

"What the hell happened?"

Despite his tone, Zoey found herself grinning in relief. Wasn't it obvious? "Thank goodness you're here."

"We sang, Daddy! And Zoey gave me candy out of her purse and I've got her mitts on my feet for socks." Lissy struggled out of her seat, scrambled heavily across Zoey's lap and fell into the open arms of her father. He buried his face in her neck for a few seconds, his arms tight around her. Zoey looked away, her eyes filling with tears.

She hadn't given him the benefit of any kind of

doubt. Not with regard to her, or his brother, or even his daughter.

"Mitts on your feet? Well, then, you can go up to the truck and get in," he ordered gruffly. "I'm taking you both home. Off you go." Lissy trudged cheerfully up the slight incline of the ditch, falling once and laughing, toward where the pickup with the snow blade was parked, the engine running, the headlights on.

Cameron wrenched the door even wider, pushing it against the snow build-up. "You okay? Can you get out all right?"

Zoey's legs were cramped and she gladly took the hand Cameron offered to extricate herself from the vehicle.

She stood shakily. "We went in the ditch," she explained, feeling a bit foolish.

"I can see that," he said, frowning. "It's icier than hell. You got the keys?"

"They're in there. In the ignition." Zoey felt the tears prickle again at the back of her throat. They hadn't been in any real danger, she supposed, and yet… She just wanted to get home, warm up and crawl into her nice soft bed and go to sleep. And have a good cry. The cake could wait until tomorrow. She heard the radio go off as Cameron retrieved the keys.

"Running the battery dead?" He held out the key-case.

His comment wiped out the good feelings she'd been having toward him. It was the final straw in what had been a very stressful couple of days.

"Damn you!" she yelled, taking a step forward and

grabbing wildly at the keys. She took a swing at his leg with her right foot and missed.

"Hey! Hold on, what in hell's the matter—"

He seized her arm and she tore it away. "Give me those keys! I'll get this damn car out of the ditch myself and drive it home. *Okay?* I can manage! A simple *thank you* for looking after your daughter would've been—"

Her voice broke and he pulled her close. Her face felt hot against the cold of his stiff canvas jacket. She didn't want to accept any comfort, but she allowed herself to lean against his chest for a second. *Why couldn't this have been Ryan?*

But only for a second. Then she was pulling away, sniffing back the tears that threatened to flood the ditch they were in. "Take your hands off me! Leave me alone—"

"Sorry." He held up both hands. "Sorry. I didn't mean anything by it. Honest. I don't care if you ran the damn battery dead. I'm just glad you're all right—"

"Your daughter, you mean!"

"No, both of you. I never should've let you go out by yourself in this weather. It's my fault."

She swayed. She felt weak as a kitten. He put his hands on her shoulders again and she stepped back.

"No, dammit. It's *my* fault. *Mine!*" She stabbed her cold index finger against her own chest. "I'm not a kid. I don't need looking after. I can drive. *I'm* the one who ran us into the ditch. Can't you even let someone run into a ditch without trying to take credit for it?" She knew she was making no sense.

He slammed the car door shut. "Let's go."

She wiped her face with the heels of both hands and followed him up the slope of the ditch as he led the way to his truck.

"I'll fetch Ryan and he can drive your car back," he said, staring straight ahead as he turned the truck around and drove toward the ranch. Lissy sat in the middle. "I'd appreciate it if you'd stay with Lissy until we get back. Or until Marty gets here."

How could she say no?

They returned at about five, and by then Zoey had regained control of her emotions. She'd washed her face, combed her hair and supervised Lissy's bath. She'd found clean pajamas and a fluffy bathrobe in Lissy's room. It was already dark, so pajamas seemed perfect. The mittens that had kept the girl's feet warm were back in the pocket of Zoey's fleece jacket, along with her new cap.

With Lissy's help—a mixed blessing—and a lot of questions from the girl, who seemed to suffer no ill effects from their misadventure, she mixed up a batch of icing. She allowed Lissy to frost the smaller of the two cakes, then sliced off a length along one side of the cakes. Both were quite tasty; the recipe would be fine.

Marty, who returned at the same time as Ryan and Cameron, immediately popped a couple of store-bought pizzas into the oven—to Lissy's delight. While anxious questions were asked and answered, Zoey slipped away to her own apartment.

It was still snowing lightly as she walked toward the darkened garage. She took small steps and trod carefully, only too aware of how useless high-fashion leather-soled boots were in this climate.

She trudged up the snowy steps and let herself in. The apartment was warm and dark, and the old fridge hummed comfortingly. She switched on the lamps and made herself a cup of tea, then curled up at one end of the sofa in the little living room. She turned on the radio to an old Bing Crosby Christmas tune, which, naturally, made her cry. Blowing her nose a couple of times, she tried to analyze her emotions, with the help of the strong, sweet tea. The tears kept rolling down her cheeks.

Okay. First: What in God's name was she *really* doing out here? Was this what she wanted—to chase after her high-school love? To prove to Ryan how grown-up she was, what a charming and desirable woman she'd become? Why wasn't she back in Toronto, being sensible, going to a play or to Handel's "Messiah," decorating her apartment for Christmas? Having dinner with friends at a good restaurant?

But, no, here she was, getting stuck in snowbanks, playing nursemaid to a motherless kid and bawling her eyes out when anyone looked at her sideways. Putting up with Cameron Donnelly's rudeness. His insinuations. His ill-humor.

If only *Ryan* had come to rescue them...

Never mind that. She had a plan, a good one. And she was sticking to her plan. She intended to give this developing romance with Ryan a hundred and ten percent of her effort. She would simply ignore his brother, who, she'd recently begun to think, was actually working against her. She'd made up her own mind; *need* his cooperation.

And if it didn't work out, the story of her Stoney Creek maybe-yes, maybe-no romance would at least be worth a laugh at next spring's reunion.

Tears filled Zoey's eyes again and she reached for a fresh tissue.

It was no use trying to make herself feel better. She didn't *want* to play this for laughs. She wanted to feel the way she'd once felt about Ryan, in high school. She wanted the passion, the romance and, even more, she wanted what she'd never had back then. *Respect.*

If, in the end, she'd given it her very best try and her Stoney Creek romantic experiment came to nothing—as could well happen—her next step would be crystal clear. She'd gracefully concede defeat, go back home where she belonged, pick up her life where she'd left off. No one need ever know.

Options were all very well, but knowing when to quit was even better.

THE MORNING OF THE PARTY dawned cold and bright. Zoey had a manicure appointment at one o'clock.

"Pink? Or Red?" the manicurist asked. "I've got a new color here called Hollyberries."

"Oh, go for the Hollyberries," Zoey said. It was Christmas, after all.

She'd spent the morning working on the manuscript. She'd finally convinced her author that a tall white man would definitely stand out on Tortola, so now the heiress's ex-husband was cruising the area on a yacht, not on the island at all. Zoey wasn't sure the murder plot would work. The heiress had been on a sailboat with a crew of seven and half a dozen friends when she'd disappeared. There were too many yachts in this book all of a sudden, and Chinchilla, quite clearly, didn't know much about sailing.

Zoey would give it some thought, but not now. After her manicure in Stoney Creek, she planned to come home, shower, do something exciting with her hair, defrag her legs, maybe have a nap—she deserved it after the midnight oil she'd been burning on the book—and then get ready for the party.

Ryan had offered to take her to the Nugents' but at half past four, just as she finished wrapping a few small gifts for the children's party, which started at six, there was a tap on her door.

"Lissy!" Zoey quickly maneuvered so that the gifts on the table weren't visible.

"Here." The little girl handed her a folded piece of paper.

"Would you like to come in?" Zoey unfolded the paper, mystified.

"Nope." Lissy shook her head. "My dad says I got to get right back and have a bath and get ready. I'm going to a sleepover at Tessa's!" She was obviously thrilled.

"That'll be fun," Zoey murmured. She read the note. It was from Cameron, handwritten—scrawled, more accurately—informing her that Ryan had been detained in town and would not be back to pick her up, after all, but that she was welcome to go to the party with him and Lissy. They would be leaving at five-thirty sharp.

"Do you want to take a note back to your dad?"

Lissy nodded importantly. "That's why he sent me. I'm the mail lady. Just like Jack Frost!"

Zoey thought she was a little wobbly with her fictitious winter characters, but never mind. She leaned against the doorjamb to pen a quick reply: *No, I will take my own car. Thank you anyway.*

"You coming with us?" The little girl looked wistful and for a few seconds, Zoey wished she hadn't been so hasty. But she preferred to retain control, including driving herself home rather than depending on a ride.

"No, honey. I'm driving. I need to practice, remember?" The little girl giggled and took the refolded paper in her snow-crusted mitten and began to make her way back down the stairs. "Is Marty going to the party, too?" Zoey asked.

"No, Uncle Ry's taking her to the airport tonight after the party so she can go to my daddy's other auntie's place. They're twins!"

Ah. Zoey had forgotten that Marty planned a pre-Christmas trip to visit her sister, Robin, also widowed, who wanted to go on a cruise with her early in the new year. Marty was such a fixture at the Donnelly house that it was easy to forget she had another life, one that didn't involve running and fetching for her nephews.

Ryan, as usual, was Mr. Helpful. She was a bit disappointed. He'd probably be leaving the party early if he had to drive Marty all the way to the airport at either Williams Lake or Prince George.

"Careful!" Zoey called, watching the child until

she'd made it safely to the bottom. Lissy waved, then trotted back up the slight hill.

Zoey stared at the blank windows of the house. Not even a string of lights, and here it was only ten days before Christmas. If she'd had any decorations, she would've put them up. What did a string of lights cost? To let a little girl experience the excitement of preparing for Christmas, the anticipation. Zoey closed the door and shivered. She was still in her dressing gown. She'd buy some lights in town next time she was in. She could always give them to the Nugents or leave them at the ranch.

Zoey's new dress was slinky purple velvet with an off-center neckline, which left most of her right shoulder bare. She decided to leave her hair loose, and softly draped. It was time for a cut, but that would have to wait until she got back to Toronto.

She took extra care with her makeup, fastened on the silver Martha Sturdy earrings her sister Tiggy had given her for Christmas the previous year and stepped back to admire herself—as much as she could—in the narrow mirror behind the bathroom door.

She liked what she saw. No more skinny little Phillips kid, although the narrow mirror did make her look nice and thin. Illusions. She struck a cakewalk pose just for the fun of it, flipped up her hair and grinned at her reflection. Even if Ryan had to leave early, she hadn't felt *this* good about going to a party in a long, long time.

## CHAPTER FIFTEEN

TO ZOEY'S AMAZEMENT, at quarter past five, just as she was about to leave, Cameron showed up at the door.

"You coming with us?" he demanded.

Zoey slung her scarf around her neck. "Didn't you get my note?"

"I thought I'd double check." She'd noticed his quick glance of inspection when she opened the door. Up, down. Up again. She fiddled with her gloves. She was wearing her cape, new black merino, over her sexy dress and she knew she looked good. His glance, no matter how cursory, warmed her. Not that she was looking for compliments from *this* man. She'd have been pleased if Mr. Furtz, the shoemaker, had noticed. *How silly women are,* she thought, *playing endless dress-up.*

"I'm driving myself," she said, pulling out her keys. "As a matter of fact, I'm just on my way. I'm supposed to help Elizabeth with the children's party."

She stepped out of the apartment and locked up, conscious of his steady gaze on her back.

"This is stupid, you know," he said bluntly. "I'm driving, I've got a four-wheel drive, we can go together. There's plenty of room."

"Is there?" This was her chance to ask if the widow was included, but she kept her mouth shut.

"Sure. Lots of room."

"Thanks, but no. I'd rather go alone."

Zoey turned and put her foot on the first step. She felt his hand on her elbow and paused. He removed his hand. "Stubborn little witch, aren't you?" he muttered under his breath.

*"Pardon?"*

"You heard me."

"The term you're looking for, I believe, is *independent*," she said firmly.

"Whatever. Look, let me go first." She saw a shadow of a smile. "Just in case you pitch downstairs wearing those ridiculous boots. Might be hard on my insurance premiums."

Zoey glanced at her footwear. Ridiculous! Well, maybe they were, but it was rude of him to comment.

She gestured for him to precede her, which he did, looking over his shoulder twice to see that she was following.

She was, clinging desperately to the handrail every step of the way. Her good kid gloves were getting wet from the ice on the railing. She was excruciatingly aware that her cowardly progress didn't do a thing to show off her new outfit.

"I'll get Gabe to put some salt on these steps tomorrow," Cameron offered, watching her navigate the last two. He held out a helpful hand when she got to the bottom, but Zoey pretended she didn't see it.

"There!" She met his eyes triumphantly when she had both feet on firm earth. Firm, snowy, slippery earth. Zoey wobbled toward her car, parked only a few feet away. She wasn't sure what was in the garage; certainly no one seemed to use it for parking. Storage, she supposed. She noted that Marty's station wagon was gone from beneath the carport attached to the house, where she usually parked.

"Marty away?" Lissy had, of course, told her that, but she felt she needed to say something conversational. He was just standing there like a stick, clearly waiting for her to get in her car and leave. Or get in her car and drive straight into the nearest ditch.

"She's in town with a friend. Ry's taking her to the airport later."

"That's nice," Zoey said lamely. She got in, slammed the door and flicked on the windshield wipers. They groaned and scraped over the ice frozen to the glass.

"Hey!" Cameron stepped over, next to the car. "Turn 'em off!"

Zoey switched off the wipers and watched as he deftly removed the ice on the windscreen with something he'd pulled out of his pocket, a credit card maybe. Zoey's teeth were on edge from more than the cold. She wanted to *leave.*

He knocked on her iced-up window. She unrolled it a few inches. Her teeth were chattering now. This flimsy wool cape she'd bought to wear with her new dress was woefully inadequate for a Cariboo-Chilcotin winter.

"Better let the car run a little," he advised. "Don't turn on your heater yet. If you do, you'll just be drawing warm air off the engine and it'll take longer to warm up.''

''Oh, I know that,'' Zoey managed.

She *hadn't* actually known that about letting the engine warm up, but it was probably good advice. She shivered violently. '''Bye. See you at the party!'' she called as cheerily as she could, waving and rolling up her window. Cameron moved away in the dark, toward the house. She noticed, though, that he was still standing outside, watching as she put the car into gear and began making her way slowly along the lane. She beeped her horn lightly just to let him know she'd seen him.

*Yo, you can go back in the house now.*

Honestly! Any woman married to a man like that wouldn't be allowed to brush her teeth by herself. She didn't envy Sara Rundle her prospects.

BEFORE SHE'D ARRIVED at the main road, she noticed Cameron's headlights behind her. She adjusted her rearview mirror to the night-vision angle. Damn!

The going was slow and she went even slower, knowing how icy it really was; she had no intention of repeating what had happened the other day. She also knew he liked to drive fast. Despite that, he adapted his speed to hers and stayed a couple of car lengths behind. About five miles from Stoney Creek, he finally pulled out and passed, with a horn blast from his vehicle. Zoey saw Lissy madly waving from the passenger window and waved back.

Finally! She could relax. Oddly, though, she missed his lights behind her. Annoying as it was to be under surveillance, there was a certain comfort in it, too. She'd never had anyone watch over her. Everything she'd ever wanted to do in her life, she'd had to do herself. Use her own wits, depend on her own counsel. Create her own opportunities.

She sighed. Cheer up, Zoey. You're going to a Christmas party, you're going to knock the socks off the man of your dreams, and if you're a good girl, you might even get to meet Santa.

WHEN ZOEY ARRIVED, Elizabeth was in a panic.

The man she'd hired to play Santa every year for Tess and Becky's combination Christmas-birthday party had shown up drunk.

"I have no idea how he drove over here. Maybe he walked or got a cab," Elizabeth told Zoey breathlessly as she took her coat and gloves. "Oh, my! Don't you look glamorous!"

Her eyes lit up briefly, but her mind wasn't really on Zoey's new Christmas outfit. "What are we going to *do?* There'll be eleven little kids here. Arthur absolutely *refuses* to get dressed up and of course the girls would know who he was right away...."

"Where's he now? The Santa?" Zoey asked.

"In the kitchen. Asleep. I made him sit there so I could pour some coffee down him and he passed out on the table. He's snoring and he's drooled all over my good poinsettia tablecloth. It's absolutely *disgusting!* I don't know *what* I'm going to—"

"We'll think of something," Zoey broke in. "Why don't you have a drink and I'll see what I can come up with." Zoey had thought that nothing could rattle her sensible, cheerful friend. Motherhood must do that to a woman, she thought. Her hopes and expectations for her children's party were so high that she was devastated by any little mishap. Mind you, a drunken Santa at a kiddies' Christmas party was a pretty *big* mishap.

"You mean *booze?* Oh, I couldn't!" Elizabeth was about to break into tears.

"Here, honey." Arthur appeared out of nowhere—wonderful man!—and handed his wife a glass of what looked like white wine. Elizabeth gulped it gratefully, the tears still glistening on her cheeks.

"Arthur, you wouldn't reconsider...?" She looked pitifully at her husband.

"No, no, no, I definitely am not climbing into some Santa suit!" he insisted. "Not even for you, darling. The mayor will be here, for crying out loud. But surely one of the other dads won't mind—"

"Ryan would do it," Zoey said, "if he were here. I know he would." He'd love to do something like that. It would appeal to his sense of fun. Where *was* he?

Elizabeth took another gulp of her wine. "Yes, he would, wouldn't he? Oh, dear," she said, handing the glass back to her husband. "That's all we need—Mommy getting pie-eyed!" Elizabeth looked as though she was going to cry again and Zoey resisted the urge to laugh.

"Where are the girls now?"

"They're upstairs getting dressed. I've still got to do Tessa's hair," Elizabeth said, distracted. "I don't want them to see this man. Arthur, we've got to get rid of him!''

''I'll take care of that,'' Zoey said decisively. ''You go do Tessa's hair.''

The man was skinny and gray, balding on top. He was wearing a huge overcoat with gaping pockets. Zoey spotted a mickey of rye in one, a cheap brand. She plucked it out—it was half-full—and poured the remainder down the sink, recapping the bottle and returning it to his pocket. He'd think he'd finished it, if he even noticed when he woke up. Arthur, she saw, looked startled.

''What, do *you* think he needs more whiskey?''

He shook his head. She bent over and poked the snoring man's shoulder. ''Hey, *pssst!* Wake up— what's his name, Arthur?''

''Les. Lester Tucker.''

''Yoo-hoo, Mr. Tucker? *Lester!*''

The man roused enough to raise his head and stare foolishly into Zoey's eyes. ''Ish it Chrish-mash yet?''

''No, you silly man. You need to go lie down for a while. Let me help you.'' She grabbed the man's elbow. She glanced at Arthur and he took the man's other elbow. ''Is there somewhere we can put him?''

''There's a guest room downstairs. He can sleep it off there.''

The two of them managed to half carry, half escort the smiling, mumbling, rubber-legged man down the back steps from the kitchen. They went past a furnace room, a games rooms complete with snooker table and shuffleboard, a bathroom, and finally into a small bedroom prettily furnished with a lacy-draped double bed, a dressing table, and a small upholstered rocker. A large Raggedy Ann doll was perched on the bed. Zoey plunked it into the rocking chair. She took off the lace coverlet—Elizabeth would die if the man threw up on it—and laid it across the footboard while Arthur hoisted the man onto the bed. Lester Tucker sighed and smiled and instantly fell asleep.

Zoey retrieved a large bath towel from the bathroom and got Arthur to lift the man's head while she spread it on the pillow. Just in case.

"You seem to know what you're doing," Arthur said.

"Been to a few publishers' parties in my time," she said with a smile.

Arthur laughed softly.

Zoey covered the snoring man gently with a blanket from the closet shelf. "Sweet dreams, Mr. Tucker," she whispered. "Poor old guy. Christmas came a little early for him, that's all."

"Damn Tucker. Quite a few people use him for their Santa parties and he generally manages to get good and drunk at one of them, but this is the first time it's happened to Elizabeth."

*Elizabeth.* Zoey thought about that as she made her way upstairs again. Wasn't the father just as concerned about a children's party-gone-wrong? Just as responsible? Or was this the mother's area? Ensuring the happiness of others. And if things went wrong, if events didn't measure up to expectations, there was someone handy to blame, too.

She recalled the many Christmas holidays when her father had held court in his easy chair, sharing a glass or two with friends, such as the shoemaker, smoking cigars and telling jokes, while her mother put the finishing touches to something she'd sewn for one of her daughters or labored until midnight making Christmas goodies, or wrapping presents, usually homemade or on-sale.

Zoey and her sisters had exchanged small presents bought from their meager allowances. As the older girls got work baby-sitting, the gifts became a little bigger—a makeup mirror or some hot rollers, or a real Barbie doll for the younger ones. Her parents' gifts, she remembered, had been more practical. Hand-knit mittens or a school book bag or a new pair of pajamas.

Had her mother resented all that extra work? On top of her shifts at the hospital? Zoey had never thought much about it. That just seemed the way it was— mothers made sure everyone was happy, whether it was a birthday party or a Christmas gift or a Sunday dinner. It didn't seem fair.

Yet, on the other hand, to have the power to create so much happiness? So many meaningful little surprises in a child's life? To be responsible for so many wonderful memories? Perhaps her mother had regarded providing those extras as an honor. Perhaps the joy on the faces of her children Christmas morning had made the midnight hours and all the sacrifice worthwhile.

Zoey thought of Lissy's dark house and resolved to buy some Christmas lights on Monday.

Upstairs, all was peace and goodwill again. The doorbell rang and Arthur answered it, admitting twin girls, with gaping front teeth and matching green and red plaid dresses, both carrying bulging fleece satchels in the shape of stars.

Elizabeth came down the stairs with her daughters, looking proud and happy. As the girls ran toward their visitors, Tessa slipped and fell and began to whimper. Elizabeth bent down on one knee and comforted her youngest, making soothing noises and showering her daughter's hair with kisses. A few seconds later, Tessa rushed off to join the others, and Elizabeth and Arthur shared a mysterious, loving look that made Zoey feel like she'd been caught eavesdropping.

She was nearly twenty-eight. Was anything like *this* ever going to happen to her?

"Where did you put Lester Tucker?" Elizabeth whispered to Zoey as Arthur went to answer the door again.

"In a bedroom downstairs. I don't think we'll need to worry about him for the rest of the evening. He's out like a light, as they say."

"How about we just forget the Santa bit?" Elizabeth suggested worriedly. "We'll hand out the presents without one. Arthur can certainly do that."

Zoey had a sudden electrifying idea. "Listen, Elizabeth—how about if I dress up in that Santa suit?" Her mind spun. "Sure, it's big, but don't you stuff it up with pillows, anyway?"

The doorbell rang and her friend rushed to answer it, throwing a startled look over her shoulder.

Hey, Zoey decided, that wasn't a bad idea. There was plenty of time to redo her makeup and dress. She practiced a low, deep, "Ho, ho, ho," and wasn't impressed.

Suddenly, there seemed to be a lot of children in the house, some drifting into the family room where Elizabeth was staging the party, others jamming the foyer, talking at the top of their lungs. Zoey noticed that Lissy had arrived with another little girl.

"Cameron!" She hurried to the door before he disappeared into the snowy darkness again.

"Yes?" He turned, his face heavily shadowed from the light over the door.

She gestured for him to come back to the door. "I need to talk to you," she whispered. He seemed puzzled. "It's important. Will you come in for a few minutes?"

"I suppose I could." He seemed ill at ease. He might as well get used to it. Lissy was going to have birthday parties and she deserved a dad who knew how to throw one. He kicked snow off his boots and stepped inside. He seemed larger than usual in the small anteroom, surrounded by children. Zoey gave him a brief glimpse of her crossed fingers. "We have a crisis in here," she whispered. "Can you come with me?"

Cameron took off his boots and followed her into the small pantry-freezer room off the kitchen, where Zoey had stashed the drunken Santa's outfit, still in its dry cleaning plastic film. There were no boots; maybe you had to wear your own.

Zoey closed the door behind them. Here, in this tiny space, with painted cupboards along one side, a humming freezer at the far end and stacks of already-wrapped Christmas gifts in boxes on the floor, he looked even larger.

And grimmer.

"We need a Santa, can you do it?"

"A Santa!" Cameron glanced at the red-and-white outfit draped across the freezer. "What the hell are you talking about?"

"The Santa Lizzie hired turned up drunk. He's sleeping it off downstairs, in a spare bedroom and—"

"Who put him there?" There was a strange expression in Cameron's eyes. As though he was actually *amused,* Zoey realized with shock. She didn't think she'd seen him amused since she'd moved to the ranch.

"I did." Zoey bit her lower lip. "Well, Arthur and I did. But now I need to find someone who'll be the Santa Claus at the kids' party. Elizabeth is so upset."

"Is this her idea? To ask me?"

"Well, no, not really." Zoey stepped back and picked up the Santa outfit. "She doesn't know I'm asking you. She says she'll just get Arthur to plain old hand out the presents." She frowned as she investigated the contents through the clear plastic. "Do you know if these things are supposed to come with boots?"

Cameron took a deep breath and put his hand on the door knob. "Well, Arthur handing them out seems like a good idea."

"Stop!" Wouldn't he even consider it? "You have a daughter here. Do you want her to be disappointed? What about all the other kids? You're going to be involved in this kind of thing someday yourself, and you should—"

"Like hell I am."

''Oh, yes, you are! You're a father and you're supposed to *act* like a father. There's more to it than just—just the original bit, you know. You're supposed to—to go to the science fair at school with her, buy all the raffle tickets she comes home with—'' She stared up at him. She felt like she was about to burst into tears and she had no idea why. ''You're supposed to take her fishing and teach her how to skate. You're supposed to dress up like Santa sometimes, dammit! Even if you *don't* feel like it.''

''Hold on, Zoey.'' He stepped forward and put his hand on her shoulder. ''Calm down.'' He glanced toward the closed door. ''I assume you don't want anyone to hear this little discussion.''

''Okay, fine,'' Zoey raced on in a heated whisper. ''*I'll* do it. You go out and do—do whatever you want for the next hour or two. I'm not going to disappoint those kids!''

She twisted her hair back and pulled on the Santa cap. It was too big, but she'd manage. Elizabeth would have bobby pins. ''Okay? Go, please—tell Lizzie I'm doing it.'' She reached up to begin unfastening the zipper of her dress. It jammed. He watched her, his expression unreadable.

''Oh, for crying out loud.'' He took off his shearling coat and threw it on top of the freezer, then started unbuttoning the tweed jacket he had on underneath. ''Leave your damn dress on. *I'll* do it.''

''You will?'' Zoey couldn't believe he'd changed his mind.

''You're too...too *short* to be a convincing Santa Claus. Plus, what about your voice? Think about it. It doesn't fit.'' He rolled up the sleeves of his shirt. ''I suppose that garb will fit over my shirt. I sure as hell am not taking everything off.''

''Oh, Cameron!'' Zoey felt like jumping up and down. Hugging him. Kissing him. Not really. But if he'd been Ryan, she would have. ''I'm going to tell Lizzie. She'll be *so* relieved!''

''This is a favor for Elizabeth, I want you to know,'' he said darkly. ''It isn't going to happen again. Ever.''

''Can you zip me back up?'' Never mind *never,* Zoey thought as Cameron struggled with the zipper she'd jammed. Finally she felt it go up the inch or two she'd lowered it.

''Thanks.'' Feeling saucy, she winked at him as she left and he scowled.

When Santa emerged from the pantry you could have heard a pin drop in the room. The children sent up a collective ''ah!'' He was perfect. It didn't matter that Cameron had complained he was sweating like hell under the pillows and all the gear he had to put on, not to mention the fake beard was driving him crazy. He was *perfect.* On his shoulder he carried the sack of wrapped gifts Elizabeth had prepared earlier, and as the children approached him, awestruck, he handed a gift to each.

When Zoey saw Lissy sitting on his knee, telling him seriously about the gifts she wanted—a Christmas Barbie, some colored chalk, a new book bag and a picture frame with seashells she'd seen in a catalogue—she was deeply moved. She was sure Lissy didn't have a clue that she was actually sitting on her father's knee.

While Zoey busied herself helping Elizabeth serve the children's meal, Santa disappeared back into the pantry, where, she presumed, he'd be getting rid of the Santa suit and slipping out the back door to do whatever he'd originally planned to do until the adult party started at nine.

This was a new, surprising, side to Cameron Donnelly. A generous side. Spontaneous, even. Whatever else happened, she and Lizzie could relax now.

It was true: Christmas really *was* for kids.

# CHAPTER SIXTEEN

RYAN ARRIVED about half an hour after most of the guests, accompanied by Mary Ellen, Edith and Tom Bennett, her fiancé, whom Zoey had met briefly the previous week. Cameron returned about the same time and came in the door accompanied by a man, a stranger to Zoey, and Sara Rundle.

When they entered the room, Zoey was dancing with the mayor. She was thrilled that Ryan came straight over to her and greeted her with a kiss, as he did the mayor's wife.

"Mind if I cut in? You're dancin' with my old girlfriend here."

The mayor bowed out gracefully and sat down with his wife. The band Elizabeth had hired, a four-piece that played everything from forties swing to Ricky Martin, had struck up a fifties jive tune.

Zoey eyed Ryan skeptically. "You want to?" She was a good dancer, and knew most younger men weren't, outside of the usual rock-and-roll gyrations.

"I'm game if you are." Ryan grinned confidently. He looked terrific in a blue cotton sweater and dark-gray dress pants.

"You're next, babe!" he called over to Mary Ellen,

who stood with her stepmother in the small circle that had gathered around the tiny dance floor.

Mary Ellen waved. Usually dressed casually, she looked sophisticated in a black, glittery skirt and wrap-over top. Edith, wearing pale pink, sat placidly in her wheelchair, looking on.

Zoey wondered if Edith ever found it depressing to see able-bodied people having fun when her own limbs so rarely cooperated anymore. According to Mary Ellen, Edith's doctor had arranged for surgery in Vancouver early in the new year. There was a small chance that she could regain some use of her lower limbs before the disease progressed any further.

Zoey realized right away that Ryan knew all the moves. Even better, he had that charming, devil-may-care attitude that made dancing with a superb partner so much fun. When the number ended, there was a brisk round of applause from the audience and Ryan swung her off her feet. The crowd laughed. Zoey noticed Cameron standing to one side, near the door, watching. His look gave her goose bumps. Surely he approved. Wasn't this exactly what he wanted—a romance between her and his brother?

Zoey took a grateful gulp of the drink Mary Ellen gave her and put her free arm around her friend's shoulder. "Plain soda, good. I'm driving tonight, so no Christmas cheer for me. Where have you been these days?"

Mary Ellen shot a quick glance toward her step-mother and drew Zoey off to one side. "Shopping. Getting some last-minute stuff done. Arranging for the flowers. You know, I don't think Edith's guessed yet, if you can believe it!'' Mary Ellen's eyes danced.

"I hope not,'' Zoey said, hugging Mary Ellen again. "The test cake turned out great, by the way. All I have to do now is keep my fingers crossed when I make the real one. No disasters, please!'' She rolled her eyes.

"I know you'll do a super job, Zoe.'' Mary Ellen impulsively leaned forward and kissed her. "Don't forget, I've tasted your Call-a-Girl cakes.''

"Well, better wait until you see the final result,'' Zoey teased. She'd rarely seen Mary Ellen look so animated. So…happy.

"I'd better go give Elizabeth a hand. You dance with Ryan.'' She'd seen the Nugents waltzing earlier and had just spotted Elizabeth hurrying in with a plateful of hot hors d'oeuvres. The party was catered, but it was just like Elizabeth to get involved.

On her way to the kitchen, she noticed Sara Rundle in the arms of the stranger who had arrived with her and Cameron. Where was he, anyway? If he didn't watch out, some other man was going to beat him to first base with the glamorous widow.

Elizabeth was in the kitchen, poking through the fridge. "Oh, Zoey! I'm glad you're here. I didn't want to interrupt you when you were having such fun. Dancing with a certain someone, I noticed.…''

She gave Zoey an arch look and passed her a platter of vegetable strips. "Where did that girl from the caterer's get to? Honestly! Could you take this out for me? How's the party going, do you think?'' Elizabeth seemed a little flustered.

"Wonderful." Zoey plucked a broccoli floweret off the tray and drowned its perfect little green head in ranch dip. "A great party, Lizzie."

When she'd delivered her tray, the mayor asked her to dance again and so did Jeff Somebody-or-other. Arthur danced with her once, and Tom Bennett led her through an old-fashioned waltz. As Elizabeth had suspected, he was an excellent dancer. She was rather surprised Cameron didn't ask her to dance, at least once, if only to be polite.

Ryan brought them all fresh drinks and Zoey sat down for a few minutes to talk to Edith. She realized she hadn't seen Cameron for a while and ventured a query when Ryan returned.

"Cam? I saw him on his cell a while ago." Ryan chose a deviled egg from a nearby plate. "Maybe he's gone over to the Robbins place. Cam's got a half-interest in a mare over there that's due to foal anyday now, and he told me the vet thought there might be problems." He stuffed the egg half into his mouth and chewed. "Leave it to my brother to run out of a party to go sit up all night with a *horse!* Why?"

"Oh, just wondering," Zoey said mysteriously. "I see he's left his date...."

"Who's that?" Ryan swung around to look in the direction she'd indicated. "Sara? That's Spence Rinaldo with her. They came together and I heard they've been seeing quite a bit of each other lately." Ryan laughed. "I think old Cam's out of the picture. Cost me fifty bucks, too. Why? You got your eye on him?" He winked outrageously.

"No!" It came out louder than she'd intended. Why

wouldn't Ryan get it through his thick head that she wanted *him*, not his brother? What kind of earth-shaking event was necessary before he'd take her seriously? He danced with her, he kissed her, he hugged her—although, of course, he hugged everyone. It was maddening!

She thought, and so had Elizabeth, that if he saw her in a sophisticated outfit, he'd forget any notion that Zoey was just a good friend from the past, that they'd been *pals* and could be *pals* again. Well, here she was, looking her best, and he still treated her like a *pal*.

She decided to ask him. Why not? She hadn't succeeded in life so far by sitting back and acting like a wallflower. No, the thing was to take charge. She felt their relationship was stuck; something had to jolt it out of the rut.

She'd start by inviting him to dance.

"Ry?" She smiled seductively and beckoned him with one long Hollyberries-painted nail. "Let's dance."

"Sure." He took her in his arms and grinned. "Hey, this is nice. No reason the gals can't ask the guys, right?"

"No." She moved closer to him and felt his arm tighten around her back. It was a slow two-step. Almost romantic.

"I've got something I'd like to say to you, Ryan."

"Hmm?"

She deliberately pressed a little closer. He couldn't miss *that*. His eyes widened fractionally. "Hey, hey, *hey*."

"Remember the spring before grad?"

He laughed easily. "Sure do."

"I used to be pretty crazy about you. I guess you knew that."

"You were?" He looked directly at her. Surely, this was no surprise!

"Of course I was. I was crazy about you, back when you wanted to date Adele. I was so jealous of her!"

Ryan's face darkened. "We were going to get married once, you know. It didn't work out."

"Elizabeth told me," she said softly. "I hope you don't mind...."

"Hell, no! It's no secret. Besides—" he shrugged his shoulders "—that was a long time ago. I got over her pretty fast. Puppy love," he added dismissively.

"I'm glad to hear that," she said. *Puppy love.*

Ryan held her gaze. "That was then," he said, with a grin. "This is now. Times change." He pulled her into an intricate turn and for a few seconds, Zoey had to pay attention.

"I—I don't think it was really puppy love for me," she managed, when she got her breath back, trying to keep the conversation on track.

"You were only seventeen! So was I." Ryan nodded at the mayor, who was dancing with his wife and had bumped into them and apologized. "We were just kids."

How could this man she was prepared to love with all her heart be so dense? Zoey raised her head and kissed him softly on the mouth. He kissed her back briefly, his eyes tender. Either he felt something for her or he was a damned good flirt.

"You know, I never should've taken advantage of

you like that," he said, suddenly earnest. "It wasn't right, using you to make Adele jealous."

"Hey, we were only seventeen," she said, reminding him of his own words. "Kids do stupid things. You think it can happen again?"

"What?" He seemed truly mystified.

"You know, young love?" She held eye contact with him. "Can it be revived? Where there's smoke, there's fire, and all that?"

"Yeah, sure it can." He held her tight for a moment and kissed her quickly on the mouth. "Merry Christmas, baby. Listen, I want to talk to you, but this isn't the time or place." He put his forefinger on her nose, an endearing gesture. "Later, when I get back to the ranch," he whispered. "Maybe tomorrow?"

Well, it wasn't exactly a declaration of undying love, but now Zoey was curious. What did he want to discuss? She could only guess. And hope.

Ryan was silent for the last few minutes of the dance, and when he led her off the floor, he leaned toward her. "The fact is, I've been thinking about the same thing you mentioned, Zoey. Young love. I haven't thought of much else since you and Mary Ellen came back to Stoney Creek."

*And?*

Ryan had already bowed grandly to their mutual friend. "You're next," he said, escorting Mary Ellen onto the dance floor.

Zoey stood by Edith's chair, sipping her lemonade, watching them. "Such a good man, isn't he?" Edith murmured. "So kind. So thoughtful. So—" she glanced up at Zoey, her eyes twinkling "—hand-some."

"Yes," Zoey returned, watching him try to cajole Mary Ellen into a polka. He seemed to be succeeding. He *is* thoughtful.

She brought out some more snacks for Lizzie, then checked her watch. Ryan was taking Marty—who was visiting a friend for the evening—to Prince George to catch her red-eye flight to Kelowna. They planned to leave at eleven. Mary Ellen was going home with Tom and Edith, and Edith had already said she'd like to leave early. Once they left, Zoey thought, the party would be over for her, too.

Finally, after she'd helped Lizzie brew some coffee and set out plates of sweets at eleven-thirty, Zoey left, too.

She drove home slowly. It had started to snow again, and the landscape was ghostly and still in the glimpses she had from her headlights. The night was pitch dark, since it was close to the winter solstice, the bleakest time of the year. On top of that, the stars were hidden by snow clouds.

Lucky for her, after all, that she'd brought her own transport. Cameron hadn't shown up again. So much for offering to take her home from the party.

She had a headache and her sinuses felt tight and scratchy. That was all she needed, a cold. Nothing like a stuffed-up nose and red eyes to look really appealing when you had romance on your mind.

The ranch house and buildings were deserted when she drove into the yard. Although the yard lights were on, the house was dark, almost hidden behind its snow-laden shrubbery and landscaping. So was her little apartment over the garage, and Zoey was suddenly struck by an enormous sense of loneliness and isolation. She had a heart-stopping sense of just how huge and empty this great Canadian landscape was, how many lonely miles stretched between her and other people. She wished she'd left on a small welcome-home light.

Of course, the ranch house *would* be dark, she told herself. Marty was away, Lissy was at a sleepover, Cameron was somewhere delivering a foal—how long did they take to be born? Probably hours and hours. Ryan was being the dutiful nephew, taking Marty to Prince George. He'd told her he planned to stay there for the night.

So she really was the only person out here at the Triple Oarlock. Not counting the dubious presence of Gabe, who was probably snoring in the bunkhouse or wherever he lived. She could hardly go down and rouse him for a cup of hot chocolate and a game of cribbage, just to have some company. Besides, he'd run like a deer, if past experience was anything to judge by.

The apartment was warm and once she turned on some lights, she felt quite differently. The Chinchilla manuscript, nearly completed, awaited her but she'd leave that until morning. She wanted to put clean sheets on the bed, which was something to busy herself with once she got out of her party garb and while she waited for the kettle to boil.

She hung the slinky purple velvet dress carefully on its padded hanger, then grabbed a handful of the fabric and crushed it between her fingers. So soft. A truly gorgeous dress. She knew it suited her perfectly—her coloring and her spirit. Had Ryan thought so? Or had he still seen her in jeans and T-shirts?

She sighed as she prepared her cup of chamomile tea. It was hard to tell. Sometimes she wished she had the nerve to out-and-out seduce him—and if he didn't go for it, she'd know, wouldn't she? At least he'd get the message she wanted him to get.

Her head was spinning. Plus feeling thick and fuzzy. Arrgh! She took a quick shower and then went to bed with another cup of chamomile tea. She looked forward to curling up with the novel she'd started reading, a new Barbara Kingsolver. It wasn't that late, only a little past midnight. But she couldn't concentrate on the novel. She kept thinking back to the party, kept seeing Ryan's handsome, teasing face. Elizabeth's tears when the Santa man had arrived drunk before the children's party. Cameron's dismay when she'd begged him to fill in. Mary Ellen's glow. If Zoey didn't know better, she'd think Mary Ellen was the woman in love, not Edith.

Zoey shut off the light. *Sweet dreams,* she told herself, cuddling down into the quilt. She didn't know how late it was when she woke up, chilled to the bone and disoriented. When she turned on her bedside lamp, nothing happened. Damn! The electricity was off again. She peered through the curtains toward the ranch house. No sign of life. Of course, who was coming home. Probably no one.

She got up. The floor was icy. How long had the heat been off? She pulled the quilt off her bed and tucked it around her shoulders and went to look for the candles. She swore when she shut the drawer on her thumb.

This was ridiculous! She'd go up and sleep at the house. They never locked their door and, besides, no one was there. Hadn't Ryan said that she should come up to the house if the electricity went off? If it got too cold in her apartment? That he had lots of room in his bed?

Well, ironically, she would do just that. Only, *he* wouldn't be in his bed. He was spending the night in Prince George. At least she knew where his room was. He'd told her. And hadn't Lissy told her, too, when she'd given her a bath once—second from the end of the hall?

Zoey pulled her jacket over her flannel pajamas, shivering as she shoved her bare feet into her new boots and draped the quilt around her shoulders for the dash across the yard.

## CHAPTER SEVENTEEN

HE WAS BONE-TIRED when he finally drove into the yard. Damn yard lights were out again, which meant the electricity was off. The business really ought to invest in a generator; they could well afford it. These power outages, three or four times a year, were aggravating but for some reason, they kept putting up with them.

No sign of the other vehicles, except Zoey's. Well, no surprise there. He wasn't sure why he'd bothered to drive all the way back tonight. He could just as easily have stayed over.

Reggie, the oldest of the dogs and still the most alert, came out to the driveway to wag his scruffy tail as the headlights lit up the side of the house.

Good old boy, he thought, stooping down swiftly to pat the aging dog's head and scratch him under the chin. The animal yawned and licked his face, then followed him to the side entrance.

He wiped his face with the back of his hand. Oh, well, he needed a shower anyway before he hit the sack. He'd been too busy for too long. This month had been crazy. Too many trips this week, too much on his mind.

He stamped the snow off his boots and felt his way

into the mudroom, accidentally kicking over something in the middle of the floor—he had no idea what. He pulled off his boots, then heard a faint mewing. Lissy's cat! He felt around his feet and there it was, soft and still so scrawny and small. Was this cat ever going to grow up? At least they knew it was a "he" now.

He put the cat down and edged into the hall, sliding on stocking feet so he didn't accidentally step on the kitten, which could be anywhere. Lissy'd never forgive him if anything happened to that cat. It was black as the bottom of a well in here, with only the glow from the pilot light of the furnace, at the end of the hall. Furnace wasn't much good without the fan. It'd be cold in the morning, but at least they had oil heat, not electricity.

Third door down, bathroom. No problem.

He stripped and stepped thankfully into the stream of hot water. The hot water system was electric but the water was still good and hot. Power couldn't have gone out more than an hour or two ago. Idly, he wondered if any of his neighbors had phoned in the outage. He'd call if it wasn't fixed by morning.

Zoey'd be freezing her sweet little butt out there over the garage, though. Should he check on her? Invite her to stay in the house? Hell, no. Leave things be. He didn't trust himself around Zoey. He couldn't make up his mind about her. And he definitely couldn't ignore her, either.

As he was toweling dry, he decided to call the power company anyway, and went, one careful step after another, into the kitchen to use the wall phone, getting the operator to connect him in the dark. The crews had already been alerted—wasted trip, and he was freezing his own butt off now.

Oh well, he'd done what he could. He made his way back down the hall, slowly, reaching out to touch the wall from time to time, to remind himself of where he was.

His room was pitch-black, not even any reflection off the snow with the curtains closed. It had to be two, three in the morning.

He dropped his towel by the door and moved cautiously forward and felt for the head of the bed. Ah!

He patted the pillow, to get his bearings, then slowly eased himself into bed. Oh, man! It had been a long, long day. He pulled the quilt over, then froze. Didn't feel right. He pulled the quilt again, very carefully. Something was preventing the sheet and blankets from moving freely. Had one of the dogs jumped up? Better not, that was a big no-no with Marty. 'Course, she'd be in Kelowna by now.

He reached out one hand.

Holy shit! Someone was in his bed.

Cautiously, he moved his hand up, then down. Whoever was there was warm—alive, at least—and— He felt a stirring in his groin. Soft, warm…a breast.

*A woman.*

He felt like one of the three bears who'd come home from a tough trek in the woods to find Goldilocks not in his chair, not at his table eating his porridge—but in his bed.

Zoey. *It had to be.*

Regretfully he removed his hand from where he'd

inadvertently placed it and held his breath as she
stirred a little. She was sound asleep. Should he wake
her up? Take the high road and send her home?

He took a deep, shaky breath. No way. This was no
accident. She was here because she wanted to be here.

Maybe this had turned into his lucky day, after all.

*SHE WAS DOZING on an inflatable of some kind, drifting
far from land. The air was warm, the sea was warm
and blue. She was comfortable and happy. When she
put her face over the side, she could see the fish smiling up at her, swimming up and kissing her toes and
her fingers that trailed in the water.*

*One came along, a huge, beautiful, iridescent jel-
lyfish, and gently pushed her off the inflatable and she
laughed as she sunk deeper and deeper into the brilliant water, not fighting it. She could breathe! Just like
the fish. They nibbled at her face and ears, tickled her
nose, unbuttoned her pajama top....*

Pajama top? Zoey opened her eyes. It was pitch
dark. For a few seconds, she wondered where she was.
Then she felt the fish again, nibbling at her skin, kissing her earlobe, breathing into her ear, touching her
breast so wetly, so delightfully....

She moved slightly, realizing then that she wasn't
dreaming. That she was in bed, in someone's bed, not
hers, and that someone was touching her, kissing her
gently. All she had to do was lie there and receive his
kisses, receive his caresses, accept his lovemaking.

*Ryan.*

She remembered everything. She'd come to the
house and climbed into Ryan's bed. He wasn't sup-

posed to be here tonight; he was staying over in Prince George. The house had been dark and still. *And warm.* She'd fallen asleep, she had no idea for how long. It was dark, the velvety darkness cupping her eyes and blinding them.

She reached out in the direction of his face and felt the roughness of his jaw, unshaven. She caught a whiff of soap, sandalwood. She couldn't make out his usual scent, his aftershave, the citrusy scent she always associated with him. His hair was slick and wet; his skin was faintly damp, damp and warm. He'd taken a shower. She ran her fingers lightly along his shoulder and arm and heard the quick intake of breath. The muscles beneath the skin were iron-hard, rigid, vibrating with tension. With restraint.

*He wanted her.*

He wanted her to touch him. As she wanted him to touch her. To keep touching her. Blindly, Zoey raised her face to his and let his mouth find hers in the dark. Hesitant, exploring. Exciting. His kiss made her senses tumble and whirl as no other kiss of his ever had done, not since she was seventeen. Perhaps they had truly recaptured the past—here, in the darkness. Finally.

Zoey felt a huge welling of relief. She'd longed for this. She'd longed for Ryan to finally see her for what she was—a warm, desirable, willing woman. She hadn't expected him tonight but he'd come back! It couldn't have been more perfect. It was fate.

He wanted her, he cared for her, as she'd always believed. He was making love to her now, this very instant. *He wanted her.* This couldn't have been any better if she'd planned it.

Zoey's pulse boomed as he kissed her, each kiss deeper, more intimate, hungrier, each stroke of his tongue hinting at what lay in store for her tonight, for them both.... She felt his hands, rough and urgent, on her breasts, teasing, stroking, driving her insane and then one hand going to her belly, below.

His head centered on her breast and she felt the tug of his teeth as he teased the sensitive flesh. She cried out and he put two fingers across her lips, silencing her. Desire, almost like pain, shot through her vitals, stabbing, insistent.

*She wanted him...how she wanted him!*

"Yes," she whispered. *"Yes!"*

But he did not reply. He kissed her again, now her mouth, now her breast, her ear, the soft skin beneath her jaw, teasing her, tormenting her with his caresses until she thought she'd lose her mind. Then she felt cold air rush over her heated skin as he moved back, fumbled. She heard a drawer open, tearing plastic, knew what he was doing.

He bent over her, took her hands in his and kissed them. One, then the other. He held her hands steady in one of his and paused. As though uncertain—after all this!—and she heard herself begging for completion. Begging him to join with her....

He pushed into her and she arched against him and cried out again as he filled her, more, more and more, until they were merged. *Yes!* She felt wet on her cheeks. Her own tears. Joy. Ecstasy.

Her heart beat like a bird's, in ten-time, a hundred-time. He pushed against her, rocked against her, thrust powerfully in response to her faint, broken cries. She heard his breath come harsh in her ear. As though he were in pain, or too moved by the pleasure, as she was, to contain it.

Then she was climaxing, crying out. He seized her mouth with his, quieting her again. Was someone in the house, besides them? The thought struck sudden terror into her heart—as if she were some teenager, caught necking with her boyfriend on the family room sofa when the parents came home early.

But she was sure they were alone. And they were adults. They took responsibility for coming together like this. Partners, lovers. Whatever they chose to be with each other.

He caught her cries, swallowing her pleasure, then groaned himself, the sound muffled as he pressed his mouth against her neck, as his body shuddered. She wrapped her arms around him, weeping. Unable to stop herself. It was too much. Too much happiness.

They lay like that for a long time. Finally Zoey's heart rate returned to something approaching normal. He moved first, dealing with the condom, then stretching out beside her and pulling her into his arms with a deep sigh. He wiped her cheeks with one hand, drying her tears.

"I—" she began, needing to say something now. His arm tightened around her shoulders. "I—I was so afraid," she whispered. "I wanted this. I wanted you to know what *could* happen between us—" She'd come to his bed for one practical reason—because she was cold and she'd assumed he was away in Prince George. But it had occurred to her more than once that if something like this *could* happen between them, then they'd know, wouldn't they? Both of them...

His arm tightened around her again, reassuring, comforting. He stroked her hair, her face, soothing her. ''Shh.''

She pressed her open hand against his chest. She couldn't stop touching him. She put her arms around him, as far as she could and held on tightly. He was so solid, so warm, so...*perfect.* He bent his head and kissed her hair. Smoothed it with one hand, kissed it again. Then he moved, repositioning himself, gathering her closer, dropping his head to kiss her face, her cheek, her nose. Softly. To bite the lobe of her ear, ever so gently.

Incredibly, Zoey felt desire again. Fierce, sudden, hot. She closed her eyes in the darkness, willing her self to be sensible. To go to sleep.

Instead, she raised her mouth to him and held his head in both hands as he took what she offered so eagerly. And this time, when he entered her, he went slowly, slowly, bringing her to glory over and over, before finally collapsing against her, taking his own reward. Zoey felt boneless and incandescent, like the jellyfish in her dreams. She felt warm, happy, powerful and, most of all, loved.

*Well-loved.*

She fell asleep in his arms and dreamed of nothing.

WHEN SHE AWOKE, it was day. Light streamed around the edges of the half-closed curtains. She stretched, her body feeling lazy and relaxed, deeply, totally satisfied. Her muscles ached, her skin tingled, her mind was clear and steady, focussed: *he loved her.* She believed what the body knew. He loved her. That was all that mattered.

She felt him move behind her, draw closer, one hand on the curve of her bare hip, his other hand cupping the crown of her head. He felt warm and large, and she snuggled against him, nestling her bottom into his hips. She was happy; she couldn't possibly be happier. She closed her eyes in anticipatory delight.

"Good morning, babe." He kissed her cheek.

*Who said that?* Zoey's eyes snapped open and she twisted her head and looked into his eyes.

And screamed.

She was in bed with the wrong man!

# CHAPTER EIGHTEEN

*CAMERON DONNELLY.*

"Omigod! What—what are *you* doing here?" She sat up and clutched the sheet to her chest. Her pajama top hung wide open!

"This is my bed. I sleep here. Mostly." He'd leaned back a little when she'd screamed. "I could ask you the same question." His face was right beside her shoulder.

Zoey scrambled to the side of the bed and leaped out before she realized she had no pajama bottoms on.

She was practically naked!

She sat back down and pulled the top sheet free, then stood up, wrapping the end of it around her. She had to think—*think!* This was a catastrophe, a nightmare, a disaster.

"Where's Ryan?"

"I don't know," he answered calmly. "Not here."

Zoey tried madly to piece events together. The facts stared her straight in the face. She'd let herself into an empty house and climbed into the wrong man's bed. Like some kind of directionally-challenged Goldilocks!

Worse, she'd made love with him. More than once. *And liked it!*

Of course, she hadn't known it was Cameron. She'd thought it was Ryan. She'd never, ever have responded that way if she hadn't thought it was Ryan. There couldn't be any question—

But, seriously, how could a woman make such a stupid error? If someone had told her a story like that, she'd have laughed. If Jamie Chinchilla ever came up with something like that in one of her books, she'd tell her to take it out. It was preposterous! You couldn't make love with the wrong man—you'd *know*.

She recollected vaguely that she *had* noticed the absence of the scent Ryan always wore, the woodsy-citrusy aftershave, but she'd attributed that little omission to a recent shower. By rights, it should have tipped her off. But why? The idea had never crossed her mind that she might be in the wrong bed. Now that she thought about it, she'd jumped to a *lot* of conclusions.

"Where's Ryan's room?"

He waved a hand lazily toward the door. "Across the hall."

"But Lissy told me where his room was! When I got her clothes for her, when I gave her a bath after we were stuck in the ditch." Zoey gnawed her lower lip. What *had* Lissy said, exactly?

"You're not blaming a kid for this, are you?" he asked, raising one eyebrow, crossing his arms across his bare chest. An attractive, well-muscled chest, with a light dusting of hair.

Was he stark naked under the sheet? Her glance fell on the crumpled white towel by the open doorway—

yes, he *was* stark naked. The tatters of packaging from several condoms lay on the bedside table....

Several? *Omigod.* How many times had they made love? She couldn't remember. This was a nightmare!

"You—you must have known! You must've known it was a mistake. You—you took advantage of me!"

He laughed. He actually *laughed.*

"Advantage of you? Hell, no. I guess I just thought *Cam Donnelly, this is your lucky night,*" he drawled. "And it was," he added, with a broad smile.

"You can wipe that look off your face," she yelled, pulling at the sheet. He hung on, maybe to preserve his own modesty, nearly causing her to lose her balance. She let go of the sheet, picked up a pillow and threw it at him. He tossed it to one side and his gaze slid down, reminding her that she'd lost her cover. Thank heavens her pajama top was relatively long.

"So, Goldilocks, why did you get into my bed, then?"

"I was cold. The electricity was off. It was freezing in my place. I—I thought no one was home here." Everything *should* have made sense. She was thoroughly confused. "Ryan was supposed to go to Prince George—he did, didn't he?"

"As far as I know, he did."

"And—and I thought I'd sleep here because I knew where his room was and I knew he wasn't coming back."

Zoey took the opportunity to snatch at the sheet and tried to button her pajama top with one hand.

"Never mind," he said. "Go ahead and use two hands. I've seen it all."

He hadn't seen a thing. Nor had she; it had been pitch dark.

"Liar!" She picked up another pillow, one that had fallen to the floor during the night, and threw it at him. He knocked it away and laughed and then grabbed her wrist and pulled her down onto the bed.

In an instant, he'd rolled her underneath him and was smiling down into her shocked face.

"Get *off* me!" She struggled to get her hands free. He held one and the other was trapped between their bodies.

He kissed her cheek, her chin.... "That's not what you said last night," he murmured, smiling.

How—how *crude!*

She yelled, "*Off!* I'd *never* get into your bed, not in a million years—"

"You did. And it was only about, let's see—" he made a great show of mental calculation "—just under four weeks after you got here, not a million years. Frankly, I didn't think it would take that long."

"I hate you!"

His mouth descended on hers, working its unique and soul-melting magic, and to her horror she stopped fighting and began to respond. She couldn't help it, he did something to her. *Something exquisite.* The feel, the taste, it brought back the night in horrifying, terrifying, wonderful detail.

Finally, he ended the kiss, at his leisure.

"Now," he said in a low voice, kissing her nose, "tell me again that you hate me, Zoey Phillips."

"I hate you," she said, but it lacked conviction. Even she could tell.

He laughed softly. "You don't. You know very well that I could make love with you again, right now, and you'd be only too happy to oblige. You'd be begging for more, just like last night. I don't hate you at all, and neither do you hate me."

Her eyes filled with tears. He was right. She was shocked, she was angry...but she didn't hate him. He'd outmaneuvered her, that was all. He'd tricked her. She couldn't forgive him for that. She turned her head away and he turned it back, gripping her chin in his fingers.

"Listen to me, Zoey," he said, his voice surprisingly earnest. "It happened. Okay? This is one thing that is *not* a figment of your imagination. No one needs to know, just you and me. You do what you have to do, but let's be honest at least." His voice lowered to a sexy whisper. "It was good between us, Zoey—*damn good.* And you know it."

She nodded. She could hardly see him, her eyes were so blurred by tears. It was true. She'd been in another world last night. A beautiful world. She'd actually believed she was in love—that she was making love with a man who cared for her, maybe even loved her, too.

The man who was *supposed* to love her—Ryan. Not this man, whom she'd decided weeks ago she didn't even like very much.

"I hate to see you cry," he said and awkwardly wiped at her tears with the side of his thumb. "But you need to know the truth. You're a willful, stubborn, beautiful, wonderful, sexy woman. A strong, feisty, stand-up lady any man would be proud to call his partner. But you're in bed with me, not my brother. You got yourself into this little screw-up and you're going to have to get yourself out—''

''I—I thought you *wanted* me and Ryan to get together.'' She blinked hard, trying to see his face clearly.

''I did. Once. But I never dreamed you'd go this far.''

''It was a mistake, dammit! I just wanted to warm up. I thought he was away!''

''Besides—'' His gaze lowered to her mouth, and she caught her breath. ''I changed my mind about you and Ryan a while ago. That first day it snowed. I realized it wasn't going to work, *couldn't* work.'' His eyes flared fire, which astonished her. ''It was plain as day to me that the entire romance plan was one-sided.''

''Me?'' Her voice was tiny. She didn't want to know. She didn't want to hear him say it.

''Yes, Zoey. You. I blame myself.''

''Why?''

''I never should've encouraged you.''

Again—taking the blame for something that had nothing to do with him. ''I made up my own mind,'' she said. ''All by myself.''

He sat up, releasing her. She sniffed and wiped her eyes on her sleeve, but the tears just kept welling up. He turned away while she scrambled for her bottoms and fastened the last button of her pajama top. She was grateful for that.

''You're just not very good at reading the signs, are you, Zoey?'' he said quietly. He sounded subdued.

"Even when they're written all over the wall. Signs that a man wants you in the worst way or signs that a man doesn't really give a damn."

What was he getting at? Was he rubbing it in? No man wanted her in the worst way.

"I see." She saw nothing. She swayed, felt like she was going to fall over, faint.

"Hey." He reached out to steady her but she shook off his hand. This was the *last* man she wanted helping her....

She closed her eyes, recalling how she'd danced with Ryan the night before—because she'd asked him. Recalling how she'd confessed that she'd been in love with him—and he'd said they'd both been kids. When she'd made it clear that she could love him again, he'd changed the subject, wished her a Merry Christmas. He'd said he wanted to talk to her—maybe to tell her what a fool she was and that it was high time she left him alone. Were these the signs Cameron was talking about?

No, Ryan was too kind a man to ever say something like that, even if it was true.

"What am I going to tell Ryan?" Her voice broke.

"Nothing." Cameron's voice was harsh. "Don't tell him anything. He's not in the picture. He never has been."

She opened her eyes. She knew he was right. One hundred percent right. And she'd been so *sure*.... She was stupid with men! Absolutely, unforgivably stupid! Always had been. Climbing into the wrong man's bed and making love with him, believing he was someone else—it was just another in a long line of mistakes. She might as well give up.

She picked up her fleece coat from where she'd flung it over the back of a chair the night before and put it on.

"Where are you going?"

"To the apartment."

He reached over to the bedside lamp and flicked it on. "At least the power's back. Your place should be warm enough."

"I suppose you'd like me to leave the ranch now that—"

"No! Don't leave." His eyes searched hers. "Stay. There's no reason to go."

There wasn't? Her eyes filled with tears again. She was a wreck. She said nothing, simply zipped up her coat with a flourish. She started down the hall and five seconds later, he was behind her, the abandoned towel draped around his waist, her quilt over his arm. She found her boots in the middle of the floor in the mudroom, tipped over. She jammed her bare feet into them and zipped them up, wobbling first on one foot, then the other. She didn't intend to say another word to this man if she could help it.

"This yours?"

"Thanks." She took the quilt from him. Why hadn't she just curled up on the sofa for the night, like a normal person?

"See you later," he said, smiling as he opened the door. But his smile didn't touch his eyes. His eyes, she realized with shock, looked dead. His eyes were as cold as the grave.

What was *his* problem? It seemed to her that she was the injured party here.

She stumbled out into a white, pristine world. She walked blindly through the fresh snow, the bright morning air, crisp and cold, and heard the ranch house door close sharply, like a gunshot. But it closed only after she'd reached the bottom of the apartment stairs and put her hand on the rail.

He'd tricked her, he'd made love to her, he despised her—*he must!*—yet he watched over her, as always. Old habits…

Zoey began to sob halfway up the stairs.

She didn't stop until her stomach told her it was time to eat. That was after noon, three hours later. She blew her nose and washed her face with cold water, then made herself a sardine sandwich on toast, meticulously taking the little innards out of the tiny fish with a toothpick. She loaded up the sandwich with plenty of mayonnaise and pepper. Drained of emotion, she ate without tasting a thing while she slowly read the last chapter of the Chinchilla manuscript. It was something to occupy her mind. Take away the images that kept tumbling through her head—of her and Cameron holding each other, kissing, making love, her smiles in the darkness, so pleased that this was happening.

How could something that was so perfect turn into such a disaster?

Because that was the bald truth: it *had* been perfect. She couldn't deny it. He'd been loving, tender, passionate, considerate. Oh, vastly more than considerate! She'd been totally and completely with him—a soul mate—every second, with every caress, with every kiss....

What did that make her? A woman who didn't know her own mind? Or a woman who, somewhere along the line, had made a big, big mistake....

She'd blink to clear her eyes, then read on.

At least with the six-foot, eight-inch ex-husband off the island—changes the author had made at Zoey's insistence—and onto a sailboat that now was a pirate yacht, the book made some kind of sense, unlike her own present and immediate future. Chinchilla's readers would be happy. The author was delivering the emotionally satisfying ending her vast audience demanded. The bad guys paid, the good guys got the rewards.

She blew her nose again. Truly, life could be stranger by far than any fiction. Sometimes you just had to live it to believe it.

HER FIRST INSTINCT, of course, was to leave. Surely that was what Cameron really wanted her to do, no matter what he'd said. Pack her bags and get on the next plane. Put this whole dreadful, humiliating incident out of her mind. Go back East. Or go to her parents' home in Rosetown for a few days. Have her mother flutter, fuss, bring her tea in bed, make sure her favorite cookies were in the tin with the big Santa face on it. Sugar cookies.

Zoey stood at the window for a long time that afternoon, gazing out at the wintry landscape. She heard a motor somewhere and wondered if Cameron was clearing the roads, yet again. How many times in a winter would that need to be done?

Then, she supposed, he'd be going to Stoney Creek to pick up Lissy and bring her home. Maybe the engine sound was Ryan's vehicle, finally coming back. She hoped not. She didn't want to face him just yet. Cameron had implied that their entire renewed courtship—hers and Ryan's—had been no more than a figment of her own overheated imagination. That it had been one-sided all the way.

Now that she was willing to look at the facts, she knew Cameron was right. He'd said she didn't recognize the signs when a man wanted her and when a man didn't give a damn.

Had Ryan really not given a damn about her? He'd been kind. Wasn't that *all* he'd been, really? Of course, he'd tried to spare her feelings. Of course, he hadn't wanted to come right out and say he wasn't interested in her, romantically. She felt so embarrassed. How could she ever face him again?

And what was Cameron talking about? *Who* wanted her in the worst way? Nobody, that was who. He was talking in riddles. Her record spoke for itself.

What made her chase down the wrong track after the wrong guy, blindly and wholeheartedly, over and over? It was the sad story of her romantic life.

Sure, Ryan had kissed her—but he'd kissed Edith Owen, too. And Elizabeth. A smooch on the lips here, a hug there. He was a contact guy. Physical. Always had been. A charmer. She'd always known that. He'd been a flirt in high school, too.

Girls like her got the wrong idea, that was all. Naive

girls. Girls who wanted too much. Girls who wanted to believe, to love…to be loved. To matter to someone, regardless of what they said about how happy they were or what a great life they had somewhere else.

Much as Zoey's bruised and frightened heart told her to pack her bags, it was impossible. She had obligations, promises to honor. She'd told Lissy she'd help her build a gingerbread house this week. In three more days the girl was out of school for the holidays. Somebody had to do a few Christmassy things with her, and Marty was away.

Then there was the wedding cake. And the wedding itself next weekend. She couldn't leave.

Besides, wasn't that what the Phillipses always did when the going got tough—left town? Started over somewhere else? Zoey had sworn she'd never do that. You never really left your troubles behind, anyway, you only thought you did.

All she could do was face up to this incredibly stupid mistake she'd made with Cameron and put it behind her. He'd said he wouldn't mention it to anyone. She believed him.

And why would he? They were both adults. They'd had what was termed a one-night stand. He wouldn't want anyone to know it had been a mistake, either. A guy had a certain reputation to maintain. He might even have assumed at first that she *had* come to his bed on purpose. Some men were just arrogant enough to think that women couldn't wait to get them into bed—

*Sure, and how would* you *know, Zoey?* Supposition,

all of it. She stopped that train of thought before it gathered too much speed.

Zoey put her cold hands—she'd been resting them on the window glass—to her hot cheeks. But there *was* one fact here. Whatever he might have believed as to the reason she was in his bed, she'd definitely set him straight. That had to hurt.

Actually, there was another fact—she forced herself to be honest. *He'd made love to her beyond her wildest dreams. He'd made her feel like the woman she wanted to be, like the woman she dreamed she was.*

She didn't want to think about that. Not now, maybe not ever.

## *CHAPTER NINETEEN*

MONDAY MORNING, Zoey had left the apartment by nine o'clock. She'd written a handful of Christmas notes and cards, including long ones to Lydia and Charlotte, and wanted to drop them in the mail first thing, plus she wanted to get to the stores in Stoney Creek as soon as they opened and buy Christmas lights. Just outdoor lights. Surely, the Donnelly household had indoor decorations stored somewhere.

After visiting the hardware store, she stopped by Elizabeth's to thank her for the party. Everything was back to normal at the Nugent household and Elizabeth was busy making more Christmas cookies.

"How do you think it went?" Elizabeth asked immediately. Zoey knew exactly what she meant.

"Oh, okay." She shrugged, then grinned at her friend. "Actually, Lizzie, I think I've been on the wrong track. I got carried away with that first love thing." She shrugged again. "Ryan and I are just good friends."

"That's all?" Elizabeth looked doubtful, but not concerned.

"That's all. I had a lot of fun at the party, though. You're right, Tom's a terrific dancer."

The conversation veered away from the uncomfortable subject of Ryan. Elizabeth seemed to accept her change of heart. Zoey had known she would. Then Elizabeth insisted she try some of her baking, so she stayed long enough for a cup of tea as well.

"I bought some Christmas lights to put on the outside of the house. Can you believe they don't have a single light or decoration?" Zoey said, pulling on her jacket. "What a bunch of Grinches! And it's almost Christmas."

"You ready for the wedding?"

Zoey nodded. "I'm doing the cake two days before and right now I'm busy with the lights and stuff for Lissy. Marty's away until the middle of the week. I hope they get a tree for the poor girl. Plus, I told her I'd help her make a gingerbread house. Well, you know, *someone's* got to do it." She glanced at her watch. "Gotta go—thanks for the cookies."

She kissed Elizabeth and went out. The sky was vivid and blue, the snow so brilliantly white, it almost hurt her eyes.

She was glad she'd told Elizabeth. And she was glad she'd never told Mary Ellen and Edith about her attempts to revive that first romance with Ryan Donnelly. At least she didn't have to drive out there to set them straight. And, of course, she was never telling a single soul exactly why she'd changed her mind...or what she'd done with Cameron.

These feelings were too new. Too raw, too painful. Not only had she been wrong about Ryan—which Cameron had bluntly pointed out—she was still confused and embarrassed about what had happened when she'd crawled into what she'd thought was Ryan's bed.

She squeezed her eyes shut to block out the memories, which poured over her like warm maple syrup.

Luckily, she hadn't seen Cameron since. She knew he must be at the ranch house, taking care of his daughter, but she'd stayed indoors all day on Sunday, had written her Christmas cards, and gone to bed early. Today Lissy would be at school. She hadn't seen Ryan since he'd returned from Prince George, which was just fine, too.

Since the perfect scenario—not seeing Cameron at all until she left Stoney Creek—was impossible, the next best was only seeing him once or twice, preferably from a distance. Across, say, a snowy pasture. She supposed it was inevitable that she'd run into him; he was, after all, Lissy's father and Zoey would be spending time with her, not to mention making the wedding cake in Marty's kitchen. In that case, she could only hope he'd ignore her, the way he always had. Just mind his own business and she'd mind hers.

She had nothing, absolutely nothing, to say to him.

WHEN SHE GOT BACK to the ranch, Ryan was waiting for her.

"Zoey! I wondered where you'd gone," Ryan said, coming down to the garage parking strip when she was unloading the vehicle. Groceries, lights, presents, wrapping paper, cake ingredients.

"Looking for me?" she said lightly. The best approach was to act as though nothing had changed, she decided.

"I'm always looking for you," he said, grinning. What a flirt! At least they could still tease each other. Be friends. He hadn't figured out that she'd wanted him as a lover, not a friend, and there was certainly no need to tell him now.

"I bought some lights for the outside of the house," she said, proud of the evenness of her tone. "Maybe you'd have time to help me put them up? Or find a ladder I could use?"

"Hey, no problem!" Ryan took a load of bags from the back seat and followed her toward the bottom of the steps. "I know Christmas isn't a big deal for us, but now that Lissy lives here, Cam ought to make the effort. Marty's given up on him. He's a stubborn bastard—you might've noticed that already." He laughed but he seemed preoccupied, alternately thoughtful and wildly pleased with himself as he carried in the bags and boxes. He kept looking at her, studying her, as if trying to see into her thoughts. She found it unsettling. Maybe this had to do with what he'd wanted to talk to her about. Surely he didn't have romance on his mind, not now!

After he'd helped her unload the car, he got a ladder and they strung the lights out, joined all the strands together—Zoey had bought enough to decorate all the bushes in front of the house—and plugged them in. The dogs went frantic, barking at the bright multi-colored lights lying in the snow like so many electric fairies. Zoey laughed.

She picked up a handful of snow and lobbed it at Ryan.

"Hey!" He ducked, halfway up the ladder with his

hands full of lights to decorate the top of the spruce tree that stood close to the kitchen window. She picked up another handful and threw it, this time with more success. It hit him on the back.

Ryan started down the ladder and Zoey shrieked and started to run. Ryan caught her as she slid in the snow and instead of jumping on her, as he'd done that first snowfall—so very long ago, it seemed—he offered her his hand and hauled her to her feet. Zoey was thankful. She'd pitched the first snowball playfully, purely on impulse, and had no intention whatsoever of flirting.

"Listen, Zoey," Ryan said, his eyes warm. "I've got something to tell you. Remember what I said at Lizzie's party? I want you to be the first to know. I haven't even told Cam."

"What's that, Ryan?" She was—she believed— prepared for anything.

"You'll never guess," he said, clasping both her gloved hands in his. "I'm getting married." He squeezed her hands so hard it made her eyes water. "Yeah, can you believe it? Mary Ellen's agreed to marry me and we're going to tie the knot next week when Edith and Tom do. It's going to be a double wedding and—"

*"Married!"* Mary Ellen! Despite herself, a tear rolled down her cheek.

"Oh, honey," he said, his shining gaze quickly turning to concern. "I didn't mean to upset you—"

"Oh, no, Ryan! I'm just—just so happy for you and Mary Ellen," she said, recovering, reaching up and cupping his face with her snowy mittens. He grimaced, which made her laugh. "I'm so happy for you both, that's all. Two of my best friends in the whole world, and I had *no* idea…."

"Oh, babe!" He pulled her into his arms. "This means a lot to me, it really does. I was worried that, uh, maybe you might've had a few leftover feelings for me." He gave her a sheepish grin.

"You idiot! That was old s-stuff. High school stuff. We were kids." She tried hard to laugh, quite unsuccessfully. "It never m-meant anything at all!"

"I'm glad you feel that way," he said, giving her an extra hug, then stepping back. "I'm so happy. Mary Ellen wants me to go into the bed-and-breakfast business with her. It's perfect for us—especially if, you know, a baby comes along soon."

"Oh, Ryan!" Zoey buried her teary face in Ryan's jacket again.

He held her away from him. She'd never seen him look happier. "This is a pretty good life here but, man! Can you imagine the *fishing* out there on the West Coast? Salmon? Halibut?"

"What about Cam? The ranch?" She knew Cameron depended on him.

"Hell, he's got Gabe and the summer gang for the heavy work and he can always hire a part-time bookkeeper. He doesn't need me." His eyes were aglow. She'd never seen him so handsome. "You're the first person I wanted to tell. I'm gonna tell Cam next, as soon as I see him."

"Let's surprise everybody," Zoey said, blowing her nose for, she hoped, the last time. "Let's get the rest of these lights up."

*Mary Ellen!* Deep down, she was pleased for her

friend. And faintly relieved, which made no sense to her at all. But, then, very little did right now.

Mary Ellen had never even hinted that she was falling in love with Ryan Donnelly. But now that Zoey thought about it, though, hadn't the signs been there?

A sudden image swept into her mind: Ryan teaching Mary Ellen the two-step, her laughter, the two of them hugging. Ryan whispering in her ear. Taking her to Prince George to shop. Had Cameron guessed? Had he known all along that his brother had a lot more interest in Mary Ellen Owen than he did in their guest at the ranch? If so, why hadn't he told her earlier?

"Where's Cam?" Ryan asked.

"I have no idea." She handed him another string of lights.

"Probably over at the Robbins place again, checking on that new foal. Hey!" Ryan turned, his arm around her shoulders. "There he is now."

Zoey watched as the too-familiar green pickup drove into the yard. She hadn't even thought of the mare Cameron had gone to check on the night of the party. The night that—oh, never mind. A lot had happened.

She felt she could face Cameron now. She wasn't going to remember that she'd seen him practically naked and—and all the rest. She was going to be cool. She was going to be unflappable. Calm. She was going to be a grown-up.

*For once.*

She watched Cameron get out of his vehicle and her knees went dangerously weak. She was glad Ryan was beside her, she could lean on him if she had to. She hadn't seen Cameron since the morning he'd walked her to the door in bare feet and a bath towel, to say goodbye. *The morning after.* Her heart thumped. He looked so familiar—dressed in jeans, work boots, lined canvas jacket, gloves tucked into his back pocket— and yet so entirely different.

Despite her resolve, she knew she'd turned a fiery red. She prayed he wouldn't notice, or if he did, that he'd attribute it to the cold and wind.

"So..." He stood in front of them. Ryan still had his arm draped around Zoey's shoulders. Cameron hadn't met her eye, which was a relief of sorts. "What's going on here?"

"Lights." Ryan waved toward the house. "Zoey bought a bunch of lights and I'm helping her put them up. A little Christmas cheer, don't you think?"

Cameron nodded. Then he looked at her. Her stomach dropped into her boots and bounced. Her hands were hot and sweaty in the cold, wet mittens. He raised an eyebrow. She swore his eyes were knowing, remembering—revealing. Seeing her stark naked, standing there in the snow. Nothing on but her fashion boots.

She remembered how grim he'd looked the last time she'd seen him, as he'd held the door for her. She couldn't—*couldn't!*—pretend nothing had happened. He was doing it to her again, making her forget her own intentions.

"I guess we've got you to thank for this, Zoey," he said casually. A pleasant, friendly tone. *Was he trying as hard as she was?*

"Yes," she gulped. "Yes, I thought the place could stand a little fixing up for Christmas. I—"

"Good idea." He smiled slightly. "Maybe I'll buy some more and we'll do the eaves, too, before Lissy gets home from school. You got time, Ry?"

He addressed his brother, ignoring her, thank heaven. Ryan agreed, and before Zoey could gather her thoughts, Cameron had returned to his truck, presumably to go to Stoney Creek for more lights, and she and Ryan were busy wrapping the shrubbery with winking and twinkling lights again.

The dreaded first encounter was behind her. Zoey felt relieved. But she also felt sad. Empty. The worst was definitely over—Ryan had told her the big news, she'd faced Cameron for the first time since, well, since she'd slept with him. Things *had* to improve from here on.

But if that was true, why did she feel so rotten?

How could any man not love her? How could any man—like his brother—stand there, his arm casually around her shoulders, talking, laughing, as though she wasn't the most glorious creature in all the world?

Would he ever get that close to her again? Not damn likely. She'd made it clear. Somehow she'd convinced herself that she was in love with his brother. He'd thought—hoped—that after they'd spent the night together, she'd feel differently.

He'd been half in love with her ever since she'd fallen into his arms at that stupid Haunted House exhibit. She'd screamed, and he'd known the absolute, bedrock truth: she *had* been scared silly. It had amused him at first and then he'd realized why he couldn't stop thinking about her. He recalled the way she'd been ready to climb into that Santa suit so the children wouldn't be disappointed. Everything about Zoey was honest. Everything you saw was true and exactly what she was.

She thought she'd been devious as hell with this hopeless plan to get something going with his brother, but he'd been aware of every little move. He still couldn't believe Ryan hadn't fallen for her. Was it because Ryan had known her for so long? But he'd known Mary Ellen Owen just as long, maybe longer, and when she'd come back to town Ryan had gone after her, hook, line and sinker.

Poor Zoey. She really didn't get it. For such a smart, savvy woman—

He shook his head. She didn't see him as a potential lover, maybe more than a lover. She only saw him as Ryan's conniving older brother, a man who'd taken advantage of her mistake, and she couldn't wait to get out of Stoney Creek and fly back East, couldn't wait to put this entire experience behind her.

Maybe she could put it behind her, but he knew the night he'd spent with her would haunt him until he died. He'd never forget how beautiful she was, even in the pitch dark, how loving and tender, how perfect they'd been together.

*And all along she'd thought he was Ryan.* The very recollection made him clench his jaw, press his foot a little harder on the accelerator. Luckily the roads were pretty empty. The only vehicles he passed were a couple of pickup trucks with freshly-cut Christmas trees in the back. People waved.

Christmas. Folks were getting right into the spirit of it.

Even Zoey. Here she was, stringing lights on his property. Doing things with Lissy. Making sure his daughter had a good time. She'd even talked him into putting on the damn Santa suit for Lissy's sake. She'd made him feel guilty and it had worked. When he'd seen Lissy's face as she sat on his knee and confessed her nearest, dearest thoughts, he'd felt love for his daughter burn in his heart like a blast furnace. He'd always loved her; he just hadn't felt anything that powerful, that unstoppable before.

Zoey'd made it happen. She'd argued and threatened and cajoled until he'd agreed, more to get her off his back than anything, and look what had come of it.

He knew why Lissy wanted that seashell frame, too, and it made him feel like a real failure as a father. He knew she had a picture of her mother and herself, when she was tiny, maybe two, taken with a Santa at some mall or other. She wanted to put that picture in the frame and hide it in her closet to look at sometimes. She'd whispered to Santa—*him*—that her dad didn't like her to talk about her mom and that was why she wanted to hide the picture, so she wouldn't make her daddy sad.

Sad? He wished he was sad about Mallory, for Lissy's sake. He was glad to have Lissy in his life again and he was sorry her mother had died. But Mallory had always been a stranger to him, even when they were married, and how could you miss a stranger?

Cameron had been grateful for the fake beard to hide his expression at his daughter's words. *Mallory had brought her back but Zoey had given his daughter to him.* He would never let anything get between them again, especially not his bitter memories. When she got that frame for Christmas—and he'd make damned sure she would, if he had to drive to Prince George to pick it up—he was going to suggest they hang it in the family room somewhere. Swallow his foolishness, once and for all. Put it behind him.

Right then, with Lissy on his knee, he knew that much as he'd fought it, he was desperately, totally, head-over-heels in love with Zoey Phillips. He'd watched her dance at the party and he'd wanted her in his arms. He'd seen her kissing Ryan on the dance floor and he'd wanted to walk over and punch his brother in the face. He knew he had to bide his time. He had to wait for Ryan to spring the news about Mary Ellen—which he'd guessed was coming soon—to clear the field.

Then…to come home and find Zoey in his bed?

Life just couldn't get any luckier. Not for him, a sonofabitch who didn't deserve a second chance with anybody, let alone a woman like Zoey.

Cameron thought back to the scene he'd just left at the Triple Oarlock. Ryan, laughing, happy, his arm draped around Zoey. *His woman.*

He knew it wasn't what it looked like. He knew there was absolutely nothing between them—certainly not on Ryan's part. And he really didn't think she was in love with Ryan, either, no matter what she'd said; she'd just let her imagination run away with her. Once she'd made up her mind to pursue his brother—he still cursed himself for his part in that stupid matchmaking plan—she'd bulldozed straight ahead.

He had to smile. That was Zoey. That was the woman he loved.

He pulled into the Home Hardware in Stoney Creek and went in to see if he could still get some of those popular icicle lights he'd seen on the houses in town. He bought a hundred feet, enough to do the front of the house and the windows. If there were any left over, they could run them along the fence.

"Merry Christmas, Cam!"

He nodded to Edgar Murphy, the old fellow who used to cook for his father, back on the family spread out toward Nimpkits Lake.

"Merry Christmas to you, Ed." He touched his hat and acknowledged Ed's wife. "Mrs. Murphy," he said, nodding.

She beamed back at him, an apple dumpling of a woman, dressed in her Christmas best.

He felt better when he got into his pickup for the return trip. Zoey didn't see things the way he did. She was humiliated and embarrassed by what had happened the other night. She didn't realize he loved her. She believed he'd taken advantage of her. He couldn't just come straight out and say he loved her now, because she wasn't going to buy it. She'd think he was just stringing her along, maybe to get her into his bed again. And, besides, she probably still thought she was in love with Ryan; she'd told herself often enough.

It was up to him to turn this situation around. To help her change her mind.

In a few days, she was leaving Stoney Creek, probably forever. That prospect scared him half to death. If she had even a shred of feeling for him, he had to know. If there was any chance at all that he could make her see things his way, he had to take it. He'd follow her to Toronto; he'd do whatever it took. Wine her, dine her, bring her flowers, do that romantic stuff other guys did.

He had to show her how he felt. Somehow he had to convince her he was serious. That this wasn't just happenstance. That she wasn't just an accidental one-night stand. That she meant everything to him.

Maybe he *should* have kicked her out of his bed, sent her back to her apartment, as he'd first considered—not "taken advantage" of her, as she had accused the next morning. Been noble.

Noble? *Nuts* was more like it. He'd had the best sex of his life that night and so had she. More, much more than that—they'd made love, in the full meaning of the term. And she knew it, too.

He'd bet the ranch on it.

That was a start. A hell of a start, in his view. And it beat wining and dining, aces to eights.

## CHAPTER TWENTY

"CAN WE PUT GUMDROPS for the windows, Zoey? It'd be like a real window if I licked the sugar off first."

Zoey pretended to consider. It was the afternoon of Lissy's last day of school. The homemade gingerbread house plan had been revised to a purchased kit with extra candy decorations, once Zoey had studied the original German gingerbread recipe Elizabeth had given her and decided it was too complicated.

"You know, I think you could be right," she encouraged the girl. "Gumdrops might make great windows. Why don't you try it?"

Lissy giggled and applied the gumdrop to her tongue several times, swallowing with obvious pleasure. "Mmm!"

Then she held the candy up to her eye. "You could even see through it, if you were small enough!"

"Okay, here's some glue—" Zoey squeezed some of the royal icing she'd rolled into a funnel-shaped piece of white paper onto the saucer in front of Lissy. They'd tried to stay tidy, but they were both covered with sugar and icing and Zoey had even found a licorice twist attached to her shirt.

But they were having fun. And that was the main thing. Even Kitty, playing with an empty paper bag under the table, knocking into their feet from time to time, was having fun.

"Daddy's gonna get more lights for us this afternoon and I'm gonna go get a tree with Uncle Ryan." The little girl's eyes shone. "We're having a real Christmas!" Zoey reached over and picked a red Lifesaver out of her hair.

"You need a bath, honey, before you go chasing around with Uncle Ry. You might end up stuck to the seat of the snowmobile and then what?"

"Yeah!"

Zoey could tell Lissy thought that prospect might prove interesting. She was surprised Cameron wasn't taking Lissy to cut a tree. Maybe this was a job Ryan was in charge of every year—if they'd ever put up a tree before.

Since Ryan had told her the big news, Zoey had seen Mary Ellen and congratulated her. It wasn't hard. Mary Ellen was ecstatic and had shyly confessed to Zoey that she'd been in love with Ryan since she could remember and she'd never dreamed he'd ever return her feelings. She was convinced that Ryan was only interested in sophisticated women like Adele Martinez and her.

*Her!* Zoey would have laughed if it hadn't been so ridiculous. "You know that was all silly high-school stuff, don't you?" she reassured her friend. "We were kids! It's history!"

"I know," Mary Ellen said softly. "I guess I was just so crazy about him I couldn't see why other women wouldn't be, too."

Yes, wasn't that always the way, Zoey thought, carefully snipping a licorice twist into sections. She was grateful no one knew how completely deluded she'd been about Ryan and his intentions. Well, one person seemed to have guessed. His brother.

Tiny candy canes worked well for fence posts. Actually, there were two gingerbread houses on the go— Lissy insisted she needed one for her apartment, even though Zoey told her she wouldn't be staying long enough to enjoy it.

"You're going home?" Lissy wailed, looking startled at Zoey's news. She wished, then, that she hadn't mentioned it until a little closer to her departure.

"Yes, I am. But there's still the wedding to go to and the big, fancy reception afterwards...."

"Do I get to go to that, too?"

"I expect so. You'll have to ask your father—"

"Ask her father what?"

Cameron stood at the door that led from the kitchen to the small mudroom. He was dressed casually, in jeans and a flannel shirt. Zoey's heart lurched into her stomach.

"Can I go to the wedding, too, Daddy? With you and Zoey? And the big, fancy 'ception?"

Zoey still wasn't comfortable when Cameron was around. These final days before she left were turning into a real ordeal. Right now, his attention was on his daughter, which was a relief.

"Sure, you can go. Your uncle's getting married, isn't he?"

"To Mary Ellen!" Lissy had been delighted at the news.

Cameron's eyes slid to Zoey. She became extremely interested in the exact placement of the gumdrop she had dabbed with icing to put down as one of the bricks in the gingerbread house's sidewalk. Did he think she cared? That she was sensitive about Ryan marrying one of her best friends? He probably wouldn't believe how *thrilled* she was for Mary Ellen.

"That's right, honey," Zoey said mildly. "Mary Ellen will be your aunt now."

"Mind if I join you girls?"

Zoey looked up. She knew she was a mess, not just from the icing and candy debris, but her hair was sliding out of its clip, too, and she hadn't dared fix it with her sticky fingers. She shook her head. Cameron sat down, next to his daughter, and across from her.

"Daddy!" Lissy was all smiles. "You can help lick off the gumdrops for me. I've got lots." She generously pushed a pile of gumdrops in front of her father and he pushed them back.

"You'd better do that, Lissy. You're good at it. How about I lay this sidewalk here, help Zoey."

Zoey looked up and their eyes met. She knew her cheeks were red. "Sure. Just put the gumdrops in a nice pattern here—" She indicated the sidewalk layout, noticing how large his hands were as he traced the outline with one index finger. Large, capable, well-shaped.

Hands that—

She squelched the thought as she tried to squelch

every thought she'd had about the night they'd spent together. She had only a few more days to get through, less than a week. And she'd get through them. *She would, she would.*

Cameron laid the "bricks" of the sidewalk for a few minutes. "You able to come over and help us trim our tree tonight?" he asked quietly.

Zoey stared at him. "Me?"

He smiled and her stomach flip-flopped, as it always did these days. "Yeah, you. Somebody else in this kitchen?"

"Oh, I—I guess so," she managed. She'd rummaged in her brain for an excuse, but couldn't come up with a thing. She'd already promised Lissy and Ryan she'd help with the tree but she had never dreamed for a minute that Cameron would be there, too.

On the other hand, perhaps she should have guessed. Since he'd gone to town two days before and returned with the Christmas lights, which he and Ryan had put up immediately, he'd spent more time with his daughter than she'd ever noticed before. Maybe he wasn't as busy these days.

He didn't seem as distant with Lissy, either. He stepped in and did things he used to leave for Ryan. Maybe it had sunk in that his brother would be gone soon—the happy foursome were going to Arizona for a honeymoon—and it would just be him and Lissy and Marty again.

Zoey could still see the child's face when she came home from school the day they'd decorated the outside of the house. When she climbed out of Ryan's Blazer, she'd stopped and stood in the yard for a full ten minutes, holding her mittened hands clasped together, her lunch box lying forgotten in the snow, her face angelic as she gazed at the brilliant display.

Zoey had had to swallow a huge lump in her throat.

Cameron's voice interrupted her train of thought. "Zoey?"

She looked at him again. "Mmm?"

"When Lissy goes off with Ryan to cut a tree, I'm going to pick up some tree decorations." He indicated Lissy, who'd gone to the refrigerator to get out a carton of milk and pour herself a glass. She was humming happily and Kitty was attacking her dangling shoelace as she walked.

"You don't have any decorations?" What kind of household was this?

"A few. Some old stuff. I'd like to get more." He smiled and applied another gumdrop. She didn't want him to smile. Not at her. She didn't want him to be friendly and nice. Why was he *doing* this? "There's always Christmas next year, right?" he murmured.

"Right."

"And the year after?"

"Right." She poked a Lifesaver into place on the roof and, annoyed, shook her hand when the candy stuck to her finger and wouldn't come off.

"Here." He reached over, removed the candy from the tip of her finger and put it on the gingerbread roof. "And," he continued lazily, "the year after that."

Zoey shot him a glance and squeezed another blob

of "glue" onto her saucer. What in the world was he getting at?

"I'd like you to come with me."

*Plop!* Now it was a lake of glue. "Go *with* you?"

"You know, pick out stuff. It's kind of a—"

"A womanly job?" She couldn't resist the jab. The reminder that he'd once wanted Ryan to get to know her more "womanly" qualities.

"You could say that," he agreed. She knew her dart had found its mark. "You'll go?"

"I—I guess so. Doesn't Marty want to do this?"

"No. She's, ah, she's busy." He looked at his daughter, who was draining her milk.

Zoey knew that Marty, who had returned from her visit to Kelowna the previous evening, was even now in her bedroom with the door locked, knitting like a madwoman. She was trying to finish a sweater she was making Lissy for Christmas. It was a delicate, white, angora thing and she still had a whole sleeve to go.

"We won't be long, will we?"

"Nope."

"Because I have other things I need to do this evening," she said loftily. It was a lie; she had nothing, absolutely nothing, planned. She was so sick of the Chinchilla manuscript she could scream and swore to herself she wasn't looking at it again until she got back to Toronto.

"Of course. I know you're a very busy woman," he said with a straight face. "I won't take up much of your time. An hour or so."

So that was how Zoey found herself, on nearly the shortest day of the year, in Cameron's truck on the road to Stoney Creek. He'd wanted to go immediately, so she'd just washed her hands and brushed her hair and tried to sponge the worst of the stickiness off her jeans.

Fleece jacket, a knitted cap to cover her hair—yeah, *that* was attractive—a pair of Marty's snowboots and some mitts in her pocket. Marty, emerging from her self-imposed exile to run a bath for Lissy and brew herself a cup of tea, had insisted she take sensible boots.

Cameron was quiet, as usual. She wondered what he was thinking. She wished she'd stayed home. He could pick out his own ornaments, couldn't he? What difference did it make, anyway? Maybe by next year, Sara Rundle would be in charge of the decorations. Ryan had said Cameron was out of the running with the teacher, but the thought that he might not be had her sitting up in the cab again, paying attention for some reason.

"I never asked, what kind of foal did that mare have?" She was glad the interior of the truck was nearly dark. Even though it was only about half past four in the afternoon, the sun had set.

"A filly."

"Was it a...a difficult delivery?"

He glanced at her. "No. The vet thought it might be, since she'd had some problems earlier, but it turned out she was fine. We just sat there, drank a little rum and coffee, kept her company."

"We?" Now *why* had she said that!

"Me and Glen Robbins. Why?"

"Oh, no reason." She pressed her right cheek against the glass. It felt good, good and cold.

"Nice sassy little filly," he mused. "Sorrel, just like her ma. Near front foot white. Her father's black, coal-black. Funny, eh? The foal doesn't look a bit like him."

"That happens." Zoey had no idea if it did or not.

He sighed. "Yeah, I suppose it does."

"So, what about this foal now? Is it yours or your friend's?"

"Mine." He shifted down for the one hill between the ranch and Stoney Creek. "I'm going to give her to Lissy. Not yet, though. Maybe the summer after next when she's halter-broke and Lissy's a little older."

Zoey thought about that. Next summer. The summer after that. These fields would be covered with grass, not snow. The cattle would be grazing, red and black. Calves would be charging around, frightening each other, their tails high in the air. The trees would be green. There'd be birds....

"You ever consider living in a place like this again?"

"No, not really," she said quickly. He'd read her thoughts.

"You're a city person now, huh? Through and through?"

"I don't think it matters much where I live." What was he getting at? "My work's portable. Most places have good and bad. There are lots of things I love about living in the city, but—" she turned to regard his profile in the dark "—there are things I hate, too."

"Like what?"

"Like being alone. Like being so far from my family. Like not knowing your neighbors." Zoey heard her voice quaver slightly and wished he hadn't asked.

"What do you love—about the city, that is?"

"I love going to High Park, watching the ducks and geese in the ponds. I love the theater, plays, stuff like that. I like good restaurants. Why are you asking me all these things?" she finished irritably.

He shrugged. "Just making conversation."

They didn't say anything else until they approached the bright lights of Stoney Creek Home Hardware was open, and next to that was a gift shop that was bound to be well-stocked with Christmas items.

He opened the passenger door for her while she was putting on her mittens, which she thought was very gallant. Cameron seemed different, somehow. Subdued. Quiet. Fewer of the hard edges he so often presented to the world.

"Where to, first?" she asked.

"Let's try the hardware."

They picked out twinkling lights, and pearly lights and lights that looked like candles with some kind of red and green liquid bubbling in them. They were expensive, but if Zoey even indicated an interest in something, Cameron pulled it off the pile and put it into their cart.

Glass baubles, crystal snowflakes, a can of artificial

snow—which Zoey said Lissy might like for spraying designs on the windows—ornaments made out of wood, ornaments made out of straw, a big magnolia wreath for the front door.

Then they went next door to the gift shop. There Cameron picked out an angel for the top of the tree. Zoey made him do the choosing—it was his tree, after all. The angel was gorgeous, with a porcelain face, a red gown and blond shining hair. She had a serene look.

*Stunned* was more like it, Zoey would've thought if she'd been feeling less charitable. But she couldn't help it; she liked everything about Christmas, including the angel Cameron selected.

"Enough?" she said, laughing up at him.

He nodded solemnly. "If you think so."

"You don't?" She was amazed. They'd probably spent over a hundred dollars already. "You're supposed to collect this stuff over time, you know. You're not supposed to go out and plunk down your credit card and buy everything at once."

"I've never bought any before," he said. "This is the first time."

"Ever?" She was astonished.

"Ever."

Cameron loaded the packages into the back of the truck, pulled a tarpaulin over them, then got in the driver's seat. "You want anything else? A coffee? I'll call home, see if Marty needs anything from town."

Zoey shivered. "A coffee would be nice." She wasn't looking forward to the twenty-minute ride home with him. He had a way of making her say things she didn't want to say, like telling him she felt lonely sometimes. That she missed her sisters, her parents.

They got their coffees, sloshed into thick ceramic mugs with help-yourself sugar packets and creamers and flimsy wooden stir sticks, at the coffee shop in the mall outside town. It was nearly deserted. Most people were shopping, not stopping for refreshments this close to the supper hour, Zoey decided, surveying the restaurant with its Christmas garlands and poinsettias. She sat opposite Cameron in a booth, then wished they'd just gotten coffee to go. This way she had to look at him.

She took a sip of the hot beverage. She'd had worse. Cameron kept staring at her, which disconcerted her enormously. Then, to her utter astonishment, he reached forward and took her hand.

"Zoey." He held her hand lightly. Her first reaction had been to pull away, but she couldn't make herself do it. "I want to talk to you."

"You do?" She curled her fingers, but he didn't release her hand.

"Yeah. First of all, I want you to know that the other night was—"

"Don't talk about the other night!" she whispered fiercely.

His eyes looked as though she'd hit him with a bucket of ice.

*"I can't stand it, don't you see?"* she went on, glancing furtively around, although there was no one

to hear them. "I feel so *stupid!* I made a horrible mistake and I—I don't blame you, but surely you can see I just want to forget the whole experience. If you're going to apologize, don't do that either! *Please!*"

He abruptly let go of her hand and picked up his coffee. "Well," he said finally, "I guess that covers everything."

"What do you mean?"

"You're telling me you don't want me to apologize. I wasn't going to. You're saying the night we spent together was a disaster. I've got to accept that, although I have a hard time believing it." He shrugged. "You say you don't blame me but I think you do. Okay, we'll forget it."

Zoey stared down at her coffee, eyes brimming. She was holding her cup in both hands. A tear dropped in. What was the matter with her? She was an emotional wreck lately.

"Zoey?"

She gazed out the window of the coffee shop, which looked onto an interior walkway in the mall. Tattered Christmas streamers decorated a kiosk that was closed for the day. Actually, when you really thought about it, Christmas was a pretty tacky time. She faced him squarely. "Yes?"

Anything he had to say to her, she could handle. If she could deal with a difficult, whiny, bossy author like Jamie Chinchilla, she could deal with anything, including a man like Cameron Donnelly.

"You're upset. I can understand that," he said quietly. "You think I tricked you, and maybe I did. But you know why?"

His eyes were anguished.

"Why?"

"Because I wanted to make love with you. I knew Ryan was out of the picture, even if you didn't. I had a feeling about what was happening between him and Mary Ellen but I wasn't going to be the one to deliver the news. Then, when you showed up in my bed like that, well—"

He reached for her hand again and this time Zoey didn't try to pull away. "Goddammit! I'm only human. When a woman I have feelings for, *strong* feelings, crawls into my bed, I am sure as hell not going to kick her out. I don't know any man who would, even if he *didn't* have strong feelings."

Strong feelings? What was he talking about? "I see," she said weakly. Why did she always say that when she didn't have a clue? "So, you were just— just overcome with lust and desire, that's it?"

"Overcome! Hell, Zoey. I've been half in love with you since you came back to Stoney Creek. I thought I'd died and gone to heaven when I found you in my bed. I hoped—" He stopped, his eyes searching hers. What did he see there? Her emotions were tumbling all over the linoleum. *Half in love with her?*

"Shit!" he muttered. "I'm no damn good at this. Let's forget the whole thing, like you said. You want some more?" He held up his cup.

She shook her head.

He grabbed the check and walked over to the cashier to pay. Zoey watched him smile, say something to the cashier, pick up a candy cane from the bowl by the cash register and slip it in his shirt pocket. For Lissy. He made a quick call from the phone on the counter, probably checking with Marty. She watched him hang up and turn toward her, frowning. "You ready?"

He'd said he was half in love with her. What in the world was that supposed to mean? He'd said she couldn't read the signs when a man wanted her and when a man didn't give a damn.

Was *this* what he'd meant? *That he wanted her?*

Zoey swallowed and stood. She grabbed her purse from the vinyl seat and pulled her mittens back on. "Hold on. Yes, I'm ready."

As ready as she'd ever be. Which wasn't saying a whole lot.

## CHAPTER TWENTY-ONE

CAMERON DIDN'T SAY anything the whole trip home and Zoey didn't know where to start. He stopped the pickup at the garage to let her out and when she thanked him, he just nodded tersely. He drove to the house and parked beside Marty's car; from halfway up the stairs, Zoey watched him carry cartons into the house. Two trips. The door slammed.

As far as she could tell—and, admittedly, the light in the yard was bad—he hadn't looked her way once.

She let herself into her warm apartment and didn't even take off her jacket when she got there. She sank onto the lumpy sofa and rubbed her face with her mittens, then took them off slowly.

Half in love with her? What did that *mean?* That same thought kept going around and around.

He'd been half in love with her for weeks, he'd said. He said she didn't read the signs when a man wanted her. What signs? He'd treated her rudely, he'd been nosy about her...her private business, he'd ignored her, he'd told her he was interested in Sara Rundle....

Somewhere in there, she was supposed to figure out that *she* was the one he'd fallen in love with?

Suddenly, Zoey felt incredibly weary. She wished she hadn't told Lissy she'd help trim the tree. Sure, she'd promised Cameron, too, but he'd understand if she didn't show. Now she had another reason to avoid him—he'd more or less confessed he was in love with her, or, as he said, "half in love," which was embarrassing for them both.

What did that mean—half in love?

Zoey fixed herself a sandwich, an open-faced Reuben that she "grilled" in the microwave. She tumbled some olives onto her plate and ate her sandwich at the table, accompanied by a tall glass of milk.

She couldn't stop thinking about the suddenness of his outburst. What had he meant to say about the night they'd spent together? He'd planned to tell her something. Now, she wished she hadn't stopped him from speaking. She wanted to know what he'd been about to say.

For the first time in many days, Zoey allowed her mind to wander back to that night. If he really cared for her, as he said he did, so much more about that night made sense.

And his lovemaking. He wasn't out for just a…a quickie. He'd wanted it to work between them. The way he'd kissed her and caressed her until she was mad with desire, mad for him…. Zoey put down the half sandwich she was holding and dropped her head into her hands. How could something so beautiful be so wrong? So false? Damn her weepiness! If it was true that he had what he called *strong feelings* for her, no wonder she'd felt so cherished and loved. *And safe.*

Her brain hadn't known who her lover was, true, but her *body* had known. Her body had responded. You could fool the mind, but you could not fool the body. Her mind had been closed to every possibility except the one she wanted to believe—that she was in bed with Ryan. The man she had out-and-out designs on, no matter what. That somehow, magically, Ryan would make love with her, thanks to the fortuitous accident of his coming back early from Prince George, and realize then that he couldn't live without her. Just like she'd hoped in high school that he'd come to his senses and choose her over Adele.

And yet, when she'd heard the news about him and Mary Ellen, her first response had been relief! Go figure.

Hold on! Just because she wasn't in love with Ryan and probably never had been, beyond a teenage crush years ago, that did *not* mean she was in love with his brother.

And, really, how could Cameron possibly *mean* what he'd said? She'd only been in Stoney Creek for about a month—during which they hadn't even spent much time together. Didn't you have to *know* a person to fall in love? Spend time together? He barely knew her!

No, he was vulnerable, that was it. He was looking for a stepmother for Lissy. She'd do, or Sara Rundle would do or any of half a dozen other women would do. How had he met and married his first wife? He'd gone to bed with her, got her pregnant and married her. Then divorced her.

*But*—a tiny voice protested—*why would he pick you, of all people, when he thought, at least at the start, that his brother was interested? Men don't do that to each other. Brothers, especially, don't do that.*

Even so, he'd chosen her out of all the women he knew. That must mean he really *did* care for her....

Zoey's brain ached. None of this made a bit of sense. She finished her sandwich and washed up, including the breakfast dishes she'd left that morning.

So what if he was "half in love with her"? These things had to go both ways. She couldn't possibly think she was in love with one man one week and in love with his brother the next. What kind of person would that make her?

A fool.

*Unless*—the tiny voice kept insisting—*you'd actually been in love with the brother all along.*

And didn't realize it?

In which case, she was an idiot, too. Zoey did her best to squelch the unsettling thought. She was getting very good at doing that.

She showered, scrubbing until her skin stung, then toweled her hair dry and twisted it into a loose French braid. She dressed in jeans and a red sweater. Applied moisturizer, hand cream, no makeup. She inspected her nails. The manicure had held up well, would probably last through the wedding. Two more days! The cake to bake early tomorrow, to decorate in the afternoon, and the day after that the wedding. Edith and Tom. Ryan and Mary Ellen.

Then, thank heaven, it would be all over and she could go home to Toronto.

*And forget.*

THE TREE WAS TRIMMED by half past eight and hadn't been the ordeal she'd thought it would be. Ryan wasn't there—it seemed he'd gone off to the Owens' to help Mary Ellen and Edith decorate theirs.

But he'd brought home a beautiful tree that afternoon on a sled behind the snowmobile and Lissy was rightly proud of it.

"We cutted it down over by the river," she announced when Zoey arrived just after they'd had their supper. She'd brought Marty's boots to return. "Me 'n' Uncle Ryan."

"It's a lovely tree. Did you pick it out?" It *was* beautiful, in its way. A wild, rather scraggly but dignified spruce tree, nothing like the ones for sale in a city lot, all clipped and groomed to shape.

When she arrived, Cameron was stretched out on the floor, securing the tree into its stand, and there was a great deal of "is it straight?" and "which way?" and "just a little more—that's it!" Marty provided hot chocolate and swore that if she almost stepped on that cat one more time, she was going to hang him from the tree for a decoration.

Lissy, of course, disagreed, and carried Kitty around for a while to keep him safe, letting Zoey and Marty do most of the decorating. The little girl seemed quite content to watch. Marty grumbled and Zoey soothed and Cameron didn't say much at all. He'd looked straight at her when she'd shown up at the door, all snowy and breathless from her dash across the yard. A warm, appreciative gaze, nothing like the deep-freeze on the trip home from town.

He'd had time to think things over, and so had she. She hoped he wasn't going to bring up the subject again.

With the lights blazing and the decorations shimmering, the tree looked truly magnificent. Then Zoey remembered the porcelain angel. They hadn't unpacked it yet. She rummaged around in the bags, found it and presented it to Cameron to place on top of the tree.

"Ooooh!" Lissy breathed when she saw the angel. "Please, Daddy, put it up. Really, really high."

Cameron obliged and after much maneuvering, which included making sure the light inside the angel was going to connect up to the rest of the tree's wiring, the angel was up, beaming down on them.

Marty switched off the overhead lights and Zoey felt Cameron's presence behind her, then his hands on her shoulders, his thumbs gently caressing the nape of her neck. She didn't dare move. Lissy was beside her, one thumb in her mouth in a sudden throwback to babyhood, one arm holding her kitten. "Oh, Zoey, isn't it boo-ti-ful?"

"It is, honey." She sensed a slight movement behind her. Cameron's proximity was doing weird things to her stomach. "It's the prettiest tree I've ever seen." Of course, she felt that about every Christmas tree every year, but there was no need to tell Lissy that.

Zoey had assumed the child would be ready for bed, but, surprisingly, Lissy asked if she'd play Scrabble with her.

Zoey caught Cameron's eye in surprise. Scrabble? Lissy was in kindergarten. He grinned and raised one eyebrow. "Up to the challenge?" he tossed out. "We play by our own rules."

"Sure." Zoey was up to *any* challenge.

"I'll get the game," Cameron offered.

Zoey cleared off the coffee table while Lissy positioned herself on the sofa. Cameron set the game down and Zoey spread out the board, making sure the tiles were all turned over so they couldn't be seen. She noticed a much-scrawled piece of paper inside the box, a score sheet, with plenty of names on it, mostly Marty and Lissy, although Cameron and Ryan were there, too.

Marty winked at her. "I'm going to do a little more of my—" she shot a warning glance at the girl "—fancywork. You have fun. She needs a little help from time to time, doncha, honey?" She bent down and kissed the girl loudly on the cheek.

"Just sometimes," Lissy admitted, nodding her head seriously. "Mostly, I can spell my own words."

This should be interesting, Zoey thought.

She kneeled down on the floor and put a tile-holder in front of her and one on the other side of the table for Lissy. To her dismay, Cameron hunkered down beside her. "I'll play, too," he said, smiling at his daughter. How could Zoey object? "Maybe I'll need some help from you, Lissy. We're not word professionals like Zoey, here."

Lissy could count, at least, and picked out her seven tiles. Cameron and Zoey did the same. Zoey got the letter nearest an "A" so she started. She felt the side of Cameron's knee pressed against hers under the low table and moved slightly. He moved, too, apparently casually, to press against her knee again.

She stared at her letters.

"Here we go." She spelled out H-U-N-T across the center square on the board. "Who's keeping score?"

"You'd better," Cameron said easily, staring at his own tiles. "I need to concentrate."

Zoey wrote their names in order. Cameron followed her, and then Lissy. The tree lights twinkled and someone had put some low music on the stereo. What a peaceful scene, Zoey reflected. Totally, happily domestic. If Charlotte and Lydia could see her now. Even Kitty was curled up, sound asleep on the sofa behind Lissy, like a cat on a Christmas card.

"Okay, here's mine." Cameron spelled out T-R-I-P, using the T from her word to form his. "Lissy?" He shifted a little closer to the girl and helped her position her tiles. P-W-T-Z-E.

"What's that?" Zoey asked.

"'Pretty,' like you!" Lissy said. "That's how you spell it, isn't it, Dad?"

"Yep." He winked at Zoey. "Close enough, honey."

Ah, Zoey thought with a smile. *That* was how the game was played. She felt Cameron's knee against hers again. She remained rock-still. He was just testing her. Teasing her. She'd show him it meant nothing.

But if that was the case, why was the room getting warmer and warmer? Zoey took off her cardigan and reached over to sling it across the arm of the sofa. It was also an excuse to move away from him and the contact under the tabletop.

"Whose turn?" she asked, noting as calmly as she could that his eyes were on her bare arms. She shivered; suddenly the room was chilly.

"Mine." Cameron made a great show of assembling his word, then helping Lissy with hers. The girl was taking the game very seriously, trying out this and that combination, some of which were vaguely wordlike. Zoey was winning by a mile.

"Okay," he said, giving Zoey a look that sent the blood rushing to her tocs and back again. "Here's my word." He spelled out M-A-R-R-Y and Zoey took a quick breath, containing her surprise.

"That's not a great use of a Y," she managed. "You could have played it for quite a few more points."

"Yes," he said, "but I have another strategy in mind. I'm not interested in maximizing my points. Not just yet."

"It's a game. Those are the rules!" *Really!* And she moved to the other corner of the table, so her knee was well away from his.

"What's the word, Dad?" Lissy asked innocently.

"Marry," Cam replied.

"Oh! Just like in 'Merry Christmas,' right, Dad?"

"That's right, honey," he said, his eyes challenging Zoey's. She felt a ripple of heat sweep through her.

"Okay, Lissy, here's your word. Right here." He used the M on his word and then put Lissy's E down beside it.

Zoey stared. *Marry me.*

"What do you say?" he asked. "How many points is that?"

"Er, it's four." Zoey gave her full attention to the score sheet. "Four for Lissy."

Aha! It was her turn. She didn't have an N to make

NO. She had an E and an S, but there was no way she was spelling YES, game or not! Yet she was tempted to play along. He'd tossed out an interesting challenge. She realized she hadn't picked up a tile from the last time she'd played.

She picked up an M. It was worth three points and she should try and play it on at least a double or a triple. *If* she was going to be sensible.... She sent him a quick look and proceeded to lay down her letters. M-A-Y-B-E, using his Y.

Cameron laughed out loud. Zoey wanted to laugh, too, but she didn't dare. Or she'd cry.

"My turn!"

Zoey edged over to help the child. "Here's a word, honey."

Lissy leaned close and whispered, "What is it?"

Zoey whispered back. "Queen. And it'll give you millions of points if you put the first letter on that pink square. You can even beat your dad. Do you want to play it?"

Lissy nodded vigorously, her eyes shining. "Zoey says we're gonna beat you, Dad," she boasted while Zoey arranged Lissy's letters, hitting a triple with the Q, which counted for 30. She felt a thrill run down her spine.

"Queen. Hmm." Cameron studied his letters. He laid down a Y next to the M from MAYBE.

My queen.

Zoey knew her cheeks were red, her eyes bright. It had been a long, strange day. She was tired. Overwrought. She wasn't the only one. Lissy put her head on her father's shoulder and leaned heavily against him, sucking her thumb.

"Time to finish up," Zoey announced. This game was getting dangerous. "Lissy's ready for bed and so am I." She added up the figures. She'd won by a mile but there wasn't a lot of satisfaction in that. "You're the winner, Lissy!"

"I am?" the girl said tiredly, popping her thumb into her mouth.

"Yep. You beat your dad and me."

Cameron stood, with Lissy in his arms. "Off to bed for you, sweetheart."

Zoey rested her hand briefly on the girl's cheek. "Good night, Lissy. That was fun, even if it was your dad's rules."

"Thanks for playing the game with us," he said.

"With you, you mean." She couldn't resist.

He smiled. "Oh, with me, it's no game. And I play for keeps. You can believe that or not."

Zoey gathered up her sweater and slipped it on. She'd carried over her own boots so she could wear them back.

"Zoey?"

She turned. "Yes?"

"Do you believe me?"

"Believe you, what?" She was playing for time.

"That with me it's not a game?"

"Yes," she said and swallowed the lump that suddenly appeared in her throat. "I do believe you. Good night."

His "good night" rang in her ears as she tossed and

turned, unable to sleep. And she had to start early to get the two cakes done tomorrow!

He wasn't kidding. He'd actually asked her to marry him in the strangest, most whimsical way. Then he'd made a point of making sure she knew he meant it. She'd never have guessed he had a playful streak in him. But he *couldn't* be asking her to marry him! He'd never even kissed her normally—either he'd grabbed her like some caveman, as he'd done in her apartment, or he'd kissed her like a lover when she didn't even know who he was. They'd had no courtship of any kind, not even a pretend one.

Yet he'd spelled out "Marry Me" and it had been no accident.

She let her mind drift back to the night they'd spent together. To the morning after, when he'd told her Ryan wasn't interested. What had he called her? Strong. Beautiful. Sexy.

*No man had ever called her that before.*

What would it be like, she wondered sleepily, to be loved by a man like Cameron?

Then she remembered: he'd also called her *stubborn.*

# CHAPTER TWENTY-TWO

GLOVES STIFF WITH COLD, Cameron broke open the last round bale he'd delivered to the herd. He forked the tightly packed bundle around a little, opening it up for the hungry steers. Their breath, thick and foggy in the cold air—the thermometer had hit twenty below this morning—surrounded him.

"There you go, boys." He felt great. He could hardly wait to get back to the house and pick up a flask of coffee. Zoey was there—*in his house*—baking her little heart out. When he'd come in for breakfast, she was already mixing up a batch of cake batter, her face flushed, her hair pinned up, one of Marty's aprons on over her jeans and T-shirt. Marty had put breakfast on the table for him. Lissy was still in bed. He'd watched Zoey work, aware that his attention flustered her. That was a good sign.

Man, hadn't he hit it right with that Scrabble game last night? Another piece of luck! He'd been angry after their talk in town and ready to say the hell with her. She had attitude problems and she definitely wasn't the only woman around.

*But she was the only woman for him.* He'd realized that when he was taking his shower before supper. He wanted Zoey Phillips. He didn't want any other woman.

Which meant he had to get back on track with her. And pronto. She was leaving the day after the wedding—two days from now. It was going to have to be the fastest damn courtship in Cariboo-Chilcotin history. And the district had seen some pretty quick work in that department over the years.

Well, he'd made a helluva good start with that "Marry Me" on the board game.

Okay, steers were fed. Ten minutes to the house. He grinned as he jumped into his pickup and started the engine.

And for her to come back with "Maybe!" Son-of-a-gun. He'd wanted to jump up and kiss her right there in the living room, under the mistletoe or not. Then pack Lissy off to bed, lock the door and make love to the woman he wanted to marry.

Of course, he cautioned himself, maybe she'd simply been missing the letters for a great big *No*.

The trailer was light with the hay gone and Cameron drove fast. He made it back in record time and parked by the house. He saw that Marty's car was gone again—she was taking Lissy shopping sometime today—and took a big breath before he walked in.

*Home alone.*

There was a time for jerking around and a time for action. He was a man of action. He wasn't going to beat around the bush with her anymore, pretend nothing had happened.

They'd spent the night together. He'd said, "Marry me." She'd said, "Maybe."

As far as he was concerned, that was a clear invitation.

ZOEY CHECKED the first batch of cakes in the oven. They looked good—so far. Twenty minutes ago, Marty had left to take Lissy to do her Christmas shopping.

She glanced at the kitchen wall clock. Quarter past ten. With luck, she'd have the cakes baked by two o'clock and decorated by suppertime. If nothing went wrong...

She heard a vehicle's engine and looked out the kitchen window.

*Cameron.*

What was he doing back here? Ryan wasn't around, but then he never was, anymore. She supposed he had last-minute things to take care of before the wedding tomorrow. Elizabeth had called to tell her she'd taken over some of Mary Ellen's duties. Mary Ellen would normally be overseeing the reception and party, but now that she was getting married herself, she needed help. Zoey, Elizabeth had declared, was too busy with the cakes to even think about doing more, so she— Elizabeth—would be happy to supervise anything that needed supervising.

Which was fine by Zoey. She hadn't slept well, and there'd been more on her mind than preparing two wedding cakes.

She went back to her bowl of batter. Each wedding cake had to be baked in two batches because a whole batch was too much to mix up and bake at one time.

She studied the recipe, which she'd taped to a kitchen cupboard for easy reference.

The side door slammed shut and a few minutes later, Cameron walked into the kitchen. He looked healthy and fit and his cheeks were red from the cold. "Coffee on?"

"Coffee!" Zoey tossed in the egg whites and turned the mixer on. "If you want coffee, you'll have to make it yourself. Marty never said anything about you coming back for coffee."

"Oh?" He sauntered over to the counter and reached into a cupboard to pull out a package of ground coffee. "Maybe that's because I didn't tell her."

Zoey gave him a surprised look. She wasn't entirely sure she liked the idea of being alone in the house with him. He was too…too dangerous to her current state of mind. She'd thought about his charge of stubbornness again and again during the sleepless night and had come to the conclusion that he was right. She had been stubborn. Ever since she'd arrived in Stoney Creek. She'd decided on a plan—to chase Ryan—and had followed it, regardless of the facts.

In the past, she'd liked to think of this particular trait of hers as persistence. Stick-to-it-iveness. But, she conceded, it could be called stubbornness, too.

She heard him run water for the coffee machine and kept her attention on the cake batter. She measured out the vanilla and stirred it in.

"Oh!" She jumped as she felt a cold sensation on the side of her neck. Cameron's arms came around her. She was glad he couldn't see her face. Her pleasure at feeling his arms tight around her, her back pressed tight against his chest, was tempered by everything that had happened in the past two weeks.

He was kissing her!

She twisted around so she could see him better and he took the opportunity to kiss her chin, to nibble at her ear.

"Cameron!" She squirmed in his arms, but he only held her more tightly. "Don't do this. Why are you doing this?"

"Mmm." He kissed her throat, and Zoey shivered. He made a low sound, sort of a laugh, deep in his throat and she shivered again, this time right down to her toenails. He kissed her ear, her cheek. She wanted him to kiss her mouth. To kiss her as he had before, to—

But he didn't. He raised his head and grinned down at her. "I think we do a lot better together, you and me, when we don't talk."

"That's—that's preposterous!" she breathed, not meaning it at all. She liked him kissing her, just as she'd liked it before. *Stubborn,* she kept reminding herself. *Don't be stubborn, keep an open mind.*

"Your favorite word. Preposterous." He released her and turned to check on his coffee, leaving her body tingling, aching for more. She turned quickly to the cake batter. Now, where was she? Had she put in the vanilla? Her mind was racing. What *was* this? What was going on here? Why was he doing this?

"Cameron. I—I think you should remember that business last night was only a game," she said, not quite as firmly as she'd hoped. "You shouldn't be—you know, kissing me like this. It's not right."

"Bullshit," he replied agreeably. "Want a cup of this?" He held up the full pot of coffee.

"It was a game, that's all!"

"I told you I don't play games. I asked you to marry me last night and you said you might. That's pretty close to a 'yes.' I figure it's my job now to convince you that you want me as much as I want you. Because I do. There's different ways of making my case. There's words, like last night, and there's action, like right now. I'm just reminding you that we have chemistry." He took down two mugs from the cupboard. "*Major* chemistry."

"I was only playing Scrabble last night. That 'maybe' was just a *word!*"

"Please, Zoey. I hate to curse in front of a lady, but you drive me to it. Do I have to say 'bullshit' again? It's only a word, too." He seemed very pleased with himself. She noticed that he had a vacuum flask on the counter and after he'd filled the mugs, he poured the rest of the coffee into the flask.

"Are you taking that somewhere with you?" she asked. It was something to say, at least. Something ordinary.

"I've got work to do. I'd love to stay here all day in a nice warm house and convince you that I'm a serious man and when I ask a woman to marry me, I mean it, but unfortunately I've got cows to look after. Any woman who marries a rancher knows that sometimes she has to take a second place to his cows." He looked up and gave her a devilish grin and she

couldn't help smiling back. Nothing fazed this man—
*nothing!*

"And his horses and his dogs and—oh, my cake!"
Zoey ran to the wall oven and opened the door.

The most enticing aroma drifted out. Caramel, vanilla, butter. Thank goodness, they hadn't burned! If
she'd wrecked the cakes.... There were two weddings
at stake.

He carried the coffee to the table and watched as
she lifted out the cakes and set them on a rack to cool.
She was conscious—too conscious—of his gaze on
her back, her legs, maybe even her bottom.

She put down the pot holders and came to the table,
standing as she put cream and sugar into the mug he
indicated was hers. "I haven't got time to stop for
coffee. I have too much to do."

"Fine. I'll just drink mine then and watch you while
you work."

Zoey regretted her refusal to sit with him. She'd
thought it would be too difficult, sitting across from
him, as they'd done only yesterday. She hadn't realized how much more difficult it was to work in the
kitchen, with his eyes on her every move. She had
some dishes to clear up, so she filled the sink with
warm soapy water.

Then she leaned against the counter, her mug in her
hand, and faced him, but that was a mistake, too. The
look in his eyes made her knees melt.

She set her cup down and began to wash the dishes.
She took her time, rinsing them carefully before stack-
ing them in the wire rack. Anything to keep from looking at Cameron.

Finally, after what seemed like an hour but was probably more like ten minutes, he stood, brought his empty cup over to her at the sink and slid it into the water.

He dropped a kiss on her nose, then lightly touched her mouth with his, picked up his coffee flask and left.

She watched him get into his truck and drive away, oblivious to the dishwater she was dripping onto the linoleum floor. Her face was hot, her lips burned, her body ached.

*She wanted him. She desperately wanted him.*

No point being stubborn. No point denying the obvious. No point pretending it couldn't happen to you, at least not twice in as many weeks. *She loved him.*

Not Ryan. Forget Ryan. That had all been a made-up, cooked-up plot hatched by that crazy idea of Jenny Springer's at the Jasper Park Lodge reunion last spring. First love, first crush. She'd made up her mind, but her heart had disagreed.

Since she'd arrived at the Triple Oarlock, there'd only been one man in her thoughts, in her dreams *and* in her heart.

*Cameron Donnelly.*

WHEN CAMERON RETURNED to the house for supper, Zoey wasn't there. Marty said she'd gone home an hour earlier to take a nap and get herself organized to decorate the cakes, which she planned to do that evening after Marty had cleared away their supper. She was running late.

Cameron ate with Marty and Lissy. Ryan wasn't around, and Gabe only deigned to join them on Sundays. Cameron couldn't stop thinking about Zoey. Earlier, when he'd left the house with his coffee, he'd worried that he was pushing her too hard, that he shouldn't have come on so strong. Still, what choice did he have? There wasn't much time. Only tomorrow and that was the wedding. She'd be leaving early Christmas Eve for the long drive back to Vancouver. Icy roads, too.

Then Toronto, and out of his life.

He didn't know what he ate. Chili? Marty was a good cook, but his mind was elsewhere. What should he do now?

He was half tempted to offer to help her finish up the cakes. That was a joke. He'd be about as much help as Lissy with a job like that. Fiddly stuff. He hated fiddly stuff.

No, it was best that he stay out of her hair. She was flustered enough with having to decorate two cakes instead of one. He knew she'd wanted him this morning: he could feel it in his bones. The chemistry, as he'd said, was there. Did she believe him about the other part? He'd never out-and-out told her he loved her. Was it too soon? He had to show her, not tell her. She'd heard enough words from enough other men, probably plenty of those fancy Toronto types she usually dated. Why in hell hadn't one of them snagged her by now? It was a miracle.

He thought back to the wonder of that night they'd spent together. She'd taken a big chance. She'd risked everything. Then she'd felt used, humiliated by what had happened. She couldn't see that what had happened might have seemed accidental but, really, it was precious. Beautiful. Meant to be.

Fate.

Then it hit him. Risk. It had worked before. Why couldn't it work again?

ZOEY FINISHED the cakes at ten o'clock. Marty had helped her with the first one, rolling out the fondant and helping her position the layers, but then she'd had to retire to her room to knit the last cuff on Lissy's sweater.

Lissy watched a video, her kitten curled up beside her.

Cameron had not shown up all evening. Zoey felt vaguely depressed. *First you don't want him, then you do—make up your mind!* She'd felt a little better after her nap and a bowl of soup. She'd been exhausted in more ways than one. The cake was a big responsibility but it was going well and she could handle that. Cameron was another story.

She'd thought maybe they'd have a chance to talk again that evening. There were some things that needed to be said.

But he hadn't even shown up.

Zoey washed the last of the utensils she'd used. The wedding cakes looked absolutely glorious. One was topped by a schmaltzy couple, gazing adoringly into each other's eyes—that one was for Edith and Tom. The other, looking slightly different with the decorations tinted and with different pedestals, was topped by a plaster couple dancing. She'd picked up several cake toppers in Vancouver, not sure which she'd use.

Tomorrow Mary Ellen, her best friend from childhood, would be married to the man Zoey had lost her heart to when she was sixteen.

Where was the man she'd lost her heart to at twenty-eight?

Zoey knocked lightly on Marty's door to tell her she was leaving and that Lissy was ready for bed. Cameron was so fortunate to have a loving, caring aunt like Marty Hainsworth to help him raise his daughter.

Zoey kissed Lissy on the top of her blond head as she passed her in the family room. The little girl was sound asleep. "Sweet dreams, pumpkin!" she said softly.

The night was clear and dark. A million stars gleamed overhead and the moon was nearly full, throwing a smooth, even glow over the land—the fences, the buildings, the pastures beyond. Funny, in the few weeks she'd been here, she'd become very familiar with the landscape. Very comfortable. Would she miss it?

*Who knows.*

*Who knows what life has to offer?*

She let herself into her apartment and hung up her coat. She'd left a light on in the living room, which had become habit. She hated going into a dark apartment. At least the place was warm. To think that she could partly attribute one of the strangest, most earth-shaking nights of her life to a power outage!

She made a cup of tea—her usual chamomile—and left it on the counter to cool as she brushed her teeth.

Then she went into her bedroom to get her bathrobe, turning on the light as she entered.

"Pleased to see me?" Cameron was lying back on her pillows, chest bare, a broad grin on his face.

"Omigosh! What are you doing in my bed?" It was a stupid thing to say, but it was the first thought that entered her mind.

"Waiting for you."

"Me?" she squeaked.

"Is there someone else in the room?" he asked, patting the blanket beside him. "It's your choice, Zoey—either you throw me out or you take off your clothes and join me."

Zoey stared at him, eyes wide, one hand over her mouth. She wanted to laugh.

"So—which will it be?"

With a squeal of laughter, Zoey launched herself at him. Somehow, in the tumultuous welcome, their mouths connected and in that connection, Zoey knew their lives were joined, as well. Joined forever.

Cameron helped her take off her clothes, which could have taken about ten seconds, but which took him a good two minutes as he kissed every inch of skin he exposed.

Finally, she was beside him in bed, in his arms. Where she belonged. Her heart was his. And so was everything else.

# CHAPTER TWENTY-THREE

THE WEDDINGS WENT without a hitch. At the last minute, Zoey and Cameron were called in by the magistrate to witness Ryan and Mary Ellen's marriage. After all Mary Ellen's planning for her stepmother's wedding, she hadn't thought to take care of the details for her own!

The reception was a total surprise to Edith. She wept when she saw the hall full of friends, the wedding cakes—two of them! the band, the flowers. When the band played its first waltz, for the wedding couples, she managed to leave her wheelchair and waltz slowly around the room in the arms of her beloved Tom.

Zoey felt the tears run unabashedly down her cheeks. "Isn't that wonderful, Cameron? Look at them—they're so in love!"

He gave her a smile and pulled her close. "Next dance is mine, sweetheart. I'm not much on the fancy stuff, but I can handle an old-time waltz or a two-step."

She nestled against his jacket and smiled up at him. He was as dressed up as she'd ever seen him and the handsomest man in the world—how had she ever thought his brother was better-looking? "Those are the really important dances," she assured him. "The rest is—"

"The icing on the cake," he finished. "Yeah, I know."

It was their private joke. They'd laughed the night before, after they'd made love, that their little tryst in her bedroom was indeed the icing on the cake.

Since he'd found a piece of fondant in her hair the next morning when he was kissing her, the phrase definitely applied.

"You're an excellent dancer!" Zoey said, when they took to the floor with the rest of the couples, after the first dance.

"And you, my dear, are an excellent liar," he said, grinning. "I have other talents, though...."

"You do," she murmured, blushing.

She'd never been happier. Marty was sitting at a table to one side, talking with some of their neighbors. Lissy was running around the adults' legs, with Becky and Tessa and several other children, getting in the way and having a wonderful time.

She met his gaze; their bodies moved as one to the music. He really was a very good dancer.

"Marry me, Zoey Phillips," he said, his voice gruff. His eyes were loving, warm, proud. "No more *maybes*."

"Why would I marry you?" she asked archly.

"Because I love you?"

"And?"

"Because you're the woman I adore?"

She missed a beat and he caught her in strong arms. "And?"

"Because I'll never meet a funnier, stronger, smarter, more beautiful, sexier woman?"

"And?" She caught her breath at his look and leaned forward to kiss him softly on the mouth.

"Or a more stubborn one. Marry me, Zoey!"

"Yes," she said, "Yes, yes, *yes!*"

The music didn't stop, but they did. Cameron pulled her into his arms and kissed her. She wound her arms around his neck and kissed him back. Her man! Her everything!

When they parted, the crowd clapped and there was a roar of laughter.

They looked at each other and laughed, too.

Ryan and Mary Ellen danced by. "Does this mean what I think it means?" Ryan asked.

"You bet it does," Cameron growled, his arms tight around her. "Now and forever."

"Forever's a very long time," she whispered.

"Didn't I tell you, Zoey?" He smiled down at her. "I play for keeps."

Dear Lydia,

You'll never guess—I'm getting married! And, no, not to my first love. To his brother! This is the best and craziest thing that's ever happened to me. I'm bringing my cowboy with me for our annual New Year's Eve get-together. I can't wait to see you and Charlotte next week and tell you all about it. I know you'll love him—I do! I think this New Year's will be one we'll never forget. Who knew where this ridiculous search for first love would lead? I sure didn't. Don't know when

the big day will be, but soon. Valentine's Day?
The sooner the better. One thing I do know, I'm
having the biggest wedding ever. I deserve it,
don't you think? I've fielded more than my share
of long shots. This is the last curve romance is
tossing me—guaranteed!

Luv,
Zoey


\* \* \* \* \*

*Turn the page for an excerpt*
*from the next* GIRLFRIENDS *book,*
*CHARLOTTE MOORE,*
*on sale in December 2001.*
*Charlotte, too, has accepted*
*the girlfriends' dare:*
*to find her first love.*
*And in her case, that's Liam Connery...*

"MA'AM?"

Charlotte shrieked and felt the goose bumps double in size all over her shivering body. "Oh—I didn't hear you coming!"

"I'm sorry, ma'am." A boy of thirteen or fourteen had emerged over the side of the sand dune from the north. He turned red as a beet. Poor kid. "You lookin' for something, ma'am?"

"My dog. She's—" Charlotte waved in the general direction of the woods to the west "—in there somewhere."

"*Your* dog?" The boy seemed puzzled. He put two fingers to his mouth and let fly a piercing whistle.

To Charlotte's amazement, a dog shot out of the trees. Maggie! Oh, no—*another* black dog emerged from the woods, right behind the first one. They ran together, occasionally turning to nip playfully and to paw each other with their front feet, then run side by side again. Neither animal headed their way.

"That's *your* dog?" Charlotte asked.

"No. Liam's." The boy looked over his shoulder, then glanced at her again. He seemed worried. "My dad's cousin."

Liam *Connery?* No. She wasn't ready to meet

him—she wasn't dressed properly. She hadn't figured out what she was going to say yet. She had a definite, much-tweaked plan for their first meeting, and this wasn't it. But it *had* to be him—how many Liams could there be in this tiny corner of Prince Edward Island?

The boy sent her another look. "Liam's mad about Scout going over the side of the boat like that—"

He stared at the two dogs, who were now running madcap along the line where the grass met the trees. Then he called over his shoulder. "Scout's here, Liam, just like you thought. He's goin' after this here lady's dog."

To her horror, Charlotte saw a man striding toward them, dressed in a camouflage jacket and carrying a— a big gun! He had another dog with him, a large brown dog with a coarse-looking coat, wavy along the back.

The conversation she'd had that morning in the diner, Sid's heavy glances exchanged with the waitress, plus his ominous comments about Liam Connery not taking to strangers skipped through her mind.

*This* was Liam Connery? The man approaching didn't look much like the boy she remembered. He was tall and powerful-looking. Dark hair—that was as she remembered—dark eyes, what she could see of them. What color *had* his eyes been? Brown? Green? She couldn't recall. A three-day growth of beard that gave him a dangerous, lawless air. Scuffed lace-up work boots, a faded plaid shirt under the open jacket. The gun slung over his shoulder. Hair in need of a trim.

He stood beside the boy—ignoring her completely—and gazed out at the dogs, frolicking halfway up the side of the hill.

"Well, dammit. Would you look at that?"

That was all he said, in a low, forceful tone. Charlotte was shivering uncontrollably. She wished she'd tied her windbreaker around her waist instead of dropping it on the sand several hundred yards back, along with her sweater and shoes. The brown dog sat attentively at the man's side, ears alert but showing no sign of joining the other two.

"Your bitch, ma'am?" He finally glanced her way. The drawled query shocked her. She wasn't used to calling Maggie a bitch, even though she knew that was the proper name for a female dog.

"Y-yes," she managed. "M-my sister's actually."

"She wouldn't be in heat, would she?"

He looked directly at her without a trace of recognition in his eyes. They were brown, shot with gold and green. A very dark brown. She shook her head. "No—at least, I don't think so."

"Good," he continued flatly. "Most people would have the sense not to let loose a bitch in heat."

"It's my sister's dog," Charlotte answered, her voice small. She decided this definitely wasn't the time to tell him she was delivering Maggie to his kennel. "I don't know why she won't come when I call...."

Liam frowned and put his fingers to his mouth, as the boy had, and let loose an ear-splitting whistle, staring intently toward the hill. No dog. He swore again.

"I don't know what's wrong with her. She's usually obedient," Charlotte said, then, irked by the man's disdain, added proudly, "She's a champ, after all."

He gave her another glance, eyes narrowed, interested—the first time, Charlotte felt sure, that her presence had actually registered with him. "Champ?"

"Show championships. A lot of them." Maybe she *ought* to sing Maggie's praises a little. The Lab hadn't made a good first impression by running off and not coming back when she was called. "Tons and tons of ribbons. Obedience trophies, too."

Liam Connery made a nasty noise in his throat and the boy quickly asked, "Want me to go get 'em, Liam?"

"Better do that, Jamie. Scout's got one thing on his mind right now and it isn't his dinner."

He turned and studied her, sizing her up—a little rudely, Charlotte thought. In the last five minutes, she'd had second thoughts about everything. First love! Scrap all her romantic little plans for a reunion over tea and cookies. This man was a lout. A *hunter*, from the looks of the gun, even though she didn't see any ducks or anything. But the gun had to be for something. He wasn't even polite. He was rude, he was bossy, and she didn't like the way he referred to Maggie as a bitch in heat, even if she was.

Charlotte was doing some serious readjusting. So much for romantic reunion stories—Zoey and Lydia would die laughing when they heard about *this*.

## HARLEQUIN *Super*ROMANCE®

Old friends, best friends...

### *Girlfriends*

Your friends are an important part
of your life. You confide in them,
laugh with them, cry with them....

# *Girlfriends*

### Three new novels by Judith Bowen

**Zoey Phillips. Charlotte Moore. Lydia Lane.**
They've been best friends for ten years, ever
since the summer they all worked together at a
lodge. At their last reunion, they all accepted a
challenge: *look up your first love*. Find out what
happened to him, how he turned out....

Join Zoey, Charlotte and Lydia as they
rediscover old loves and find new ones.

Read all the *Girlfriends* books! Watch for
*Zoey Phillips* in November, *Charlotte Moore* in
December and *Lydia Lane* in January.

### HARLEQUIN®
*Makes any time special* ®

*Together for the first time
in one Collector's Edition!*

**New York Times bestselling authors**

# Barbara Delinsky

# Catherine Coulter

# Linda Howard

# Forever Yours

**A special trade-size volume containing three
complete novels that showcase the passion,
imagination and stunning power that these
talented authors are famous for.**

Coming to your favorite retail outlet in December 2001.

HARLEQUIN®

*Makes any time special* ®